REVIEWS OF TH

"**The Collingwood Series is Canadian historical fiction at its best,** reviewing events that took place in 1950s and 1960s Canada, an era when racism was often unacknowledged."

–Diane Donovan, Donovan's Literary Services

"**A wide-ranging novel** that will provide much food for thought and discussion among any with an interest in the foundations of courage, convictions about equality for all, and how a nation handles (or mishandles) its immigrant influx and their absorption in and contributions to society."

–Midwest Book Review

"**A poignant, evocative, and engaging read...** Engrossing and elegant, Fillis' second installment in the Collingwood Series explores relationships, endurance, desires, and means of survival. Fillis skillfully captures the pain of loss and the resiliency of the human spirit, and his crisp prose keeps readers turning pages fast. This fascinating coming-of-age journey, focusing on the strength of family and friendship, forgiveness, redemption, integrity, racism, and issues of immigration, will appeal to a wide readership. Fans of historical fiction will be enthralled."

–The Prairies Book Review ★★★★★

By George Fillis

A HEART TO SURVIVE
first novel in the Collingwood Series

AN UNEXPECTED FATHER
second novel in the Collingwood Series

UNPUNISHED CRIMES
third novel in the Collingwood Series

SHAVANO
a short story

Author's website:
GeorgeFillisNovels.com

Author's Note: the Collingwood Series should be
read in chronological order and not as individual
stand-alone titles because of the background of
events, characters, and storylines.

George Fillis

UNPUNISHED CRIMES

third novel in the Collingwood Series

Though inspired by true stories and real characters, this is a work of fiction and of the author's imagination. References to real people, events, scenes, conversations, dialogue, establishments, organizations, or locales are intended only to provide a sense of authenticity and are used fictitiously. The views and opinions expressed in the book are those of the author only and don't necessarily reflect or represent the views and opinions held by individuals on whom those characters are based.

Unpunished Crimes / George Fillis

ISBN: 978-1-7359372-4-3 (Print)
ISBN: 978-1-7359372-5-0 (Ebook)

Printed in the United States of America

Publisher: Bluerock7, LLC.
Book Design by Berge Design
Cover Image by Doug Burlock Photography

To my wonderful wife, Karen, thank you for being the love of my life and for your collaboration and encouragement.

And to Dr. Lew Spurlock for his friendship and literary mentoring.

Contents

"Keep your face to the sunshine,
and you can never see the shadow."

Helen Keller

Chapter One

Collingwood, Ontario | 1966

In my foolishness, I had lived as if all the days of my life were still to come. As if being Chinese in a white domain was not hard enough, events to come threatened to shatter my world.

It was after midnight on a Sunday in late March, and I was sound asleep in our bed when Caitlin shook me, and I opened my eyes.

"Something's wrong!" she said with a tremble in her voice.

Turning on the lamp and seeing red-stained sheets, I looked at Caitlin and said, "Oh my God! Is our baby dying? I'm calling an ambulance right now. Are you in pain?"

"No. I want you to take me to the hospital and stay with me."

With that, she started sobbing and was inconsolable as I bundled her in warm clothes.

"What's happening to me? Please, God, don't let me lose our baby."

After I helped her into the car, I ran to the driver's side and threw open the door. I could barely get the key in the ignition as my hands were shaking so much, but once I got the car started, I jammed the gear into reverse and slammed my foot on the accelerator. The tires complained about the abuse, and thankfully there was no one on the street at this time of night.

The night was cold with freezing rain, and the car fishtailed several times on the way to the hospital, and each time Caitlin gripped my arm and whimpered. When we finally arrived, after what seemed an eternity, I slid the car at an angle under the portico and ran into the Emergency Room shouting for help.

A middle-aged woman with brow line glasses and a name badge that read 'Mary Petain' sat at a desk, looked at me, and calmly said, "What seems to be the problem, sir?"

"My wife needs help. She's pregnant and bleeding."

She looked unperturbed and said, "Well, why don't you bring her in?"

I couldn't believe her attitude, but I ran back out to the car, and as gently as I could, helped Caitlin into the ER where we stood in front of Miss Petain's desk. She had several framed photos, a full ashtray, and an open cigarette package aligned on her desk that looked like it marked boundaries of her control.

She didn't even look at us when she said, "What seems to be the problem, honey?"

"I'm bleeding," Caitlin sobbed.

When she finally looked up she exclaimed, "Oh, you're white! Take a seat."

"Look, Miss Petain, my wife needs to see a doctor now!" I shouted as blood rushed to my head, and I was about to explode.

"Sir, if you don't calm down, I'm going to call security." When I didn't reply, she continued with a small smile, proud that she had put the Chinaman in front of her in his place.

Caitlin had managed to control her tears but was still taking deep breaths in between frequent gulps to hold back her emotions.

After Caitlin told her about the bleeding, Petain looked at me and said, "Sir, only the patient can be here. Take a seat over there." She pointed at several empty rows of chairs behind us.

"She's pregnant and bleeding and needs to see a doctor right away!"

"Sir, take a seat."

When I banged my fist on the desk, the startled attendant pushed back in her chair, and her cheeks turned red. "Sir, keep your hands on your lap, or I'll call security."

Glaring at me, she added, "You've driven her here, so go take a seat and wait for your…your…woman. It's your choice, eh!"

She didn't want to call me Caitlin's husband.

"Listen to me, Miss Petain, I own Merchants Bank, and I'm a member on a Federal Parliamentary Commission, and I know…"

Caitlin put her hand on my arm, squeezed it, then said in a meek voice, "He's my husband, and I want him here."

I held my tongue and didn't want to upset Caitlin further as Miss Petain avoided eye contact with me. "Oh, I see," she said as she raised her pen to her mouth and looked at Caitlin. "Before you can see the doctor, we need to complete the admissions process."

This was ridiculous, and I started to say something, but Caitlin patted my arm and said, "Please, call Dr. Franklin, my obstetrician."

"The on-duty doctor will see you first, and he'll call Dr. Franklin if he's needed."

Caitlin gritted her teeth and squeezed my arm, warning me not to speak.

After completing the paperwork, Miss Petain said to Caitlin, "Take a seat in the waiting area. Someone will be with you soon."

I helped her to a chair and kissed her still wet cheek. When I sat, she put her head on my shoulder.

The yellowed wall clock read 1:25. After what seemed like an eternity, a young nurse came with a wheelchair, and I helped Caitlin up. The nurse said, "Thank you. I have her now."

"May I come with her to see the doctor?"

"I'm sorry, you're not allowed. Only family."

Caitlin said, "This is my husband, and I want him to be with me."

The nurse cleared her throat, glanced toward me, then looked at Miss Petain, who was watching with a stern expression, then she said to Caitlin, "After the doctor has examined you, he'll consult with your husband about your condition."

When I looked at Caitlin and saw the pained expression on her face, I met the nurse's gaze and let go of Caitlin's hand. They disappeared behind heavy metal double doors with a sign, 'Medical Staff Only.'

I walked outside to move the car, and when I returned, I paced the floor and watched the clock. I was the only one in the waiting area. Miss Petain stopped her paperwork and stared at me with a frown on her face. As much as I tried to control my emotions, my blood was boiling.

This was the same hospital where I waited on doctors treating Julian and Catherine for heart attacks. There had been little respect toward me then, as well as now. I was so worked up that I could feel my heartbeat. Prepared to confront Miss Petain, I took a step in her direction. On this cold and frightening night, I needed to choose my battles. Arresting my emotions, I stopped and stared back.

She blinked her eyes, and when I didn't back off, she pushed her glasses up on the bridge of her nose, lowered her head, and returned to her paperwork.

I sat and watched the clock on the pale green walls and tried to stop my feet from bouncing. I needed courage and faith, but it was difficult to find it at two in the morning, waiting by myself and not knowing what was causing my wife's bleeding.

Caitlin was in her sixth month of pregnancy, and all of her checkups had gone well. Her excitement about the baby was contagious. Every few days, she bought children's books, and when we nestled together in bed, I would read aloud, then Caitlin would sing to the baby. The first time our baby moved, I was amazed by the wonder of life that was forming within her. It was the life of our child, but now I sat and prayed that Caitlin and the baby were okay.

I never imagined marriage or children until I met Caitlin, and at thirty years old, I was becoming a father. We had interesting conversations over names. When Caitlin suggested naming a girl after my mother or a boy after my grandfather, I didn't want them to struggle with integrating into Canadian society, so I told her that I loved Mother and YeYe, but didn't want our child to have a Chinese name. I asked her to consider Catherine, our dearest friend, or if it was a boy, to name him after Julian, my adoptive father. In the end, I said I would defer the baby's name to her, and she glowed but told me it would be a mutual decision.

Unable to sit still, I stood and paced as I considered whether the threats and actions by Tak could have stressed Caitlin and contributed to her bleeding. It had been a few months, and as far as I knew Tak was still in jail in Ottawa for his attempted murder of us in the Ottawa Train Station. And then, there was the ever present threat of Dung wanting revenge against us for Tak being in jail. I tried to keep these concerns out of any conversation with Caitlin, and she was not one to express her worry to me. The thought that it was too early in Caitlin's pregnancy for the baby to be born kept repeating in my mind.

I wanted to call someone for reassurance, and the first person that came to mind was Virginia, Julian's nurse, but she had returned home to Nova Scotia a few weeks ago. Catherine would want to help, but I didn't want to wake her in the middle of the night with her heart condition.

When I found a payphone in the lobby, I called Caitlin's mother. When I told Maureen what happened, she said they would come right away. Time seemed to crawl while I waited, so I sat, picked up one tattered magazine after another, and thumbed through each without finding anything of interest until I heard, "Winson."

It was the deep raspy voice of Caitlin's father, Kierian Mulroney, who bellowed like he was still barking commands at the shipyard.

Maureen's soft, high-pitched voice sounded like Caitlin when she said, "How is she?"

"I haven't heard since the nurse took her into the examination room over an hour ago. I'm waiting for the doctor."

Maureen put her hand on my arm and squeezed. Caitlin had her mannerisms.

"They took her back a few minutes before I called you. They won't let me be with her."

"Why not?"

"Because he's Chinese," Kierian said in his blunt manner. Maureen glared at him, then said, "What happened?"

As I recounted events, the doors swung open, and a tall, light-skinned man wearing a green smock approached us, looked at Kierian, ran his fingers through his already disheveled hair, then addressed Maureen. "I'm Doctor Tremblay. Are you Caitlin LeBlanc's family?"

"Yes, we are, and this is Winson, Caitlin's husband."

He glanced at me and said, "Caitlin and the baby are resting comfortably. Her bleeding is from cervical polyps, which can occur during pregnancy. We gave her a local anesthetic and the bleeding has stopped, but she experienced some mild contractions, so we would like to keep her in the hospital for a few days for observation. Dr. Franklin should be in to see her before his office hours this morning."

"Are the polyps cancerous?" Maureen's voice fluttered, and when I heard the word cancer, I tried to regain control of my nerves.

"We'll biopsy them, but most often they're benign."

"Did you remove them?" I asked.

"We don't feel it's necessary and don't want to jeopardize her pregnancy."

Maureen said, "Thank you, Doctor," and when I asked, "Dr. Tremblay, can I see her?" he turned and walked away. I knew he heard me because Maureen gave me an embarrassed look. Although I had come to expect this behavior, it stung under the circumstances.

"You should get some sleep. It's been a long day for you and for all of us," Maureen said.

"I want to see Caitlin before I leave. Let's check with the admissions attendant."

When Miss Petain saw the three of us standing in front of her, she tried to ignore us.

"Excuse me, Miss Petain, can you tell us about Caitlin LeBlanc's status?"

She thumbed through some papers and said, "Your wife's in the process of being moved to a hospital room, and it'll be hours before she'll be allowed visitors."

As we stepped away, Maureen said, "Why don't you go home and try to get some rest, eh?"

I knew I wouldn't be able to sleep, so I said, "I don't want to leave her, but I'll go clean up at home and return to the hospital before seven."

"Then I'll come back at nine and stay with her through the afternoon. Now, go." Maureen said.

∞

Two days later, Caitlin returned home and was lethargic. The good news was that Dr. Franklin said Caitlin and the baby were both fine, but we remained anxious for the three days until we received a negative lab report on the biopsy.

The next night at dinner, as Caitlin picked at her food, she forced a smile and said, "Kathleen came to see me today. This weekend she's going to her family's cottage on Pine Isle. It's a small secluded island in Georgian Bay. Most every summer growing up, I'd go with her for a few weeks. Her husband, Patrick, has been traveling for work, so she invited us to join her, to rest and relax. It would be good for me to be there, it has always been a place of comfort for me, and Dr. Franklin said it was okay for me to slowly return to normal activities. Can we go?"

"It's a difficult time for me to be out of touch."

"We'll be back before you have to fly to Victoria for the Chinese Benevolent Association meeting. It'll give you time to prepare your speech."

"Sweetheart, this week, the Ministry of Finance informed me of an interim examination at the end of the month. They spent a week auditing our books during the last exam and investigated hundreds of our customer accounts. We are in the process of preparing for them. I also have scheduled customer meetings, and on Thursday I'll be in Ottawa for the semi-annual meeting of the Immigration Committee with a full agenda."

When I saw her expression fall like a bridge crumbling into a river, I said, "You should go, as long as Dr. Franklin approves. The time with Kathleen will be good for you."

"If he says yes, can you at least come the second week or for a weekend?"

I hadn't told her about the increasing loss of bank customers we had been experiencing and my concern about the deposit to loan ratios that the examiners would scrutinize. If I told her everything that was going on at the bank, she wouldn't want to go, and a change of surroundings in a safe place with her best friend from childhood could do her good. So I said, "It will be good for you to spend time with Kathleen, and there will be another time when we can go together."

"You act like the bank, the exam, and these meetings are more important than our baby and me. There'll always be problems and excuses."

The look on her face pierced my heart, and she seemed to look right through me as she said, "We've been through a lot of turmoil over the past few months, and I want us to spend time in a sheltered and quiet place together."

When I sighed, she added, "Kathleen can show you pictures and tell you about the island. Maybe you'll change your mind and come for a few days."

"I'd be open to that." I tried to appease her even though I knew I couldn't leave the bank and let the staff deal with the examiners.

When we went to bed that night, she turned away from me, and when I awoke in the morning, we weren't touching.

∽

On Thursday, when I came home at noon to check on Caitlin, Kathleen was with her in the breakfast room having tea. I greeted Kathleen, kissed my wife, and sat next to her.

"May I pour you tea?" Kathleen asked.

"Please."

"Rhoda came this morning with freshly baked scones. Would you like some?" Kathleen extended a plate, and I took two.

As Kathleen passed jam and added milk to the tea, Caitlin said, "We're talking about Pine Isle."

"Winson, I want you to join us because you both need time away. So please, come and stay with us."

Caitlin took my hand in hers, and when our eyes met, said, "Sweetheart, I realize you must attend the meeting in Ottawa and have issues at the bank, but come the following week, even if it's just a few days?"

I looked away. My heart wanted to go, but my mind argued against it. I looked back at Caitlin and said, "When are you planning this trip?"

"We'd like to leave tomorrow or Saturday," Caitlin responded. "Come for a week. Do it for yourself? The bank will still be here when you return," Caitlin pleaded. "It's so remote, and you won't be bothered by anyone."

"I wish I could, but there's no stand-in for me."

"Do it for us!" Caitlin dropped her head, then looked for support from Kathleen and said, "Show him the pictures and tell him about the island."

"My grandfather bought the island years ago. He and his brothers built the cottage out of pine logs felled from the property. A long front porch overlooks a sandy beach and sheltered bay. Inside are four bedrooms and a large living area with a dry-stack stone fireplace that goes from floor to ceiling. The house is surrounded by a forest of birch, maple, and pine trees with hiking trails and pinkish-gray granite outcroppings all over the island. It takes about an hour to walk the perimeter trails." She showed me photos as she spoke.

"Winson, you love nature." Caitlin's voice was soft and kind, with the inflection she used to get her way with me. "We can take walks, and you won't hear any phones or customers complaining. Pine Isle is amazing and is part of an archipelago of over 30,000 islands."

I closed my eyes and reconsidered. "Caitlin, you're right, the rest would be good for both of us, and I want to go." I shook my head and added, "But I've a full calendar of meetings, and I need to get out in the community and understand what's…" I stopped short of telling her that we were losing customers.

"You were shaking your head before you even answered. You've never permitted yourself to play. First, the civil war in China took that away from you and then the trafficking ring. You didn't even take a day off when we got married. Life is more than work." The more she raised her voice, the lower my spirit sank.

When I saw her chin dip and her lips pressed tight, I said, "I'll make every effort to join you for the last weekend."

The corners of her mouth started to turn up as Kathleen said, "If your circumstances change, you can always come sooner. We don't have phone service, but if you want to come, contact my parents, and they'll get word to me through Mr. Gerow, who lives on an island close to ours. When he boats to Penetanguishene for supplies at the general store, he calls my parents when I have a message for them, and if they have a message for me, they leave it with the store. So you can always leave a message for us by calling my mother. I'll leave you her phone number."

∽

Before sunrise Saturday morning, in constant light rain, we drove two hours to the Penetanguishene harbor. Caitlin was quiet during the ride. When we parked at the dock, I loaded the luggage and supplies into the small boat, and when I finished loading, I held an umbrella over her, and before she stepped onto the boat, I slipped my arm around her to kiss her goodbye, and she turned her cheek away. I held her arm as she got onto the boat, but everything seemed misaligned between us, and I didn't want to leave her this way.

Then I helped Kathleen into the boat, and she took hold of my arm and said, "I'll take loving care of her. Let me know if you can come early. Otherwise, I'll plan to pick you up here Friday at about ten."

I forced a smile as I untied the dock lines, then watched the boat pull away from the dock. The rain was soft and almost transparent against the morning light as I watched the boat until it was out of sight. It was as if I was standing along the boat's railing back in Hangzhou as I departed home and watched my family disappear in the distance. I don't know how long I stood in the rain, but my clothes were soaking wet when I got back to the car.

As I turned onto the road that led away from the harbor, the rain let up, and I was thankful to see the sun peek through the clouds, but I already missed Caitlin and regretted not going with her. Could I rearrange my schedule to spend a few days on the island? Was the bank more important than Caitlin and our baby? Would she stay angry with me the whole time she was on the island? My mind went through a litany of doubts.

On the drive home, massive thunderhead clouds spread along the ridge of the Blue Mountains and I saw one cloud that looked like a dragon ready to swallow the mountain. I was exhausted and imagining forms in the sky where there were none.

That night, a violent storm hit Collingwood, with high winds and rain. It was a long time before I fell asleep and was awakened by someone or something assaulting me. I woke gasping for air and realized it was only a dream. Hail was hitting the windows, and the fluorescent clock showed it was only three.

My heart was racing, and the sweat on my shirt was cold against my skin.

Chapter Two

Sunday

The storm had continued through the night with gale-force winds that knocked out electricity and phone service. I rose before dawn, went out to inspect any storm damage, and saw limbs scattered across the sidewalk and driveway. After several hours the sky turned crystal blue, and the temperatures dropped as the north wind was chilled coming off the lake. I put on old clothes, a heavy coat, and gloves to clear away the debris surrounding the house. The physical labor took my mind off Caitlin and problems at the bank for a few hours.

As I was piling up the limbs and debris, I heard a whiny, nasal voice from behind me, "Hey boy, where's the owner of the house?"

I turned and saw a slightly built man dressed in black pants and a heavy parka standing on the entry walk. He had a pencil-thin mustache, long sideburns, and salt and pepper hair. "Who are you looking for?"

"The man who lives in this mansion."

"Who should I say is calling?"

"Benjamin Saez."

Saez was the name of the cousin who Julian excluded from his will.

"Who are you?" he asked as the intensity in his voice rose.

"Winson LeBlanc."

"Julian LeBlanc is my cousin, but he never mentioned you. Just because you change your name, do you become French?" He laughed, raised his voice and said, "Where's the old man?"

"He passed away."

"Well, well. I heard a rumor to that effect."

My dislike for him rose as he looked around at the property and smirked.

"Then this is my house." He looked me up and down, then arched his eyebrows and rubbed his chin with thin pasty white fingers. "Maybe you want to work for me? I'll need a yardman for a place this large."

He stepped to the side of me with a gloating smile and looked at the house with greedy eyes.

"You should call on Mr. LeBlanc's attorney."

"Who's that?" He spit out the words.

"Clive Owen, of Owen and Owen Barristers."

"Where is he?"

"His office is on Hurontario Street."

"Well then, that's what I'll do."

He looked around at the yard and said, "Now you do a damn-good job cleaning the place for me."

With a slight limp, he walked around me and started to take the stairs, but before he reached the front door, I called out, "Mr. Saez, you'd better speak to Mr. Owen before you enter the house."

"Don't tell me what to do, boy. I can go where I want in my house."

"It's not your house!"

"Well, if it's not Julian's anymore, it belongs to me."

"No. It goes to his son."

He cast me an evil eye. "Joseph was his only son, and the kid's dead."

"I'm his other son."

"He doesn't have another son. His john didn't work after his accident." His face hardened, and he hissed, "Get off my property now."

I furrowed my eyes, tightened my muscles, and prepared to fight. "Julian legally adopted me and left the house to me in his will. You can verify that information with Mr. Owen. Now please get off MY property."

"Julian wouldn't adopt a Chink. You know nothing about us."

"You're Jewish and came to Canada from Warsaw. You have three sons and started Bear Oil Company."

He took a step back as if I had struck him in the face. I walked up to him, looked firmly into his cold eyes, and said without hesitation, "Mr. Saez, I will call the police if you don't leave the premises now."

He pulled on his collar, arched his eyebrows, and leered at me. "You stupid fool. You better start looking for a laundry job." He glared at me and added, "When I'm through with you, I'll have more than my revenge against Julian and his... new son. You'll wish you never left China."

He turned, walked down the steps to his car, and I watched him drive toward town. He was heading to Clive's office, even though it was Sunday.

∽

Later in the day, there was a knock on the front door.

Surprised to see Clive, I said, "You must have had the pleasure of meeting Julian's cousin, Mr. Saez."

"My misfortune to be working at the office on a Sunday. He walked up as I was locking the door and asked me who the Chinese yardman was at the LeBlanc house. I replied, 'Julian's son, Winson.'"

"I'm pretty sure he didn't say Chinese."

"As a matter of fact, he called you something in Yiddish, and when he said you were a squatter, I told him you inherited the property from Julian. He demanded to see the will, so I invited him in, pulled the file, and let him read it. I could have told him it was public record and to go to the Courthouse on Monday, but thought it best to be up-front. When he read the clause that said he and his family were specifically excluded from any inheritance, he turned purple. He started bellowing that Julian was incompetent, and he would be contesting the will's validity."

"He was forceful with you like he was with me."

"I told him he would be wasting his money, that Julian's body had failed him but not his mind. Saez raised his voice and said he knew you and Caitlin lived with Julian and that you exercised undue influence over him. He also called me names in Yiddish."

"What did you do?"

"I gave him my card and showed him the door. The last thing he said was 'I'll take more from him than he stole from me.'"

"What does that mean?"

"Don't worry about Saez. Julian's will is legal and sound, although he can always apply to the court to contest it. Julian often called him a gonif."

"What does gonif mean?'

"It's Yiddish for a thief or swindler."

I was lost thinking about his threat and what a lawsuit could do to the bank's public image if it became known that my ownership was being questioned. It startled me when Clive took hold of my arm and said, "What's wrong? Are you okay?"

"I'm sorry, it's what Saez told you. How did he know so much about Caitlin and me? What will happen if he does try to make trouble either in court or personally?"

"Enough of that. I'll manage whatever Julian's cousin attempts," Clive interrupted.

When I saw the compassion in his eyes, I nodded and said, "I appreciate how you stood up for me."

"It's my pleasure. Julian would be proud of how you conduct yourself and honor him."

I thanked Clive, walked him to the door, and stood on the porch as he walked away. I wanted to tell Caitlin about Saez, but there was no phone service on Pine Isle, and I didn't expect to hear from her. Kathleen said Gerow made trips ashore every few days for supplies and would pick up whatever they needed, and I considered leaving a message but decided not to concern her with Saez's visit or his threats. I was lonely without Caitlin and started thinking of getting away to see her even sooner.

I didn't want to return to an empty house, so I sat on the porch where Julian liked to watch people and cars. There were times when Julian wanted Scotch, and sometimes he'd ask for a second shot. On those days, he looked sad, and I wondered if he was thinking of his wife Ruthie because that was how I was feeling about Caitlin.

Because of my relationship with Julian, I had inherited the business he built and a beautiful home. It was more than I could ever have imagined. I realized if I lost the house and bank to Saez, but still had Caitlin and our child, I would consider myself wealthy and fortunate. I was finding more reasons to spend time on Pine Isle with Caitlin and Kathleen.

As the wind picked up, I marveled at how a gentle breeze with a touch of dry coolness could be such a pleasure.

Chapter Three

Monday

Struggling to sleep, I woke at four-thirty in the morning, showered and dressed, walked to the bank in pitch darkness, and arrived at half-past five.

Twenty minutes after the bank opened, Peggy knocked on my door and asked, "Sir, may I have a word?"

"Please come in and have a seat."

"Late Friday, Mr. Drott was in the teller line and asked Anita what he needed to do to close his accounts. She asked if there was anything wrong. He wasn't specific but said it concerned his business. He's been a customer for many years, so I thought you should know."

"Thank you for telling me. I met with Mr. Drott earlier last week and everything appeared to be okay, but I'll give him a call."

I knew he'd been purchasing wood from *Imperial Lumber Company* and wondered if Dung was pressuring him to move his banking away from Merchants as a tactic against me.

As I stood in the doorway of my office and watched the lobby, I noticed a reduced level of customer traffic throughout the morning for a Monday and decided to speak to each teller about customer comments and satisfaction. Each was encouraging, but several said they had been asked to close accounts, including Collingwood Terminals Limited, a bank customer since 1938 whose 100-foot grain elevators were a conspicuous Georgian Bay landmark. I was concerned that losing their business would be a harbinger of bad news.

It was after lunch when Peggy knocked at my door again and said, "Mr. Stromberger is here to see you."

I didn't answer right away when Peggy said with a pained expression, "Sir, do you want me to deal with him or should I tell him to come back another time?"

The concern on her face was understandable with the attrition of accounts over the past weeks.

"No, Peggy, I scheduled a meeting with Mr. Stromberger and apologize for hesitating. I was thinking about Mr. Drott and don't' know what's going on behind closed doors, but I have a feeling that this community does not trust a Chinese banker."

"Sir, there's no one more honorable or professional than you."

"Thank you for your kind words."

"The staff feels the same as I do, Sir."

I forced a smile and said, "Thank you. Please escort Mr. Stromberger into my office."

When he walked in, I stood and greeted him as warmly as possible. "Mr. Stromberger, it's good to see you. Would you like tea?"

"No, thank you, I won't be here long, but I do have a matter to discuss with you. Do you mind if we close the door?"

"Of course, and please have a seat."

He looked around my office while I closed the door and tried to control my anxiety.

"I had lunch with Sander Drott on Saturday. He wanted to speak with me in private."

As I sighed, he paused and studied me, and I braced myself for what he had to say.

"You're my friend, and I think you should know that one of Drott's major customers is pressuring him to move his accounts from your bank. When he told them he'd been banking with Merchants for decades and was satisfied doing business with you, they inferred that they might consider moving their cabinet business from him if he didn't move his banking."

I took a deep breath, then turned my head and looked out the window, as I realized that it wasn't Dung pressuring him. In all likelihood, Hollis Fitch of Simco Shipbuilding was threatening to move his cabinet business. I heard rumors that he targeted me because of what Julian and I did regarding the *Montebello* accident, which caused Simco to lose profits when they created a disability fund for injured workers. I didn't know how much more I could take between the unscheduled bank audit and customer accounts transferred to other banks. I was in a vise, and the pressure was tightening.

"Thank you for telling me about Drott. You're a friend and a well-respected member of the business community. Unfortunately, the bank has been losing a considerable number of depositors. On Friday, Drott asked a teller about closing his account. I intend to call on him later this afternoon. Have you been approached to move your business accounts from Merchants?"

"I have received no personal pressure to move my accounts, but I know of several merchants who said certain individuals have called on them. I'm here to offer my help."

I took a deep breath and exhaled as his words buoyed me.

"Over the weekend, I met with Drott and several other merchants and reminded them that if it weren't for Julian loaning us money when no one else would help us start our respective enterprises, none of us would be in business today. I told them what you and Julian did to help those injured in the *Montebello* launch and how you supported families whose husbands were killed or severely injured and got them settlements. You should have seen Drott. His face turned red as a tomato, as he lit his pipe, pulled on those suspenders of his, stomped around, and told the group he would reconsider moving his accounts."

"Thank you for your support." I fought to restrain my emotions.

"Drott called me yesterday morning to say he thought he would have to comply with his customer's demand, but when he reviewed the contract, there was a termination clause. So he decided to tell the customer it was their option to terminate the contract. He said he was better off accepting the termination penalty instead of putting up with their coercive gambit. Hopefully, the other merchants will follow his lead."

My throat tightened, and I had trouble getting words out. "That was good of Drott."

"Then we did a little brainstorming and decided to spread the word to our suppliers and customers to inform them about what you and Julian did to help the community and to encourage them to move their banking to Merchants."

I put my hand over my mouth, closed my eyes, and sighed.

"Winson, are you okay?"

I rose from my chair, and as I walked around the desk, Stromberger rose. I faced him, extended my hand, and trembled out the words, "Thank you, you're a loyal friend. I've been going through a challenging time, and your encouragement and support are important to me."

As I took deep breaths, I could feel my eyes welling up. It was comforting to know a few people were on my side. When he left, I walked to Drott's.

He was upstairs in the embalming area. When he saw me, he approached with a smile and extended his hand to shake mine. "Are you here to apply for your old embalming position?"

I laughed and said, "I may need to if I continue to lose more accounts."

"I vow to you that won't happen if I have anything to do with it."

He pulled on his suspenders when I thanked him.

Chapter Four

Tuesday

It was two o'clock Tuesday afternoon, and I was in my office when I heard shouting in Mandarin. I rushed into the lobby and froze when I saw Peggy standing in front of two men.

One was a tall Chinese man wearing a black silk shirt and matching coat and slacks. His black hair glistened from oil, and he was smoking a cigar. The other man was big and even taller, wearing khaki pants and shirt. I recognized them immediately.

The last I knew, Tak was in jail in Ottawa after being apprehended by undercover officers for his attempted murder of Caitlin and me. He had wanted to kill me before I escaped from Dung's logging camp in British Columbia, but here he was standing in my bank lobby with Eng. I couldn't believe what I was seeing and a chill coursed through me.

When Tak saw me, he pointed at the floor in front of him, shook his finger, and said in Mandarin, "Tao Wen Shun, come stand here in front of me."

He was demonstrating his supremacy by telling me to come to him. Peggy turned and placed her hand across her chest.

He was raising quite a commotion, and my staff had terrified expressions on their faces. Two women customers clutched their purses and hugged them to their chests as they hurried out the front doors. Fortunately, there were no other customers at the time. I moved halfway toward them and, not wanting to jeopardize Peggy's life, motioned her to move away, and out of the corner of my eye, saw Anita walk down the stairs to the safety deposit area. I hoped she was going to get Gene, our security guard.

All the staff watched as Tak waved his arm and motioned me. Then, in Mandarin, he said, "Come closer."

I responded in Mandarin, not wanting the staff to understand whatever Tak was to say, which I anticipated would be malicious. "If you want to talk, as long as you're not armed, come into my office where it's private."

"I'm always armed, but I won't shoot you here, even though I want to. But there will come a time when I kill you and your wife."

Then Gene came and stood by my side. He was a tall, lanky man, a decorated WWII Army Sergeant who had served in a segregated unit.

Looking around the bank, Tak sneered and pointed, "I'm standing in your own house, and your workers are terrified."

Gene had his hand on his holstered gun as he looked at me for a signal. I shook my head at him and said to Tak, "How did you get out of jail?"

He mocked Gene as he looked at Eng and pointed to Gene's gun and chuckled. "No one can keep me behind bars."

He looked at Eng again and said, "Police can't hold me, and you'll pay dearly for what you did to me. I know where you live and work."

This was my place of business, and I refused to be intimidated by his threats. I remained silent, and it seemed to infuriate him as his face hardened, and he put his hand into his right coat pocket as Gene released the strap on his weapon.

Needing to defuse the situation, I asked, "Let's stay calm. What do you want?"

"You tried to take away my freedom, I should have killed you at the station, but I have ways to make you lose something even more precious to you than your life. You'll soon see."

He shook his fist at me.

My heart pounded like it was about to burst when they turned and left. I was shaking but tried not to show it as sweat covered my body.

"Sir, are you okay?" Gene asked.

"Thank you for standing with me. I'll be okay, but stay here for a few minutes."

I looked around and said, "Everyone, take a deep breath. I'm going to call the police. We still have a bank to operate, so please go back to work. I'll meet with everyone at closing and tell you what I know."

My first call was to Clive, who said he would call the police and ask for an officer to be posted at each entrance to the bank if Tak returned, and would try to find out how he was released from jail. Clive cautioned me to be on high alert and suggested I start driving instead of walking around town and take Gene with me whenever I could.

I called my friend and Parliament Member, Ellen Jerome. It was with her help that Tak had been arrested in Ottawa. She was shocked to hear that Tak had been released from jail.

I told her I couldn't understand how a court could have allowed his release after the attempted murder of Caitlin. She said someone must have persuaded or pressured a judge to allow for a bond to be posted on some legal technicality. I said Dung had his political connections, and his tentacles reached into all echelons of the government. Miss Jerome said she would make inquiries on how Tak had obtained release. However, if it was legal, there was nothing she could do about it. Her comment was distressing. At the least, Caitlin and I should have been notified of his release since the murder attempt was against us and Tak wanted revenge.

I held a staff meeting to explain my background with the trafficking ring and the events in Ottawa that led to Tak's arrest. I didn't know how they would react, but one after another expressed their support and understanding.

My biggest concern was Caitlin, and I didn't know how to break the news of Tak's release to her. I needed to be by her side and considered going to Pine Isle as soon as possible. But in a way, I was glad she was with Kathleen and out of harm's way and beyond their reach.

Gene insisted on driving me home after work, and I kept looking for Tak and Eng along the way. I asked Gene to walk around the house with me as we checked all the doors and windows before I unlocked the back door and we went inside.

Clive called that evening and said, "The police put out an all-points bulletin on Tak for the threats he made at the bank today but could not assign guards around the bank to protect you without a charge and evidence against Tak. You could hire security guards."

I thanked Clive and didn't tell him that cash was tight due to the loss of customers. So I postponed hiring additional guards and relied on Gene. Mostly, I was hopeful Tak would be arrested before Caitlin came home, as she was my main concern.

Chapter Five

Wednesday

Wednesday morning as the bank opened, Peggy told me that Ari Green, who owned Christie's Boutique, was in the lobby with two other gentlemen, wanting to see me.

"Please take them to the conference room and offer them something to drink."

I closed my eyes and prepared for what I feared I would hear.

When I walked in, Green said, "Winson, I want to introduce you to Max Gilpin, who owns Gilpin's Hardware, and Oscar Mote, who manages the fish hatchery."

I forced a smile as I shook their hands and said, "It's a pleasure to meet you. Were you offered tea or coffee?"

"Thank you. Peggy offered, but we met earlier for breakfast and only have a few minutes. Oscar, why don't you go first," Green said.

He cleared his throat, and I didn't know what to expect. "Winson, we've been talking to other businessmen. Most of them don't know how much you and Julian have contributed to our community," Mote said.

"Townsfolk don't realize that what you and Julian did forced Simco Shipbuilding to offer disability payments to their workers. They think Simco volunteered to provide added benefits. Hans Stromberger set me straight on those facts over the weekend. My cousin broke his back and couldn't work, and he and his family struggled until they received compensation for his injuries. I appreciate what you did," Gilpin said.

"Now that we have the facts, we want to tell others and hope that spreading the word will calm some people in town and even send new business your way," Mote added.

I nodded my appreciation.

Green stood up, took a gentle hold of my arm, and said, "Hollis Fitch and the Metzgers are speaking to certain groups in town, including us, about moving our accounts and loans, but we'll not have any of it. You and Julian stood by us when we needed it. Now it's our turn to stand by and support you."

"We know it impacts the bank when customers close their accounts and move deposits, so tell us who is closing their accounts, and we'll go talk with them," Gilpin said.

I swallowed hard, trying to control my emotions, and wanted to accept their backing in the worst way, but I needed to adhere to privacy laws and banking regulations.

"I don't know if it's legal to do that because there are privacy issues, but I can contact customers who close their accounts and tell them they can speak to each of you. I appreciate your sentiments and efforts. Your support means the world to me right now."

Gilpin nodded his head and shook my hand, then Mote clasped both my hands in his and started to say something but choked up. As he continued to hold my hands for a few moments, it was as if I heard Julian's voice whisper in my ear, "It's a display of compassion. They're feeling your pain."

"I lost my brother-in-law in the accident. What you and Julian did has helped my sister and her children survive," Mote said.

My voice trembled as I gutted out a heartfelt thank you. After they left, Peggy came into my office and asked, "Sir, is everything okay?"

When I told her about the meeting, her eyes welled up.

I rose out of my seat, walked around the desk, and said, "I appreciate how you have supported me. Thank you."

"You made me feel valued when I was being abused by Taylor and Cheek, then went out of your way to stand up for me with Mr. LeBlanc, and were always thoughtful of my feelings and circumstances. I will always defend you and have your back."

"Peggy, I appreciate you more than you know."

∽

It was almost noon when Clive stood in my office doorway and said, "May I come in?"

I came around the desk to shake his hand. "You never need to ask. Would you like something to drink?"

"No, thank you. I'm having lunch with a client in half an hour."

"It's been a good morning. I have been concerned about a loss of accounts and this morning several customers came to see me, and offered their support and said they would spread the word to the community about Julian and my efforts to get Simco to provide compensation to workers injured in the *Montebello* accident."

"That's great. Who was it?"

"Ari Green, Max Gilpin, and Oscar Mote."

"I remember when Julian financed their business loans when other local banks had turned them down. Julian believed in their character, and it's good to see them support you at this time."

"They asked to speak to any customer who was closing their account. I told them I appreciated the gesture but I couldn't provide names due to confidentiality concerns.

"Julian would be proud of you Winson, just as I am." His voice was tempered. "Let's close the door?"

"Certainly."

Looking at him sitting across from me, his expression turned serious as he reached into his tweed sport coat, pulled a folded piece of paper from his pocket, and handed it to me. As I opened it, he said, "I received this certified letter a few hours ago. It's from Benjamin Saez's attorney. Saez has filed a notice of objection with the court. He's contesting the will."

I adjusted my position in the chair, but I couldn't get comfortable. After reading the document, I laid it on the desk, pondered the implications, and asked, "What should I do?"

"I'll oversee the litigation and court hearings. I believe the court will rule that he has no grounds to challenge it, but we'll have to go through the legal process."

"It states that he's challenging based on testamentary capacity, valid execution, lack of knowledge, and undue influence." I read from the notice.

"Those are specific grounds for his challenge."

"I assume I'm the undue influence."

Clive nodded.

"It says he's filing liens."

"While you're in litigation, the liens will cloud title on your assets which were part of Julian's estate. It will prevent you from selling or borrowing money against the bank or the house until there's a ruling from the court that would release those assets."

"When I had the confrontation with him at the house, I saw seething anger in his eyes. There's a darkness in him. There must've been more history between him and Julian.

"Julian never said anything good about him and made a point of having me write an exclusion from his will, as if he expected pushback from Saez."

"Well this is not unexpected because of what Julian told me of his history and conceit. It just comes at a difficult time."

Clive arched his eyebrows, looked at me with concern, and said, "I'll manage him. You have enough worrying about issues at the bank and Tak."

"Thanks. Tomorrow, I'll take the evening train to Ottawa for the Immigration Commission meeting. I'll be back late Thursday night."

Chapter Six

Friday

Friday morning at the bank was uneventful, and I was thankful for a slow day. For a break, I took a walk and was back in the bank before hearing the noon whistle at the shipyards when Anita entered my office and said, "Sir, this envelope was left with a teller. It's addressed to you."

It was sealed, with no return address or stamp, and had my name on it. I pulled out a letter opener, cut the edge, and slid out a handwritten note that read:

> **If you want to discuss an opportunity regarding your bank, meet me today at 4 p.m. at Coppers Pub in Creemore.**

I considered calling Clive but didn't want to bother him on what might amount to nothing, and besides, I wanted him to focus on the Saez lawsuit. I was concerned the meeting might be a setup because the note was anonymous but I wanted to go if I would receive helpful information. Creemore was over the mountain and about twenty-five kilometers away. Since Tak had threatened me and was out of jail, I didn't want to go alone, so I called Gene into my office.

"I have a meeting in Creemore this afternoon. Can you drive me there about 3:30?" I asked.

"Yes, sir, if you don't mind driving that far in my old pickup."

"The vehicle doesn't matter. We can take my car. I want you to go with me. I received a message and don't know who or how many will be there. Please bring your gun, just in case?"

His eyes widened. "Yes, sir, and I'd prefer to drive my truck. It might be old, but she runs like a top."

Gene's truck was a dark blue Ford F-150 with fancy silver hub caps and in pristine condition. I climbed into the cab, and when Gene started the truck, the low growl that came from under the hood was witness to the power that lived there. I looked at him with a smile and said, "Very nice truck."

His smile reached from ear to ear.

We drove through Collingwood, and I noticed the curious stares from passengers in the cars around us. The pair of us, me in a suit and Gene in a uniform, a Chinese and a Black person, riding in a shiny blue truck with fancy hub caps. We must have been a noteworthy sight.

South of town, Gene took the side roads through farms and fields amidst serene rolling hills with subtle beauty and a picture book quality until we came to the Township of Creemore. Anita had told me Creemore had Irish roots, and its name meant "*big heart*." It was a small village tucked away in the Mad River Valley and surrounded by the Purple Hills. The village's history dated back more than a century to when it supplied a growing Toronto with lumber and hogs. Driving into town, there were four old church buildings along the main street and a mix of brick and wood-framed buildings with Victorian architecture.

Three men in denim bib overalls with mud-caked work boots sat on a bench alongside the road. One of them pointed at us, and the other two stood up as they watched us drive past.

Coppers Pub was a converted house at the far end of town set amidst tall pine trees. Gene parked away from two cars in the parking lot, and we scanned the area before getting out of the truck.

"Do you want me to wait outside?" Gene asked.

"I'd like you to come in, but not knowing their policy about accepting you or me because of our skin color, it may be a short visit, so wait here." I looked around and said, "Keep an eye out, and if I'm not back in fifteen minutes, come in after me."

He nodded and said, "I saw those guys we passed in the overalls."

"If you see them again, come inside for me. We both need to stay alert."

When I entered the pub, it was empty except for a bartender washing glasses and a man sitting alone at a table. The man's dark eyes locked onto me. He smoked a pipe, wore a pin-striped suit, and had a dark-red prominent birthmark high on his left cheek. He sat tall in his chair and gray hair curled up around his ears like ducktails.

I approached him and said, "Excuse me, but are you meeting Winson LeBlanc from Merchants Bank?"

"Take a seat."

I had never seen him before and hesitated before sitting.

"I've been waiting for you."

"Who are you, and what's the opportunity you wanted to discuss?"

He remained silent as he looked at me.

"The answer to any person's riddle lies in the past."

I was puzzled at his statement. We stared at each other until we were interrupted by the bartender, who could have been a professional fighter judging from his thick neck and massive shoulders.

He placed a glass of whiskey in front of the man across from me, who said, "Thank you, Conner."

Looking at me with furrowed brow, Conner said, "Is the darkie outside yours?"

"His name is Gene."

"They won't be here long," the mystery man said.

The bartender shrugged his shoulders without asking if I wanted a drink, turned, and left the table.

"You don't know me, do you?"

"No, Sir."

"I'm Darwin Avant, the president and owner of First Simco Bank and Trust."

I looked at Avant and his thin lips twisted into a smile. He lifted his glass with his right hand and circled the rim with the index finger of his left hand. His hands were covered in liver spots. I watched him without saying a word.

"Tell me something close to your heart."

When I remained silent, he sipped his drink and took measure of me.

It was an uneasy few moments until he set the glass on the table, grabbed the arms of the chair, and said, "I called you here to make an offer. Bank regulators are coming from Ottawa to examine your bank's books in a few weeks. I contacted them and am prepared to take over your bank this weekend and reopen it Monday morning as a branch of Simco. We can conduct a peaceful transfer, and if you're cooperative in the transition, there'll be some cash for you."

"Excuse me? What are you saying?"

"I know the status of your capital accounts, the deposit runoff you're experiencing, and the examiner audits from last year."

"How do you know? That information is private."

"When Taylor was president of the bank, he made me aware of certain issues, as well as how you accounted for bad debts," he snickered.

"Taylor? You're in contact with him?"

He looked away.

"He's a criminal, and warrants are outstanding for his arrest for what he did when he was employed at Merchants Bank."

He sipped his drink as he stared at me.

"If you know his whereabouts, you need to contact the police."

"You have immediate and pressing problems."

"We passed all audits and are in compliance, even after Taylor embezzled funds from us."

"You're losing deposits, which could turn into a run on your bank with just a tip to the newspapers. What I'm offering is a clean transfer of ownership to save you embarrassment."

I pushed my chair away from the table, preparing to stand up.

Avant narrowed his eyes and said, "You don't want to turn into another Home Bank? You'd become the second institution to fail in Canadian history."

I searched his face and saw no compassion, only a brutal coldness.

"I want a response!" He hit the table with his glass.

"I don't know where you got your information, Mr. Avant. Merchants Bank is solvent. Like I said, if you know of information on the whereabouts of Taylor, you're obligated to report it."

"You don't' tell me to do anything, ever."

"It was Taylor that embezzled funds and is wanted by the Ontario Provincial Police."

"You're out of your element, boy!"

"I can let the OPP know about our conversation, and I'm sure they would question you."

"Your story would be a figment of your imagination, your word against mine, and who do you think they'd believe?"

He squeezed his empty glass and, in a demanding tone, said, "Conner!"

"This conversation is over." I rose as Connor delivered another whiskey.

Avant narrowed his eyes, then downed the drink, took a billfold out of his coat pocket, dropped it on the table, and said, "My family has been in banking for three generations. It should be Canadians that run our banks." He stood and once again looked me over. "Who do you think you are? If it was me, I'd impose another Head Tax on you people, just like we did after the railroad was completed."

We locked eyes as if two bulls were confronting each other.

"My offer stands until Sunday night."

As I walked away, Connor looked at me like I had sullied his pub.

Outside, Gene was leaning against his truck, and when he saw me, he came around, opened my door, and said, "From the look on your face, it must've been a rough meeting. Is everything all right, Mr. LeBlanc?"

"Thank you, Gene, for being here. It's time for us to go someplace more pleasant."

The encounter stuck in my mind as we drove back to Collingwood. I didn't want to be alone after meeting with Avant, and his words, 'who do you think you are,' kept echoing in my mind. I was a Canadian citizen like Avant, and I owned a bank, a house, and was married to a Canadian woman. We all breathe the same air, and our hearts pump the same red blood to our bodies. As a people, why couldn't we be accepting?

When we were near the bank, I said to Gene, "Can I buy you dinner at the Towne Terrace Café?"

"Ah, Sir, I don't think that's a good idea."

"We'll be together, and I'm friends with Sandie, the owner."

"I don't want to push my luck, and besides, my wife is expecting me for dinner."

I could see how uncomfortable Gene was, and I understood his concern about the reaction we might receive, and it drew me back into reality.

"Sir, to be safe, how about I drop you off at your car?"

I nodded and said, "I understand."

When he stopped, I thanked him and decided to walk the short block to the Towne Terrace. Sandie greeted me warmly and led me to a corner table. As was my habit, I scanned the room and saw Drott sitting alone at a table, and there were several hefty men in khaki work clothes drinking pints at the bar.

"Where's Caitlin tonight?" Sandy asked as she brought me a menu.

"She went with Kathleen to Pine Isle."

"The islands are gorgeous, and the water is so blue. Why didn't you go?"

When I shook my head, she bit her lip, put her hand on my shoulder, and said, "Let me bring you today's special. It's freshly caught Walleye and comes with clam chowder. It'll warm you up, and tonight it's on the house."

I fought the urge to not let her treat me and remembered that Julian told me to accept the goodness of others. "Thank you, Sandie. I appreciate your kindness, and Caitlin appreciates you and the flowers you share with her from your garden."

Her eyes became glassy, then she flashed a bright smile and took hold of my arm. Her cheerful countenance and attitude were refreshing and needed after the Avant meeting.

As she disappeared into the kitchen, the front door creaked open, and in walked Hollis Fitch, Simco Shipbuilding's CEO, and with him was Jay Metzger. Fitch pointed at me and whispered something to Metzger, then they went to the bar and spoke to two gruff-looking men drinking beer, who turned and stared at me.

Metzger and Fitch cast disdainful looks toward me as they left the café. The two gruff-looking men rose from their barstools, walked in my direction, stood on either side of me, glared at me in an intimidating manner, then sat at my table.

I pushed my chair back when I smelled their sweat. The man on my left put his elbows on the table, and a curved pewter medallion around his neck fell out of his shirt. He leaned toward me with liquored breath and said, "You don't belong here Chink. They don't allow yella in this part of town."

The other man had bloodshot eyes and slurred, "You best leave now, and don't stop until you get your ass back to China."

After driving through Creemore and meeting with Avant, I lacked emotional reserve, and my patience was thin. I tried to process the situation before reacting. I didn't want to create a scene or cause a problem for Sandie. It would be safer to leave, but I had enough abusive behavior for one day. I saw myself standing on a line of self-respect which I didn't want to cross. "You can have a brown egg and a white egg, but when you crack them open and put them in a pan, they're the same."

"We'll crack you wide open," the one on my left said as his hands formed fists. My muscles started tingling, and my pulse raced as I tried to slow my breathing. I looked for Sandie, but she was still in the kitchen, and I glanced at Drott, who quickly looked away. I was about to rise and prepare to fight when two other men who were bigger than those at the table came from the bar and surrounded the table. I kept my eyes on the two at the table to avoid getting sucker punched. The larger man put his hand on the shoulder of the man on my left and said, "Hey guys, what are we doing here?"

The man standing to my right snickered and said, "Don't brush against him, or your skin 'll turn yella like his, eh!"

The man sitting on the left leaned away and nodded in agreement as he took a drag on his cigarette.

"My blood's red, just like yours," I said.

The medallion man leaned within inches of my face, and I saw his crooked teeth as he raised his voice. "Your blood will run like a pig's!" He seethed and slapped his right fist into his palm while his friend picked up my spoon and stubbed out his cigarette on it, then dropped it in front of me.

The larger man said, "Do you gentlemen know who this man is?"

"Yeah, a yella-bellied Chink," the man on my left snickered.

"His name is Winson LeBlanc, and you'll have to fight with us first, because of what this man did for our community and even for you."

"He's just a Chink."

"You know about the disability fund we have at the yard, the one that pays us if we get hurt on the job?"

"What about it ?"

"We wouldn't have it without Winson's efforts."

"What's that got to do with anything?"

"This man is the reason our families will be taken care of if something happens to us."

"No shit?"

"If you ever mistreat him, you'll need to deal with plenty of shit from us. Now, treat this gentleman to a pint!"

The man on my left rubbed his chin and meekly said, "Sorry, Sir. I'll tell the barkeep to bring you a pint on us."

The bearded man said, "Now that was pints, the best black stuff, Irish champagne, on you, right?"

"Pints it is, the best in the house," he mumbled.

As they left the table, the bearded man said, "Sorry about that, and also what I did to you years ago, eh."

I silently repeated his words, "Did to me years ago?" I looked closer. Who was this man? In the dim light, and with all that was happening at the table, I hadn't recognized him, but it was the man Caitlin's father sent to beat me, and who abused me at the yard, and who now came from nowhere to save me from a fight.

"Sullivan?"

"Yep."

"I don't understand."

"What don't you understand?"

"What you just did."

"Why did you fight Simco Shipbuilding?"

"It was the right thing to do."

"You answered your own question, eh."

I put my elbow on the table, rested my chin on my hand, and marveled at the change in him.

He nodded, then winked at me, and when the bartender brought me a Guinness, he said, "Another time and place, and I'll drink with yah, eh." Then he picked up the cigarette butt lying in front of me and left with his friend.

I took a few swigs of beer, mulled over the turn of events, and thought of how we become locked in our own belief systems and what it takes to break through those barriers to bring about change.

Then a shadow fell across the table, and when I looked up, Drott was standing before me and said, "Winson, I couldn't help but overhear the conversation between you and those men. I should have been more like Sullivan and come to your rescue. But I was…"

"It's okay. I understand."

"May I sit with you and pay for your dinner?"

"You don't need to do that, but it would be my pleasure to dine together."

Drott proceeded to tell me more of the behind-the-scene tactics of some people in town that pressured him to move his bank accounts from Merchants.

"Can you tell me who?"

"Others like Metzger and Fitch. If you've lived here as long as me, you know who hates most anyone who isn't white."

"What about Avant?"

His eyes darted around the room, and he gave a quick nod. He leaned toward me and whispered, "Did you know that Simco Shipbuilding asked Fitch to resign?"

"No, I didn't. How do you know that?"

"I sold cabinets to them and was told by their purchasing manager."

"Do you know why?"

"I'm sure it was over the compensation fund they had to establish to make payments to those injured from the *Montebello* incident."

When Sandie brought out the Walleye, she waited till I took a bite, then smiled and said, "How's everything?"

"Delicious, thank you."

Looking at Drott and then Sandie, I said, "And I appreciate having good company."

❧

Spending the weekend without Caitlin was distressful. She had only been gone a week, yet I had so many things to talk to her about. But most of all, my heart ached for her. I never considered there would be someone to hold my heart and fill the void in my soul, but she did all of that as well as lift me off the ground when we fell in love.

Catherine was always there for me, so I went to see her and shared what was happening at the bank, Tak's surprise visit, Saez's lawsuit, the Avant meeting, and the encounter at Sandie's. She was supportive and encouraged me to go to Pine Isle and to take time to rest, and when I didn't respond right away, she said, "The circumstances will still be the same whether you go to Pine Isle or not, and it would give you time with Caitlin."

Looking at the piano bench, I remember how this petite blind woman would put her arms around me and teach me the fingering with her hands on mine and how she would listen to me speak and patiently correct my English. She had one of the kindest hearts and purest souls I've ever known. Being with Catherine was my safe haven.

With her wise counsel, I decided to contact the Grahams to make arrangements to go to Pine Isle Thursday morning. When I spoke to Mrs. Graham, she said she would make arrangements to have Kathleen pick me up at the dock in Penetanguishene at ten o'clock. I was excited about taking a few days off and being with Caitlin and began to feel that my life was again under control. I spent most of the weekend cleaning house, preparing for the trip, and anticipating the time with Caitlin.

Chapter Seven

Monday

At six-thirty Monday morning, I went to see Clive to tell him about the meeting with Avant.

Seeing me, he laid the *Collingwood Times* he had been reading on the table and said, "Good morning, I have bagels, and the kettle's on."

"Thank you, I'll have tea."

"Have you seen today's paper?"

"No. Why do you ask?"

"It's not good news." He turned the paper so I could read the headline:

Is Merchants Bank Solvent?

His chin rested on his hand while I read the article. When I looked at him, he ran his fingers through his hair and asked, "Any truth to this?"

I shook my head as I cradled my cup of tea with both hands. "You know about the audit we had due to Taylor and Cheek's embezzlement and the notice of an irregular scheduled audit in a few weeks. Recently, I have been concerned about withdrawals and have met with customers to understand and address their issues. I told you about my meetings last week with Stromberger, Drott, Gilpin, Mote, and Green, and I have been encouraged that we have opened several new accounts and have new loan applications in process."

"So some of their facts are correct, but the context is false. If customers lose confidence, then a run on deposits starts, and it's hard to stop it."

"My grandfather used to say that a rumor goes out of one mouth and into many ears."

"That's quite discerning."

"The timing of this article is too coincidental. I had a meeting with Darwin Avant, President of Simco Bank and Trust, late Friday. I received an anonymous message to meet someone at the Coppers Pub in Creemore. Since I didn't know who I was meeting, I took Gene with me, and he waited outside. When I walked into the pub, I didn't know who he was, and he spoke in riddles for a few minutes. He eventually introduced himself, then made comments about speaking to Taylor, our examiner audits, a run on deposits, and then informed me that he knew bank regulators were coming from Ottawa to examine our books again. He said he arranged the audit and offered to quietly take control of the bank over the weekend and reopen today as Simco Bank. I rejected his offer, told him Taylor is wanted by the OPP, and he was obligated to report Taylor's location to the police."

"Did he say anything else?"

"He said that Canadians should own banks, and the Canadian government should put a head tax on Chinese like they did after the railroad was built. He threatened that a depositor run on the bank could occur with just a tip to the newspaper."

"Like a casual leak to a reporter."

"He also said if I repeated what he said, it would be his word against mine, and who would anyone believe?"

I lifted the paper and looked to see which reporter authored the article.

"Your suspicions are correct about Avant. You met with him Friday, refused his offer, and Monday morning, this *Times* headline appeared. It is intentional meddling to undermine and injure you. But if it precipitates a deposit run, there'll be little, if any, stock value. The Ministry of Finance will take over and bring in another bank."

"Avant alluded to that outcome."

"It smacks of political maneuvering."

We sat in silence for a few moments.

"Clive, what about Avant talking to Taylor?"

"We don't know Taylor's whereabouts, and it would be hard to prove their collusion, but they certainly know each other and have been in communication. We might consider contacting the OPP regarding Avant's disclosure of conversing with Taylor. It would go on record."

"Avant said that his family has been in banking for three generations. Could he have advocates within the Ministry of Finance?

"I don't know, most likely yes."

"Can you speak to the *Times* reporter who wrote this article or the editor, so we can provide the facts and ask for a retraction?"

"I'll contact the newspaper and see what I can do. In my weekend mail, I received notice from Saez's attorney, and he has recorded liens on your assets to cloud title until the will contest resolves. This action restricts your selling stock or borrowing to shore up the bank's assets, not that you would want to, but it's an issue that we'll need to monitor."

I sat in silence to consider the impact of the lien filing. Finally, Clive refilled our cups and said, "The timing of this headline is like throwing out chum in shark-infested waters for the regulators and for anyone you approach to raise capital. Let's hope it doesn't create a run on the deposits."

"Our books are in proper order, so I'm not concerned about the audit unless we lose more customer deposits and face a liquidity crisis. I'm doing all I can to stop the deposit drain. Last week, I met with customers and received a lot of encouragement. I have already put some of my personal funds into the bank to bolster our capital requirements."

"You might want to keep some personal funds separate or in Caitlin's name for protection. I'll contact the *Times* today and pursue a retraction. I need to work on the Saez lawsuit and try to get an early court date. Once it's resolved, the liens can be released. I'll also call the OPP about Taylor and Avant. Call on me at any time if you need me to meet with you and any customers."

I thanked Clive, walked out of his office, and leaned against a wall as the recent events cascaded through my mind. I wondered about Caitlin's reaction to hearing all that was unfolding but didn't want to burden her with more problems, and I hesitated to tell her about Tak's release. Hopefully, there would be some resolution before my trip to Pine Isle on Thursday.

Returning to the bank, I called a staff meeting, discussed the article, and assured them that the news reporter was misinformed. I instructed the tellers, if any customers asked about the bank or the article, to be polite and call me so I could speak directly with them.

Chapter Eight

Tuesday

Tuesday mid-morning at the bank, Peggy knocked on my door, "Sir, may I have a word?"

"Come in and have a seat."

She started fidgeting with her clothes, and when our eyes met, I said, "Is everything okay?"

"I received this letter in the morning mail." She laid an envelope on my desk addressed to her at the bank and postmarked from Newberry, Michigan, with no return address.

"Please read it."

I pulled out one sheet of plain white paper. In irregular printed letters, it read:

> **Soon you'll be sorry you sided with the Chinaman. The time is coming when he will lose everything dear to him and LeBlanc isn't around to save him or you.**

"Oh, Peggy! I think we both know who this is from?"

"Who else would it be but Taylor?" She gripped the arms of the chair, and her face turned red as she looked me in the eye and said, "I am so angry with Taylor, his conduct is meant to intimidate, and I'm fed up and won't stand for it."

"Let's call Clive and the OPP and tell them about this letter. Taylor is still wanted in Canada for embezzlement and if we know he is in Michigan, the U.S. will restart searching to find him."

Her eyes darted about the office.

"You're exceptionally talented, professional, and knowledgeable about bank operations. Any banking organization would value you, but I want you to spend your career with me at Merchants Bank."

"Thank you, Sir. I appreciate your confidence in me. I wouldn't want to work with anyone else."

When I called Clive and told him about the letter, he asked, "Has anyone handled the letter or envelope?"

"Both Peggy and me. Why?"

"The OPP will want to examine them for fingerprints, so don't touch the paper without gloves."

After I hung up with Clive, I called Detective Inspector Albert Picard with the Ontario Provincial Police, who oversaw the Taylor and Cheek embezzlement. He was out, so I left a message, and Peggy returned to her duties as head cashier.

My mind raced, thinking of how Taylor could be working through Avant to destabilize the bank.

Picard called later, and after I told him about the letter and the meeting with Avant, he sent an officer to collect the envelope and letter. He asked me to write detailed notes of the Avant meeting and conversation. He said he would contact the Michigan State Police and request they post notices throughout the Upper Peninsula for anyone with knowledge of Taylor or Cheek to contact the police.

Vengeful people, who feel they have been harmed, do desperate things.

∽

I was in my office about one o'clock when Peggy approached me with a request from an Asian woman named Lysa Wu, who asked a teller if she could see me and was waiting in the lobby. I told Peggy to bring her into my office. She was a striking woman, tall and thin, dressed in a fitted green print dress, who looked to be in her early twenties. Peggy introduced her and turned to leave, but I asked her to stay while we talked and to leave the door open.

Miss Wu looked at Peggy, then spoke to me in Mandarin, "My name is Lysa Wu. I'm from Timmins and am a friend of Wei Lei."

She had striking emerald green eyes, unusual for most Chinese, with long lashes, which she batted at me while handing me a note. It was from Wei Lei, written in Mandarin. It asked me if at all possible to help Lysa and her family.

She had a perfect complexion, stylishly coiffured dark plum hair, and long red fingernails, but wore little jewelry and no rings. "Tell me, Miss Wu, how do you know Wei Lei?"

"Please, call me Lysa." She crinkled her small flat nose. "We worked together cleaning houses in Timmins." She looked more like a fashion model than a cleaning woman.

"Do you know her boyfriend?"

"You mean her husband? Yes, I know Kai. He works in a mine." She looked away and, in a faint voice, said, "You're right to question me. I wouldn't trust someone I've never met, but Wei Lei said because of what you experienced with Kai in Vancouver, you would have a heart for my family's plight."

"Why do you say that?"

"Dung and Tak are after my family and me. Wei Lei said you would understand." Her large and arresting eyes became glassy. "We have no one else to turn to."

I shifted in my chair as Peggy watched and looked uncomfortable, probably because we spoke Mandarin.

"How did your family become involved with Dung?" I asked in English.

Her eyes shifted toward Peggy, then back to me as she responded in Mandarin. "Father worked in a small general store, and mother was an artist. We left China because he didn't want to live under Communism. Father chose to leave first, and we followed. He arranged for the same agent he used to provide false identification and transportation for us. It was frightening for my mother and me on the trip. We didn't know we would be forced to work on the ship. When we got to Vancouver, we met Tak and Dung before seeing father. He had been cooking at the work camp, and after we landed, Dung forced my parents to work in restaurants to pay their debt."

"By the look of your hands and nails, you don't look like you cleaned houses in Timmins."

She put her hands in her lap.

"Mother worked with Wei Lei in Timmins, and I…"

She bit her lip, pulled back into her chair, and appeared agitated as she glanced again toward Peggy.

"Would you like tea or water?" I said in English.

"Water, thank you."

"Peggy, please bring Miss Wu a glass of water."

As Peggy left my office, Lysa carefully wiped her eyes with her fingers, and her eye liner smudged on her cheek. I pulled a handkerchief from my pocket, handed it to her, and as she leaned forward to take it, her sleeve pulled back enough for me to see two marks on the inside of her right wrist. It was two Chinese letters, in a combination I had seen before on women at the Hangzhou docks. YeYe told me it was a branding mark of the sex trade.

When she noticed my eyes on her arm, she pulled her sleeve to cover her wrist, changed position in her chair, and glanced around the office.

"You don't have to let anyone own you," I said.

"What do you mean?" she asked while blotting the area under her eyes.

"I know what your tattoo represents."

She looked over her shoulder toward the door, then looked at me and whispered firmly, "I was only thirteen when Dung violated me. I was forced to take care of men after that." Her voice trailed off.

"We do what we can to survive," I said softly.

She took a deep breath and seemed to hold it as she remained silent until I asked, "Where did you live in Canada before Timmins?"

"We lived in Chinatown near Vancouver while paying our debts, but in 1960 the RCMP, with the help of police brought in from Hong Kong, started raiding businesses looking for illegals like us. We had paid our debt to Dung but feared that he would report us to the RCMP for a reward, so we fled BC along with many others who called it the 'Driving Out.' After moving from city to city, we ended up in Timmins, where we were free until Tak and his men appeared a few weeks ago."

Her story was like mine. When Peggy returned and handed her a glass of water, Lysa seemed bothered. I didn't know what to make of this, so I asked in English, "How can I help you?"

She took a few sips, looked at Peggy, then replied in Mandarin, "Wei Lei mentioned something about an immigrant fund." She lowered her eyes, then dropped her head as she whispered, "Any assistance you could offer my family would be appreciated."

She wouldn't have known about this program unless she spoke with Wei Lei, but I needed to process what I was seeing and hearing, so I said, "Let me consider your situation. Any payments from the immigrant fund must be approved by a board, which meets once a week."

She folded her arms and exhaled.

Remembering my own struggles, I sympathized with her and said, "We can process a financial request if you fill out an application and provide contact information."

She took the forms I handed her from a file on my desk, looked them over, and said, "I move around a lot."

"Are you in town for a few days?"

She nodded, and when she caught my eye, she looked at Peggy, then leaned toward me and said, "Discussing my family's situation in front of others is difficult. Is it possible to discuss our matters in private?"

From my own experiences, I recognized the pain of talking about personal difficulties with those who never experienced our type of circumstances. It took Catherine and then Julian and Caitlin to help me work through those emotions. I paused to consider how to respond, then said in English, "I am married and prefer to discuss business here at the bank. And if needed, either Peggy or I can help you fill out the forms."

Lysa nodded, then rose, bowed before me, and said in Mandarin, "I apologize if I have offended you in any way, it was not my intention."

I rose, met her bow, and said, "I understand much of what you and your family have endured, so let me see what we can do for you."

She faced Peggy, bowed, and walked out.

Peggy was wide-eyed as she looked at me, shrugged her shoulders, and said, "I didn't understand a word she said."

"Miss Wu spoke in Mandarin. It's our native tongue."

"Was I supposed to bow?"

"It's a custom in China but unnecessary in Canada."

"Is that how women dress in China?"

"Only a few dress like Miss Wu. I want you with me whenever she returns to the bank."

"What did she want?"

"She had heard about Julian's immigrant fund. I would like you to work with her if she returns."

"Yes Sir, of course."

I had no way of contacting Wei Lei or Kai to verify her story, and it added to an exhausting week with all my other pressures. I also wondered if Dung and Tak had found Kai and Wei Lei in Timmons.

∽

It was near three o'clock when Peggy came into my office and said, "Lysa Wu is in the lobby again asking to see you."

I was surprised and hadn't given much consideration to what I could do for her and her parents, but remembering the anxiety I endured, I didn't want to put her off.

"Bring her in."

"Before I get her, we had two more customers close their accounts today. They refused to meet you and demanded that the accounts be closed immediately. I'm not sure how you want us to manage these situations."

"Who were the customers?"

Peggy named them.

"Schedule a staff meeting at 3:30, so we can have a discussion of how to respond to customers who are reacting to the *Times* article."

As Peggy turned to walk out, Lysa stood in the doorway, and I was concerned that she overheard our conversation.

Peggy said to her, "I asked you to wait in the lobby."

"I'm sorry, I was anxious and misunderstood. I need to speak with Mr. LeBlanc."

"Peggy, it's okay. Please, both of you, take a seat. Miss Wu, would you like tea?"

She shook her head and pulled folded application forms from her black leather handbag and gave them to me. Her eyes watched my every move as I looked through her responses and noted her Timmins address. I spoke about the purposes behind Julian establishing an immigrant fund and the need to discuss her situation with my co-trustee to see if funds would be approved to assist her family.

"How long will that take?"

"I can't say for sure, but it will involve several discussions and might generate additional questions."

She rose, but in her voice, I sensed something had happened since our morning meeting, so I asked, "Before you leave, I have a question."

She sat and put her purse in her lap.

"Have you been contacted by Dung or Tak since we spoke this morning?"

Without delay, her face hardened, and her body stiffened.

"I know Tak has been in Collingwood recently. Are you still working for them?"

"Thank you for anything you can do for my family."

She wasn't going to answer my question. I chose not to press the issue. "Where can I contact you?" I asked in a quiet voice.

"I'll get back to you."

She didn't bow as she hurried out the door. Peggy looked at me with surprise, then followed behind her. By Lysa Wu's manner, she was concealing something.

～

At the staff meeting, I thanked everyone for their understanding and discussed our efforts to retract or correct the newspaper article. I informed them of the support I'd received from several businessmen who would be promoting our bank to the community. I asked that any customers requesting to close an account be referred to Peggy or me. If they refused, tell them it's Bank policy and tellers do not have authority to close accounts. I addressed questions and mostly assured everyone that we would come through this situation stronger.

I wanted to believe what I was telling them.

Chapter Nine

Wednesday

Early Wednesday morning, I met with Clive, who said, "I talked with the reporter who wrote the article and asked how he obtained the information, but he refused to discuss his sources. Then I asked him how he knew about the deposit withdrawals and the bank audit when Taylor was president. Again, he refused to provide his sources or evidence to verify facts. When I wanted to meet him and provide facts that refuted his article, he hung up on me in mid-sentence."

"What can we do?"

"Send a certified demand letter asserting that the Time's article made false statements of fact and that Merchants Bank would suffer financial harm as a result of their article and demand a retraction."

"What if that brings no response."

"We may be forced to file a lawsuit against the newspaper. We will sue under the *Slander Act* for defamation that slandered our reputation. As a defense, they will claim protection under the Canadian Charter of Rights and Freedoms, which guarantees the right to 'freedom of thought, belief, opinion, and expression, including freedom of the press,' but this right is not absolute."

It was not in my nature to sue, so I said, "I don't want to bring a lawsuit against the *Times*."

"It's something we have to consider to protect the bank. If we don't' protect ourselves, they will continue to publish these types of articles."

I walked to the bank in a dreary fog, and an hour after we opened, Peggy brought me the morning mail. In the mail was a faded cream-colored envelope with no return address but a Collingwood postmark. Inside was a note written in Mandarin which read:

> *If you value your family, meet me alone in Tobermory on Wednesday, 6:00 PM. There will be a telegram at Western Union with directions.*

I knew the note was from Tak or Dung, so I called Clive and read the note to him.

"What do you know about Tobermory?"

"Not much. I know it's at the tip of the Bruce Peninsula and the site of numerous shipwrecks."

"It's quite remote, about 180 kilometers from here. With Tak out on bail, you need to avoid places like Tobermory and focus on going to Pine Isle tomorrow to be with Caitlin."

"Sounds good, but what should I do with the note?"

"There's a new police chief, Kirkpatrick. I talked to him about Tak. Let's take him the letter and see if he has an update on Tak after your encounter at the bank."

The Chief wasn't there when we arrived at the police station. We left the note for him and a translation in English. Clive said he would follow up with Kirkpatrick Thursday morning and for me to enjoy my trip to Pine Isle.

∽

Other than the note I received in Mandarin, Wednesday had been a good day, and I was encouraged because we had made three new loans, two customers had reopened their accounts, and several others were considering moving funds back to the bank. It was late evening, and I was in Julian's office going through correspondence when I heard a loud knock at the door.

When I answered, I was surprised to see Kathleen's parents.

"Mr. LeBlanc, may we have a word?" Mrs. Graham asked.

"Please come in."

"This is my husband, Frank."

"Please call me Winson." When I reached out to shake, he pocketed his hand.

"Please call me Clara."

"Let's talk in the parlor."

Mr. Graham looked around and said, "Fancy place, eh. LeBlanc made a lot of money, charging immoral interest on his loans."

I turned toward Clara, a slender woman with bony cheeks, and said, "I just finished packing for Pine Isle. Please have a seat. Would you like something to drink?"

"We won't be here that long, and you won't be going to Pine Isle," Graham snapped as he sat in a winged back chair, gripped the arms, and avoided eye contact with me as he looked around the room.

He reeked of cigarette smoke, and when he took a pack of Player's out of his shirt pocket, I cleared my throat and said, "I'm sorry, Mr. Graham, but we don't smoke in the house."

He glared at me, then pulled a cigarette out of the package and said, "Do you have an ashtray?"

I stared back. He was a stout, middle-aged man with a barrel chest and short neck and treated me like a lower-class person in my own home.

You could have cut the tension with a knife when Clara said, "Frank, they don't smoke in the house. Remember, Caitlin's pregnant, and they're trying to protect the baby."

He grunted and said, "But she's not..." he stopped and scowled at her before putting the cigarette back in the pack.

Clara was sitting on the edge of the sofa with clasped hands in her lap as she said, "We're here about Kathleen and Caitlin."

"Is everything okay? I hope they're having a good time."

"They're not on the island," Frank snapped.

"What?"

"They've disappeared!" he added.

Without warning, it was as if the moon ceased to orbit the earth, and the world stopped its orbit around the sun. I put my hand over my mouth, and it took a few moments before I came to my senses.

"How?"

Clara said, "I left a message on Sunday for Cornelius Gerow, our neighbor, to have Kathleen pick you up Thursday morning. He called back this afternoon and said that he stopped by Pine Isle on Tuesday on his way back from Penetanguishene and the girls weren't there, but the boat was docked, and the house was open, so he left a message on the table. Then he returned today to check on them, and the same dishes were on the table, and the message was still there. He was concerned, so he went back to the mainland to call us."

I stood and paced about as I tried to process what she said. "Could they've gone to another island?"

Graham stood up and snapped, "Dumbass! Cornelius said they're gone, as in missing! I knew better than to let Kathleen travel with your wife," and he sneered the words "your wife."

I took a step toward Graham with my hands balled into fists, and I was filled with rage. My anger and frustration were about to explode. He was about a head shorter than me. He came at me with one arm in front of his face to block any blows and swung at me with the other fist.

I grabbed his arm mid-swing and pushed him back.

Clara yelled, "Frank, Winson, stop it."

I had to clear my head and could feel the blood drain from my face. I paced about and then stood in front of Graham and said, "What do you mean?"

"You know perfectly well."

"No, I don't. Explain it to me."

"People around here don't like one of ours marrying your kind."

My jaw clenched, and I stepped toward him as I critically repeated, "Your kind! Your kind!"

"Frank! No! Mr. LeBlanc, Winson, please stop. That's not what he meant. You must understand that he's upset. Kathleen's our only child."

"You're wrong," he shouted. "That's precisely what I meant!"

He stepped toward me again, and I welcomed it as my pulse accelerated until Clara stepped between us, with both arms extended. She was in a dangerous position, and instinctively, I knew to step away.

He glared at me with a cold emptiness. "They're missing because Caitlin married you. I don't understand what was in Caitlin's mind. Her parents were furious over what she did."

His face and throat were turning red.

"My wife had two miscarriages and a still-born girl. I'll never forget the tiny casket I made with my own hands for her. It looked like a shoebox. Kathleen's our only surviving child! If anything happens to her," his voice caught in his throat before he was able to go on, "I hold you responsible!"

Clara took a firm grasp of his arm, pulled him into her, and kept herself between us. In a calm tone, she said, "Now, Frank. We're here to tell Winson what we know. The girls' safety is what's important. Nothing else."

Without moving my eyes from his and with my fists still clenched, I said, "What can we do?"

"I told you it was a waste of time to come here. This…this idiot can't be any help at all," he huffed, stomped his foot, took a firm hold of his wife's arm, and said, "We've already said enough! Let's go."

He pulled her with him as he walked toward the door.

"Wait! Wait! Have you contacted the police?" I asked.

Clara stopped in the doorway, lowered her head, looked at me with tears welling in her eyes, and said, "We're driving to Penetanguishene to report them missing to the OPP."

She looked flustered as she said, "We'll let you know if we hear anything."

"I'm going with you."

"Hell no!" Graham said.

❧

My wife and Kathleen were missing. Missing! I couldn't believe it. Pine Isle should have been the safest place for Caitlin. Instead, distress erupted into anguish that exceeded anything I had ever experienced since leaving Hangzhou. I closed my eyes and kept shaking my head because this time of our lives should have been the most hopeful.

My heart was pounding, and I was full of rage at Graham and what was happening to Caitlin and Kathleen. 'What can I do?' kept repeating in my mind as I paced back and forth. Caitlin was seven months pregnant. No one knew where they were. Suddenly the room was too hot, and then I was shivering. Like it or not, I was yoked with the Grahams in a terrible mess.

Trying to collect my thoughts, I needed to settle my emotions and clear my mind. I needed an intervention. I needed Julian and headed for the office. All I could think of was to sit in the chair across the desk from where Julian sat. Then I leaned forward, turned his framed picture to face me, looked into his eyes, and spoke to him out of my distress.

I beckoned him to speak to me. I waited, then closed my eyes, focused on breathing deeply, and told myself to relax more each time I exhaled. I repeated this cycle until I could visualize water flowing over a cliff, falling slowly from the effect of gravity. After a few minutes, I became aware of a calm falling over me like rainfall.

I pulled from my memories and experiences with Julian and knew I had engaged my imagination when I heard Julian say, "This calls for a drink. We need some Scotch!"

I smiled as I rose and opened the cabinet, picked up the Macallan, took out two shot glasses, set them on the desk, then poured one for Julian and another for me. I looked at his picture, and his eyes were clear as a young man's.

"Julian, I raise my glass to you, l'chaim!"

"L'chaim. Take the shot for me, as well as the other for you," I heard him say.

I drew in a deep breath and paused. What I heard was his voice, his tone, his inflection. It was as clear as when we talked together.

I took the shot and it burned all the way down. When I opened my eyes, I looked at his picture and saw his smile. Of course, no one would understand what was happening, nor could I explain it, but none of that mattered.

I wiped my mouth, reached across the desk where I had placed his shot, raised it to him, and said, "L'chaim."

Then I heard him say, "The assistance you require in this situation will come from a Yiddish concept I spoke to you about that means accepting goodness, compassion, and mercy from others. You need to be still, remain centered, and accept what people will do for you."

"But you taught me that your father was a man of action, and I should be that way too."

"It's in your nature to take action, so this will be difficult for you, also because you are a giver, not a taker, but in this situation, you need to accept help. You can't get through it alone."

I was numb, and my eyes were blurry, but I knew he was right.

"Circumstances have robbed you of choice, and you're not in control. Like me after my accident, you'll be dependent on others and not yourself. And, because of your good name, 'Shem Tov,' others will come to your aid."

I heard his words and understood their meaning, but it went against my grain and was foreign to my instincts.

I looked at him and heard him repeat, "Trust. Trust. Trust."

I closed my eyes and thought of Caitlin, our baby, and her delicate condition. I didn't want to go through life without her. She is my rock, my foundation, and my safeguard against hardship and adversity.

"Call Clive," his forceful tone jarred my thoughts.

"But it's almost midnight."

"Call Clive, now." His tone was resolute. "Tell him I told you to call."

"If I tell Clive that you were speaking to me, he wouldn't believe me."

"Call!"

I looked up Clive's home number in Julian's address book, picked up the phone, looked at the clock, then at Julian, looked at the clock again, and then back at Julian. Taking a deep breath, I dialed. When I heard Clive say hello, I said, "Clive, it's Winson. I apologize for calling so late, but Caitlin's missing."

He must have heard the tremble in my voice because he said, "I'm coming over right now. Are you home?"

"Yes. I'm sorry…."

"Julian would've told you to call. I'll be right over. Put the kettle on."

I sat for a few minutes, picked up the empty shot glasses, went to the kitchen, put the Scotch on the counter, and brewed the tea. I added a log into the fireplace to keep the chill out of the air, turned on the outside lights, paced near the front door, and watched out the window for Clive. When I saw him walking up the front steps, I opened the door, and he embraced me.

I rambled until Clive put his hand on my shoulder and said, "Let me take off my coat. Let's sit at the kitchen table, and you tell me what's happened."

We went into the kitchen, and I poured two cups of tea. My hands were shaking so bad that the tea was spilling from the pot.

"Let me do that for you," Clive said as he reached for the teapot.

I told him about the Grahams' visit earlier in the evening and that the neighbor found the boat docked, but Kathleen and Caitlin weren't on the island. I also related what had taken place over the past few weeks, from the hospital visit to driving Caitlin and Kathleen to Penetanguishene.

When I paused to catch my breath, Clive looked over at the bottle of Scotch and said, "I think we need something a little stronger than tea."

"I already had a couple of shots with Julian. Would you like one?"

When Clive's eyebrow arched, I realized what I had said and recognized how comfortable and transparent I was with him, but would he think I was an idiot? My concern evaporated when he said, "Julian used to do that with me on occasions when I needed his advice."

The tension in my shoulders eased.

"Now, pour us both a drink," he said.

As I filled the shot glasses, he said, "Tomorrow morning, we need to meet with Chief Kirkpatrick, the newly appointed Police Chief I told you about. He can contact the Penetanguishene OPP and obtain a copy of the missing persons' report, if one was filed after the Grahams visit. But tonight, we need to brainstorm all the possibilities of what might have happened."

"When Tak came into the bank, he said he knew where I lived and worked. He could have had someone following us.

But I don't know how they could find Caitlin on Pine Isle. Do you think it was Tak?"

"It could be, but don't jump to conclusions."

"Tak also said that I would lose something very precious. I should've gone to Tobermory. Maybe Caitlin is there."

"Beating yourself up won't help the situation."

Taking a sip of Scotch, he said, "Maybe the girls went with someone to another island. We'll ask Kirkpatrick if he can send men to check both Pine Isle and the adjacent islands."

"The Graham's didn't think that was a possibility."

He looked at me and must have seen something in my face as he said, "Pour us another shot."

After drinking the shot, Clive said, "The police can't do anything for forty-eight hours after someone is reported missing. It's going to be difficult waiting for information, news, or a ransom note."

"Ransom note! This can't be happening!"

"Stay with me now."

"Maybe the note we took to the police station yesterday was a ransom note. The Grahams think Caitlin and Kathleen disappeared sometime yesterday morning, and I received the note about meeting in Tobermory today. I should've gone to that meeting tonight. Maybe Tak wants to trade me for Caitlin and Kathleen."

"Let's take a step at a time and prepare for meeting with Kirkpatrick in the morning. He'll want a list of possible suspects."

Clive studied me for a few moments and said, "Get a notepad and write down anyone who could have a motive against you, Caitlin or Kathleen. We'll detail what any motives might be."

This was unsettling, but I knew it was something I had to do. He pulled a pen from his pocket and handed it to me, and I picked up the notepad by the kitchen phone.

"I don't know anyone with an issue or grievance against Caitlin."

"Then focus on you."

"Start with Tak and Dung. They're angry that I escaped from the work camp. Tak has threatened my life numerous times. They still want money from me even though I paid my debt. I guess you're never free from a trafficking ring."

"You should put Saez on the list."

"Taylor and Cheek, and possibly Compton. They hate me for discovering their embezzlement scheme."

"And Peggy got that threatening note."

"What about Darwin Avant. He was certainly threatening at our meeting in Creemore, but would he kidnap my wife to get the bank?"

"He's a manipulative character and certainly has his sights set on Merchant's Bank, but I don't think he would kidnap to get it. He's done a lot of damage with his leaks to the newspaper."

"I'm still going to put him on the list."

"Is there anyone else who has had it out for you?"

"Maybe the Metzger's. Jay's been a thorn in my side for years."

I turned the pad around for Clive to see my list. Running his finger down the names, he looked at me and said, "Good start. What about Hollis Fitch? When we forced the shipyards to create a disability fund, and it cost them profits."

"Did you know that he was asked to resign from Simco Shipbuilding?"

"Where did you get that information?"

"From Drott, he heard it from one of the Simco's purchasing managers."

"Maybe there is justice in this world. Definitely include Fitch."

"Okay."

"Anyone else you think of, add them to the list. Let's call this our working list of suspects. We must consider all possibilities, and Kirkpatrick will work through them and eliminate one at a time. We'll be proactive, even if we need to hire a private investigator, but waiting on others will be hard for you."

"Should I call my Parliament friend in Ottawa, Miss Ellen Jerome?"

"We need to utilize all available resources, and I'm certain she can assist in some way."

I closed my eyes for a moment, and Clive said, "I can stay here with you tonight, or we can meet first thing in the morning at my office with Kirkpatrick."

"I appreciate your friendship and support more than you know. I'll be okay by myself. I already feel bad about calling you at this late hour."

"I would have been offended if you hadn't, and from now on, you call anytime for any reason. Let's meet at my office at seven, and I'll call Kirkpatrick to meet us before you go to the bank. In fact, we should plan to meet every morning at my office until we find Caitlin. Agreed?"

"Agreed. Thank you."

He put his hand on mine as if to consummate the agreement.

Before leaving, he took firm hold of my arms and said, "I meant it when I said to call me anytime."

"Thank you for your support. If you hadn't come over, I might have drunk myself into a stupor."

"We'll get through this together." He patted me on the back, and I watched him walk to his car. When I closed the door, a shadow seemed to fall across me. The house was empty and so was my heart.

In the bedroom, I opened the dresser and pulled out one of Caitlin's nightgowns, held it to my face, and caught a scent of her. The loss of hope pierced my heart. From the moment I met Caitlin, my world shifted, and now, it was shifting again. What would I do without her?

When I picked up our wedding picture, I held it in my hands and clutched it to my chest. I leaned against the wall and slid to the floor, my legs buckling beneath me, and wept.

When I composed myself, I went into the parlor, sat at the piano, and read the music piece Caitlin had been working on, then ran my fingers over the keyboard. I played the first duet Caitlin and I had played for Catherine from memory. When I came to Caitlin's part, I couldn't go on. Without her, it was as if my life was over, and nothing else seemed important.

My mind was in a spin, and I knew I had to think of something else. So I told myself to process what had happened during the day, quiet myself, and try to rest until I met with Clive and Chief Kirkpatrick in the morning.

After a hot shower, I crawled into bed and tried to slow my breathing and relax my body but couldn't fall asleep. My eyelids were like sand against my eyes, and the silence in the room was deafening. My mind raced as I reached for Caitlin and pulled her pillow to my chest, praying that she was safe and would be found.

Watching the clock slowly tick past every hour and hearing every sound of the night and creak of the house in the wind, I struggled to stay in bed, but sleep was futile. Sound sleep would not happen until Caitlin was found. Always touching and in contact with each other, we maintained a sense of where each of us was. But now, I was clueless.

It was still dark when I walked outside and smoked one cigarette after another, and my stomach cramped as every bad memory seemed to come after me. Why didn't I go to Pine Isle with Caitlin? She's the most important person in my life; why did I put the bank first? Why did I let her go when she was obviously upset with me? I wish I could turn back the clock.

Our lives are like the leaves of rice plants in the wind, blown in different directions by forces we can't control. If the wind is strong enough, the whole plant can be torn from the ground. Could I withstand the storm around me without Caitlin?

Finally, I determined to set a place at the table for Caitlin until she returned. I had to remain positive if I was going to survive.

Chapter Ten

Thursday

Walking in the early morning darkness, it was cold and damp. When I entered Clive's office, I smelled freshly brewed coffee.

"Morning, Winson. I knew you'd be early. Coffee's ready."

"Good morning Clive, and thank you for last night."

Clive stood in the kitchen pouring coffee into an oversized mug and said, "Chief Kirkpatrick will be here in a few minutes. When I called him at six this morning, he was more than willing to come by before going to the station. Kirkpatrick is a veteran with a solid reputation. Maybe he'll move Sargent Ellarby to traffic patrol. I'm still angry about Ellarby investigating that bogus rape charge against you. There had to be someone who put him up to it, like the Metzger's."

"We need to add that to the list to tell Kirkpatrick."

"I stayed awake thinking about Caitlin and our strategy. Bet you didn't sleep either. We should consider hiring a friend of mine, a retired undercover Toronto detective turned Private Investigator living in Midland. He's an avid fisherman who knows the 30,000 islands."

"Great idea."

"I'll bring it up with Kirkpatrick."

He handed me coffee and pointed to an open container on the counter. "My wife baked maple scones for us this morning.

She was preparing the dough when I got home last night. Take a plate and try one."

I had no appetite, but I took one to be polite, then a second because they were delicious and might help absorb last night's Scotch. Clive's grin exposed his dimples as he offered a napkin and said, "You liked it!"

"Please tell your wife they're wonderful."

"You have icing on your upper lip," he chuckled.

I wiped my mouth and replied, "I haven't met your wife. What's her name?"

"Her birth name is Eleanor Sue, but everyone calls her Bitsy. You'd better take another napkin," he started laughing as I wiped more icing from my lips.

"These are delicious. Is Bitsy a baker?"

"She could be, she loves to cook, but by training, she's a psychologist." He looked into the distance with a look of affection. "She's only 5'1" and of small frame, hence her nickname. She's cute as a button, with a pleasing personality, and most people adore her."

"She sounds like Caitlin." Saying her name made me turn away to hide my emotions.

"Both of our wives are gracious ladies who have never had an enemy."

"My mother has something in common with Bitsy. She was one of the few women in Hangzhou with a university degree. She used to teach science and math before Mao took over China. Does Bitsy still work?"

"Not anymore. She volunteers her services to those in need who can't afford to pay. She's therapeutic in all her relationships. When I tell her she's the best thing that ever happened to me, and it was my lucky day when we met, her reply is, 'The luck of the drop of the stork.'"

When we heard the front door open, we went to the reception area, where a tall man with a lean physique and sharp facial features removed his hat and extended his hand to Clive.

"Chief Kirkpatrick, thank you for meeting us so early in the morning. Let me introduce you to Winson LeBlanc, the President of Merchants Bank and a good friend."

Attired in crisp uniform, he extended his hand as he approached me.

"Nice to meet you, Mr. LeBlanc," he said with a pleasant smile.

"It's my pleasure, Chief Kirkpatrick. Thank you for coming so early, and please call me Winson."

Kirkpatrick's speech was slow and deliberate, and his handshake was firm and impartial. It seemed every step he made was measured and thought out.

"How about hot coffee or tea and a maple scone? My wife has been baking."

"Coffee, please."

"Black or with milk?"

"I'll go with you. I drink my coffee with milk and a lot of sugar."

They both laughed as we all walked into the kitchen. After getting coffee and scones, we entered the conference room. Clive offered Kirkpatrick the head of the table, and I sat across from Clive.

Kirkpatrick stretched his long legs out in front of him, and said, "Winson, I understand from Clive that your wife, Caitlin, and her friend, Kathleen Chorley, were vacationing on Pine Isle and Kathleen's parents, the Grahams, reported them missing at the OPP office in Penetanguishene. He also said you are working on a potential suspect list. What can you tell me about their disappearance and any events leading up to today?"

He opened a spiral journal and took notes as I went over everything Clive and I had discussed the previous evening. I gave him the list of potential suspects and told him that Caitlin is seven months pregnant.

"I have the letter you received about the meeting in Tobermory. We are checking it for fingerprints, but I doubt there are any since it went through the postal service and you opened it without gloves."

"The meeting was supposed to be in Tobermory yesterday at six o'clock. I should've gone. Maybe they have Caitlin and Kathleen."

"By the time I got the note, it was too late to send detectives to Tobermory. Tak is certainly a suspect since the note was written in Mandarin and he made threats toward you in the bank. He's wanted for questioning and we're circulating photos of him to local precincts."

"What do you make of receiving the note in Mandarin the day after Caitlin and Kathleen's disappearance?" Clive asked.

"We can't assume anything yet." There was a pause of silence until he said, "These types of disappearances typically follow a pattern. Their disappearance might be voluntary, or there could've been an accident, with or without witnesses, or a crime of kidnapping committed for various reasons, often for financial gain. If it's a kidnapping, there'll be some communication and demand for compensation in return for the release of the women. There was no request for ransom in the Tobermory note.

"Initially, we'll search for Caitlin and Kathleen and look for any evidence that may lead us to their whereabouts. Tell me everyone who knew about their trip to Pine Isle?"

"Kathleen's parents, Catherine DeVeaux who teaches with Caitlin, and I assume Kathleen's husband, Patrick Chorley. Caitlin probably told her parents, Maureen and Kierian Mulroney, but I'm not certain."

"In most circumstances, if the intent is for financial gain, there'll be more than one perpetrator, and they'll present a demand for payment in the next few days."

Kirkpatrick's thought process reminded me of Julian and Clive's. I was comfortable with his approach but nervous as he studied me.

"Winson, the hardest thing for you right now is wait on the police to conduct their investigation," Clive said.

Kirkpatrick added, "This is what we're trained to do. You need to contact us immediately if you receive any message or communication from anyone concerning your wife and Kathleen. Don't touch any potential evidence with your bare hands. From now on, everything we discover becomes evidence, so keep that in mind."

When he said, "Everything becomes evidence," it echoed in my mind, and I determined to keep a note of everything. Julian had taught me the journaling process when we investigated the ship launch accident. It was an activity to help me stay focused and keep my mind off my distress.

"My office will be contacting the OPP office in Penetan-guishene to get a copy of the missing persons' report. There is normally no activity until adults are missing for forty-eight hours. With your permission, we can request the file be moved to Collingwood. We have a larger staff than Penetanguishene, and the ladies both reside in Collingwood."

"We would like you to oversee the investigation for Caitlin. Do we need Patrick Chorley or the Graham's approval for Kathleen?" Clive asked.

"That will be between our office and Penetanguishene. I'll be in touch with you both this afternoon after we meet with Mr. Chorley and the Grahams, but now I need to get to the station to open our investigation."

"I know a Private Investigator, who lives in Midland, and his knowledge of the 30,000 islands might help in a search," Clive added.

"I'll keep that in mind. But we usually use our own assets."

"Chief Kirkpatrick, I hope it's appropriate, but I'd like to call a Parliament Member, Ellen Jerome. She protected us with undercover officers who apprehended Tak when we were threatened in Ottawa."

"Absolutely, she may be able to add resources to assist our search. Ask her to contact me." He handed me his card.

Kirkpatrick was a no-nonsense sort of fellow, and I liked him right off. As I left Clive's office and walked to the bank, it was as if every sense of my life was diminished by more than half, and the low clouds and dampness seemed to weigh on me.

At the bank, I went into my office and called Ellen Jerome. I left a message with her secretary, and Miss Jerome returned my call around noon. When I told her about Caitlin's disappearance, there was a moment of silence.

"Miss Jerome."

"Winson, I'm so sorry. I'm in shock. As soon as we end this call, I'll contact the Ontario Provincial Police to request a special investigator from the Toronto office named James Milner, with whom I've worked before. He's top-notch, among the best we have, and I'll ask him to meet with your local police chief first thing tomorrow morning."

I thanked her and called Clive to inform him of our conversation.

"I am glad you called her. I'll let Kirkpatrick know about Milner. Now I have a message from Bitsy. She's expecting you at our house for dinner tonight."

I stumbled on my words, not knowing how to reply.

"You're hesitating. We won't accept no for an answer. Besides, Bitsy's already working on a menu, and you have no choice in the matter. Will six o'clock give you enough time to freshen up after work?"

"Clive, I appreciate the offer, but…"

"It's casual, and she's looking forward to meeting you. See you at six?"

"Thank you."

I didn't want to disappoint him or be disrespectful, as I knew they were doing this to support me.

When I got off the phone, I called Peggy into my office and told her about Caitlin and Kathleen. She put her hand over her mouth and gasped, then wanted to do something to help, but there was nothing any of us could do except wait on the police investigation. I asked her not to tell anyone since the police did not want the media to know because Kathleen's husband had not been notified.

I went through the day in a daze and, on my way home, stopped at a shop for flowers to give to Bitsy. When I walked into my house, I expected to hear Caitlin greet me when I called her name, but there was no answer. The only sound was my solitary voice. As I walked from room to room, I wondered how I would survive without my soulmate. I was incomplete without her. When I entered the nursery, my body began to tremble with fear for Caitlin and our baby. Were they alive? What if she started bleeding again and needed a doctor?

My muscles tightened and my face burned. If she was kidnapped, I wanted to kill the abductors. My anger startled me, and sweat beaded on my face. I needed to shower and was thankful that Clive forced me to be with him and Bitsy for dinner.

Clive's home was a two-story red brick house with a charcoal slate gabled roof located several blocks from his office. It had a wraparound cedar porch and a stained glass entry door and transom.

When I rang the bell, the door swung open, and I was greeted with, "Winson, it's so good to finally meet you. Please come in. Our home is your home."

"Mrs. Owen, it's a pleasure to meet you, and thank you for the invitation." She extended her hand, and when I took it, she clasped it with both her hands.

"It's Bitsy. There are no formalities here. I'm so sorry to hear about Caitlin's situation."

I had no words to respond, so I handed her the flowers, and she thanked me, took my arm, and escorted me into the parlor. She was even smaller than I anticipated, with short brown hair and a ready smile that reached all the way to her soft brown eyes.

"Please make yourself at home. Clive will be here in a few minutes. He has spoken so much of you for years that I feel we're already friends."

"You're exceedingly kind."

"May I get you something to drink?"

"Thank you, but I'll wait on Clive."

"If you'll excuse me for a moment, I need to put these flowers in a vase and check on dinner." She looked at me with a warmth that helped me to relax.

When she left the room, I wandered over to the fireplace and looked at the photographs on the mantle. When she returned and saw me looking at the pictures, she came alongside me and said, "The picture you're looking at is our daughter Ally, with her two children. It was taken on her youngest daughter's fourth birthday."

"Who's the clown next to them?"

"Would you believe that's Clive?"

I started laughing, seeing Clive with a red ball for a nose, orange hair, and huge feet.

"In China, we only celebrate the 1st, 10th, 60th, and 70th birthdays."

"That's very interesting."

"The last birthday we celebrated was YeYe's, I mean, grandfather's 70th. We ate long noodles for longevity."

"I'll bet you miss him."

"I love YeYe, we did everything together, and he and mother raised me."

"How close were you to your father?"

I paused while I mustered the energy to describe our relationship. "Let me say, it was distant. Father had troubling experiences from the war against Japan and never opened up to me or expressed emotion."

"I read of Japanese atrocities committed against the Chinese. Perhaps he suffered from trauma due to the conflict."

As my throat tightened, I managed to choke out the words, "China was another life for me."

When our eyes met, I shifted uncomfortably, looked around the room, pointed to another picture, cleared my throat, and said, "That's a nice picture of your family horseback riding."

"It was at one of the horse farms in the foothills of the Blue Mountains."

"Caitlin wanted to take me horseback riding on several occasions, but I never made the time, and now…."

She gently took hold of my arm. "I know this is a tough time for you."

I heard footsteps on the stairs, and Clive entered the room. Bitsy said in a quiet voice, "I want you to know that I'm here for you."

"I appreciate that."

"Winson, I apologize for not greeting you on your arrival, but I see that you've met my better half."

He shook my hand and put his arm around Bitsy. The Irish fisherman's sweater he was wearing contrasted with his usual business attire.

"I see Bitsy is showing off pictures of our children and grandchildren. She's a terrific mother and grandmother. I'm so proud of her."

She smiled at him the way Caitlin would with me.

"She was the quintessential first child who never did anything wrong and was a significant role model for our children."

"Clive, enough of that." They looked at each other with warmth, grace, and an ever-present twinkle in their eyes.

We enjoyed a wonderful dinner, and my nerves started to relax. When I complimented Bitsy on dinner, she said, "I inherited the love for cooking from my mother. I don't know how to cook in small quantities, so I hope you'll be able to join us often. In fact, I'm cooking something special Sunday evening. Will you and Caitlin join us?"

I looked at Clive, and he cracked a smile and had a glint in his eye, taunting me to dare say no. I was so comfortable in their presence that I said, "It would be our pleasure. Is there something we can bring?"

"Just yourselves."

I thanked her, and she kissed me on both cheeks, and I did the same. It was nice to talk about Caitlin in the present tense.

Clive walked me to the door and said, "Kirkpatrick called to set up a meeting with him and a special investigator named Milner, whom Miss Jerome sent to assist us in the investigation. They will meet with us in his office at seven o'clock in the morning. Come by my office, and we can walk to the police station together."

"I appreciate being invited for dinner, even if you forced me to come. I enjoyed meeting Bitsy. She has a special aura about her, and Caitlin would enjoy her company."

He laughed and said, "She's a special lady. See you first thing in the morning."

On my drive home, I sensed that Julian was responsible for the closeness of my relationship with Clive.

Chapter Eleven

Friday

Caitlin and I had laid in bed only weeks ago, listening as we often did to birds singing to announce the sunrise. She often placed my hand on her tummy to feel our little one kick. At times I could even see the baby move. Lying together was one of the simplest and yet greatest gifts that fate had bestowed.

But now, when sunlight streamed through the windows, the quiet in the house was devastating. It was only broken by my cry for the one who was no longer lying next to me.

The trafficking ring had robbed me of my youth. Was I now to be deprived of my life with Caitlin and our child?

I was a solitary man in a big house without Caitlin, Julian, Virginia, or Rhoda.

∽

I arrived at Clive's office Friday morning, and we walked together to the police station. Chief Kirkpatrick stood in the conference room next to another man and said, "Winson and Clive, let me introduce you to Inspector James Milner."

Milner was trim, medium height, and without any distinguishing features, but he wore black and white shoes which were quite bold. As I walked toward him, Kirkpatrick said, "Inspector, this is Winson LeBlanc, husband of one of the missing women."

"Inspector Milner, I contacted Miss Jerome and want to thank you for joining the investigation," I said.

"Fine lady, Miss Jerome. Glad to help her anytime," Milner replied in a high nasal voice.

Milner tended to hold his head high, giving him the appearance of looking down his nose at everything. It made me think he was trying to imitate Winston Churchill. When I extended my hand, he gave a soft handshake and said with a brief smile, "Pleasure."

Milner shook Clive's hand the same way and sat at one end of the conference table with Kirkpatrick at the other end. Clive and I sat next to each other.

Milner gulped his black coffee like it was water, then lowered his head, and opened a folder lying in front of him. His shoulders were stooped as he leaned over the material, inches from his face.

Kirkpatrick started the discussion. "Since Caitlin LeBlanc and Kathleen Chorley were reported missing in Penetanguishene and the disappearance occurred on one of the 30,000 islands in Georgian Bay, the investigation could be a maritime issue. However, since both women are missing from Collingwood, I contacted the maritime authority and the Penetanguishene Police Chief and asked both to allow us to take charge of the investigation. After they agreed, I sent Detective McGee with two officers to search Pine Isle yesterday.

"There was certainly evidence that the women had been there. Their suitcases were still in the bedrooms, there were dishes on the table, and there was a note on the table from Mr. Gerow advising Kathleen to pick Winson up in Penetanguishene on Thursday morning. So our guess is the women disappeared sometime before noon on Tuesday. There was a boat at the dock, which matches the description you gave of the boat that belongs to the Grahams."

He pulled papers out of a file, placed them in front of me, and said, "Winson, you need to file an official report regarding Caitlin, and Patrick Chorley needs to as well for Kathleen. We've been unable to contact Mr. Chorley, so I called Kathleen's father, Frank Graham, who said Chorley works for Ontario Marine Insurance, travels the Great Lakes region, and comes home on the weekends."

"If you'll complete these forms, we can get the investigation officially moved to Collingwood."

Having to declare Caitlin officially missing caused my hands to shake so bad that I couldn't even pick up the pen.

"Let me help," Clive said as he steadied my hand with his own.

I provided a complete description of Caitlin and details regarding the last time I had seen Kathleen and her, including the date, time, and location.

"Do you have a photo of Caitlin?" Kirkpatrick asked.

When I opened my wallet and pulled out our wedding picture, I slumped in the chair.

"Milner, do you have anything to add?" Kirkpatrick asked.

"I've four items. First, the OPP office in Penetanguishene hasn't started an investigation since the women haven't been missing forty-eight hours. Still, by Detective McGee's report, it appears the women are missing. I'm going to Pine Isle to inspect the island myself, and I also plan on meeting with Mr. Gerow. Second, I'll have the maritime division check adjacent islands for any witness accounts of the two missing women. If nothing materializes, we'll expand our investigation to the marinas along the coastline. Third, I'd like to talk to Mr.

Chorley. From what Mr. Graham said, he doesn't even know his wife is missing. Fourth, the Tobermory note, which I'll discuss shortly."

"Didn't the Graham's report Kathleen missing in Penetanguishene?"

"Yes, and that report will be transferred to us if it's okay with the Grahams. If the Grahams haven't been able to contact Mr. Chorley, is it possible that your wife and Mrs. Chorley are with Mr. Chorley, and no one is missing at all?" Milner asked as he looked at each of us.

"No, because Kathleen said Patrick was going to be out of town for two weeks. That's why Caitlin went with her to Pine Isle," I said.

"Ontario Marine should know how to reach him. We'll contact them today. Now regarding the Tobermory note, Chief?"

"We were not able to lift any prints off the Tobermory message. Yesterday, after our morning meeting, I sent detectives to the Western Union office and retrieved the message. The instructions were for Winson to meet the sender at the Grotto."

"What's the Grotto?" I asked.

"It's a cave south of Tobermory, on the eastern side of the Bruce Peninsula in the National Park. It's a long walk through a dense forest," Kirkpatrick said.

"Chief, you should've sent Winson, used him as bait, made sure he was seen around Tobermory, and then used a disguised Chinese detective to go to the Grotto. But it's too late now," Milner added.

"Absolutely not. I don't want to consider using Winson as bait," Clive said.

"If it's Tak or Dung who'll meet him, they'll know what he looks like, so it has to be Winson," Milner insisted.

"Well, it's a moot point because Winson didn't go to Tobermory," Kirkpatrick said.

"If Tak and Dung were behind this meeting, Winson needs to be the bait to draw them in. Let's see if he gets another note," Milner said.

"If I meet with Tak, he'll kill me."

"How do you know that?" Milner asked, raising his voice.

"He told me so when he was in the bank lobby, and he had the same enraged look he had when he pulled a gun on us in the Ottawa train depot and on me in the logging camp years ago."

"We'll protect you this time." Milner puffed up like a bird.

"Like you kept Tak in an Ottawa jail for attempted murder?"

"I don't know about that."

"Like the RCMP has shut down Dung's illegal activities?"

Milner said nothing.

"You'll need to find another solution. I will not let Winson be bait," Clive said.

"It's not for you to opine counselor," Milner's tone was terse, and he turned his body away from Clive and me.

"Enough, Milner. You're not running the department. I am. Remember, you're here on loan from Toronto. Understood?" Kirkpatrick asked.

Milner looked away, marked some items on a sheet of paper, then looked at me and said, "We'll be issuing an all-points bulletin for your wife and Mrs. Chorley, and if anyone you know has seen them or has knowledge of their whereabouts, they're to contact me immediately." He pushed copies of the bulletin across the table toward Clive and me.

"I want to go to Pine Isle with you," I said.

"No. It's a crime scene. Anything else?"

"Do you think receiving the Tobermory letter the day after their disappearance might be important?" I asked.

"Don't know. I need to learn more about Tak and Dung. At this point, any information could be important."

"Winson, can you show us on the map where their logging camp was in British Columbia?" Kirkpatrick asked.

Kirkpatrick pulled a map from his folder, and I first pointed to the section of the river that it was on and then to Chilliwack, the closest town. Kirkpatrick said he would contact the Chilliwack police station.

There was further discussion, and it was decided to contact and collaborate with the RCMP office in Vancouver regarding Dung. But when I told them of Dung's judicial and political connections in Vancouver, it led to further discussion.

Before Clive and I left the police station, I told them about Lysa Wu's visits to the bank and her connection to Dung and Tak. There was something in my gut about her. Kirkpatrick wanted to question her and said he would initiate a search to locate her. If she came back to the bank, I was to immediately let them know.

"What can we expect?" Clive asked Milner.

"The first forty-eight hours are critical because that's when investigators have the best chance of following up on leads and before people's memories start to fade. As time goes on, there are fewer "breadcrumbs" to follow.

Clive looked at me with a sorrowful expression like he wished he hadn't asked Milner.

"If there are no more questions, thank you for your time, and contact us if you hear anything," Kirkpatrick said.

Clive and I left without further discussion, and I had an overwhelming urge to smoke to relieve stress.

∽

About an hour later, I was at the bank when Detective McGee knocked on the door to my office and introduced himself. "Chief Kirkpatrick told me to tell you that missing person's police reports were issued throughout the province of Ontario, and calls are being made to family, friends, hospitals, and jails. He wanted you to have this."

McGee placed an envelope on the corner of my desk and turned to leave. He paused when I said, "Thank you." But he didn't turn around to face me before departing.

When I opened the report and saw my wife's photograph below the title, 'Missing Person,' I found myself in a twilight state where nothing was as it should be.

No sooner had McGee left when Peggy brought my mail. I flipped through the stack and saw the same faded cream-colored envelope with no return address. I immediately called the police station.

When Milner took the call, I said, "In today's mail, I received another envelope with no return address like the previous Tobermory note."

"Have you touched it?"

"No, but my assistant handed it to me."

"I'll come right away, but keep it isolated."

I sat there imagining what the message contained, and minutes seemed like hours. I was relieved when Milner walked in.

"Where is it?"

I pointed to the mail stack. Milner pulled white gloves out of his briefcase, put them on, gently slit open the envelope, and pulled out a note. Again, it was written in Chinese characters. He unfolded it and said, "Can you translate this?"

"Yes."

"I'll hold it while you read because I don't want you to touch it."

"It's in Mandarin and reads:

> *It is in your best interest to meet me alone, 6:00 PM tonight in Tobermory. Same Western Union location for instructions. No police. Your future is at stake.*

"Can you tell anything from the writing?"

"No. I'm going to Tobermory this time."

"Not my decision. Chief says no," Milner said in a clipped tone.

"My wife is missing."

When I banged the table, it startled him, and he used the phone to call Kirkpatrick. After considerable discussion, Milner ended the call and said, "We'll arrange for an undercover Chinese detective to go in your place."

"It must be Tak. Can't you arrest him for possession of a firearm while he's out on bail?"

He looked at me quizzically. "I'll consider issuing a warrant, but you and any witnesses will need to fill out a police report for the encounter you had with him in the bank."

"That would be Peggy and me. We can follow you to the station and start the paperwork."

He grunted, put the envelope in his briefcase, and said, "Bring Peggy and meet me at the station."

Peggy and I filled out the paperwork, and when we returned to the bank, Anita came to me and said, "Mr. LeBlanc, that Asian woman that was here a few days ago, came in and asked to see you. I told her you were out and asked if she wanted to leave a message. She said she would come back later."

I called Milner, told him about Lysa Wu, and suggested she might be a go-between for Tak or Dung.

All he said was, "Noted."

∽

Just after noon, Milner called and requested that I meet him with the Grahams at three o'clock at the police station. I arrived early and was sitting by myself in the conference room when Milner came in, opened a file, and read silently from a report.

"What's come from the searches?" I asked.

He didn't look up, as he said, "Georgian Bay is like a sixth great lake, and searching for Caitlin and Kathleen is difficult and complex," then he continued reading the document.

I sat in silence until the Grahams arrived. Clara smiled and greeted me while Frank Graham glared.

Milner broke Graham's stare as he said, "Mr. and Mrs. Graham, thank you for providing information on your island and providing access to the cottage. Officers went to Pine Isle Thursday, and I went yesterday to investigate the scene and meet with Mr. Gerow. We're hoping to find eyewitness accounts of your daughter and Mrs. LeBlanc."

Graham put his fists on the conference table and leaned toward him, staring at him intently while he slowly said, "My wife and I wanted to go to Pine Isle Wednesday night, but the Penetanguishene police officer told us not to go because it was a crime scene. So what did you and your men find on our island?"

"The officers took pictures. Let me show all of you the photos."

He laid them out on the conference table for us to see. Seeing Caitlin's suitcase and her clothes on the bed, I cringed.

Clara gasped when she saw the pictures.

Graham grabbed her free hand, then stared at me as he said, "This is your fault."

She jerked her hand back from his and said, "Frank, this isn't Winson's fault."

I was surprised at her statement as he blurted, "Shut your mouth."

Milner intervened, "This meeting isn't about placing blame. We're looking for evidence that leads us to find the women and those who abducted them."

"Abducted," Graham grunted. "Who would abduct Kathleen? She doesn't have any enemies."

Milner cleared his throat and said, "Mr. and Mrs. Graham, we don't know enough about the circumstances and we're trying to gather more information. Speaking of which, we've been unable to contact Mr. Chorley. We've left a message in his mail slot to contact us as soon as possible, and we've contacted Ontario Marine who said he'd been in Thunder Bay and Sault Ste. Marie. Apparently, he's due home this weekend. Have you heard from him?"

"He sells marine insurance throughout the Great Lakes, spends most weeks traveling, but seldom calls, and when he does, it's to speak to Kathleen. But he can't call her on Pine

Isle because there's no phone. We provided this information to Detective McGee yesterday afternoon," Clara said.

"Why are you spending time looking for Patrick when you should be focused on Kathleen?" Graham asked.

"Most kidnappings are for money, so we'll need to know if he or you or Caitlin's parents or Winson are contacted." He looked at his writing tablet, made some notes, and said to the Grahams, "Please look at these photos again. Is there anything unusual or out of place?"

When Graham looked at the photos, he put his hand over his mouth, looked at Clara, and said, "Those marks on the front door are new. We don't normally lock the cottage while we're there, but I imagine Kathleen locked it at night."

"Our on-site inspection confirms there was a forcible entry," Milner said.

A shudder went through me as I imagined several men kicking in the door. When I thought of my seven months pregnant wife being brutally manhandled by her kidnappers, I burned with anger and swore to myself that I'd kill them with my bare hands. But I didn't want to continue with those images.

"Were there signs of struggle?" Graham asked.

Milner took a few moments to answer. I had to hold my legs still with my hands and bit my lower lip, waiting for his reply. Finally, he shook his head and said, "All we have are these photos, and we can't recreate the situation from what we have."

"There's usually a throw over the sofa and another on the chair. We use them as cuddle blankets when it gets cool at night. They're both missing, and the chair appears to be out of its normal alignment," Clara said.

Milner flipped the page of his notebook and cleared his throat, "Do any of you know anyone who might have a motive to harm these ladies?"

Graham crossed his arms and said, "Everyone who ever met Kathleen became her friend. She didn't have an enemy in the world." Then he stared at me, and his face reddened.

"Caitlin, like Kathleen, always treated everyone with kindness and respect," I said.

"But what about you? There's bound to be someone angry with you." Graham snapped.

"You're a bigot who looks down on me because of my race."

"Bigot! Where do you get off calling me a bigot when you're just a pissant chink!"

"Gentlemen, let's focus on the facts," Milner said. "First, we sent notices to all the marinas along the Georgian Bay archipelago. With thousands of miles of shoreline, it's difficult to visit every marina in a brief time. In addition to the islands, fishing cabins present exceptional opportunities to keep victims captive.

"Second, rangers in seven provincial and national parks have been made aware of the disappearance and were asked to watch for the women."

"Do you have any leads?" Clara asked.

"We received a few leads. Nothing positive yet, but we're following up on any information we get.

Milner looked at the Grahams and said, "Mr. and Mrs. Graham, I want each of you to list anyone that comes to mind as a possible suspect. I don't care how remote the possibility. I'm going to check on a few things and will return in about twenty minutes."

"What about him?" Graham said, pointing at me.

"He's already given us a list, but he can review it and make any changes."

"I'll bet it was long. That's where you should start the investigation."

"Please cooperate, Mr. Graham, and work on your list."

"Can we have a private room to do this?"

Milner looked at Graham and said, "Follow me."

Before Clara left the room, our eyes met, and she gave me a faint smile.

I glanced around the spartan room before reviewing my suspect list, but there was no one else to add.

I was in a lonely place.

⁂

My journey to Collingwood and my time in the area had unexpected twists and turns and was anything but settled. Jackson, Catherine, Caitlin, and Julian had turned my life around, but now Julian and Jackson were dead, and my dearest Caitlin with our child was missing. My dreams were shattering like Mother's crystal water pitcher just before I was forced to leave my home in China, and I was losing my grip on hope.

All that mattered to me was finding Caitlin. Dealing with banking issues only temporarily took my mind off her. Without appetite, I worked, went home, drank Scotch, and the few hours I could sleep provided but a brief respite from a persistent numbness.

My patience was drying up, and I was losing focus at work. None of the police leads were productive, and I couldn't contain the feeling that I needed to be doing something constructive.

Without Caitlin, I was unhinged. But then my internal voice heard Julian's comment, "You weren't meant to do this by yourself. You need others to help you through this situation."

My first thought was Catherine, and it was time to tell her about Caitlin. Catherine had been my rock from the moment I met her. I could talk to her about anything, and she loved Caitlin almost as much as I did. So I headed to the Lawrence house.

I opened the front door and didn't hear piano music. Catherine usually gave lessons on Friday afternoon. When I peeked my head into the parlor, she was knitting in her rocking chair and wearing her favorite sweater. I heard her melodic voice, "Winson, what are you doing here? You're supposed to be on Pine Isle with Caitlin."

"I should've come sooner, but I've been preoccupied."

"I can hardly wait to see Caitlin. Why didn't you bring her with you?"

I cleared my throat and couldn't find the words to tell her.

"You know I have a sense about you because you're in my heart, and we're part of each other. Give me a hug, and tell me what's going on. Are Caitlin and the baby okay? I've been praying for both of you, but she's been on my mind for days."

I hugged her, and when she clutched my arms, I choked out the words, "Caitlin and Kathleen are missing."

"Oh, God, no!"

"The neighbor on Pine Isle told the Grahams on Wednesday afternoon, and they told me Wednesday evening. The police are investigating, and a special investigator from Toronto in charge. They suspect a kidnapping, but there's been no ransom note."

I barely got the words out of my mouth when she reached for my hand. After a few minutes, I collected myself and said, "I apologize for not coming to you sooner, but the days and nights have become one, and I've gone from one crisis to another."

She paused to consider all that I had shared, then closed her eyes and said, "Winson, I'm so sorry, and I'm at a loss for words."

There were moments of silence until she said, "Let's have tea and talk. Go put on the kettle."

Surprised by her request, I went into the kitchen, and while steeping the tea, I started to feel my shoulders relax. I was comfortable in the Lawrence house with Catherine. It possessed good memories for me.

I returned with tea and sat next to her. She sipped it and rocked in her chair. When she stopped, she said, "Tell me what you feel?"

"What's happened to Caitlin is because of me."

"It won't do any good to blame yourself or to fall apart from worry. That alone will crush you. There's nothing for you in the place where pity resides."

My eyes welled with tears, and then they ran down my cheeks. When I reached in my pocket for a handkerchief, she said, "It's good to cry, let it go."

I wept. It was easy to release my emotions with Catherine.

She kept rocking, and when my grief ran its course, she said, "We can't control what happens to us, but we can choose how we think and how we react."

"I don't understand what's happening. Everything's a blur. All I think about is the sweet girl I fell in love with who possesses a beautiful spirit. She's gentle, kind, and affectionate.

Why would anyone harm her? God alone knows when, if, we shall see each other again."

"Then, we'll leave it in His hands."

Her presence and words settled my spirit. We sat for a while in silence, and then I said, "Julian spoke to me."

"What did he say?"

"Wait for and accept compassion from others."

When I paused, she said, "Go on."

"Julian said that I needed to wait on the goodwill from others to help me through this situation. It's based on a Yiddish term that means mercy or empathy."

"Julian's right. I rely on you to do things for me. Sometimes it's difficult for me but necessary to accept help."

"But I can't be idle. I need to do something."

"It doesn't mean you become passive. On the contrary, you can still take the initiative. What do you want to do?"

"I want to go to Pine Isle and investigate for myself."

"If I were you, I'd do it."

"But the police said it's a crime scene and don't want me or the Graham's to go."

"Have they inspected the island?"

"Yes, twice."

"Well then, if you go now, it shouldn't contaminate the scene."

"But I don't want to disrespect the authorities."

"Don't sit still like an envelope without any address on it. Just go. And remember, I want to know what you discover."

She tickled me, and we didn't say much else, but sitting with her was therapeutic.

When I was ready to leave, she said, "I've had to struggle with grief and concluded that it's not a sign of weakness. It's the price of love."

"I promise to keep you informed." I hugged her and whispered, "I love you," in her ear.

"I love you too. Always have, always will."

On my way home, I kept repeating, 'Always have, always will. Always have, always will.'

Finally, hope arose from somewhere, and I had a plan of action, and it ignited an energy in me.

❧

When I got home, I called the Grahams, and thankfully, Clara answered the phone.

"I can't think about anything except Caitlin and Kathleen. I'm going to Pine Island. If you're going, we could travel together if you'd like. But I have to go no matter what. I have to see for myself where Caitlin was last."

Clearing her throat, she said, "I...I don't think it would be a good idea for us to go with you. Frank is too upset. I'm going to the market in a few minutes, and I'll drop it by your house with the coordinates on how to get there. You're home, aren't you?"

"Yes, yes I am. Thank you."

When Clara arrived at my house, I asked, "Do you know where I can hire a boat to take me to the island?"

"Go to the marina where you took Kathleen and Caitlin. Talk to the harbormaster. I know there are boats for hire, but they can be expensive for a full day's charter. You'd better go early in the morning if you want to find a charter."

Chapter Twelve

Saturday

Early Saturday morning, I drove to Penetanguishene, and when I pulled into the parking area, my spine tingled as I took in every detail of the place where I had last seen Caitlin. I headed to the harbormaster's office, and the man behind the counter said that it was a busy sightseeing and fishing day for charters, but he had seen Chad Finnegan of Finn's Fishing Charter earlier, and he might be available for a full day's charter for a couple of hundred dollars.

Leaving the office, I carefully noted the surroundings as I headed past the boat launch. The harbormaster's directions led me through a series of wooden docks toward the slip for Finn's charter. As I walked along the dock, I noticed men cleaning fish and tossing the guts into the water. The ducks and cormorants were eagerly waiting for their share of the spoils, and it shook me like a bad omen.

I stood on the dock adjacent to the slip for a sixteen-foot bay boat below an old weathered wooden sign that read *Finn's Fishing Charter*. A tall, bearded man with sun-darkened skin and deep wrinkles was near the stern, wiping the interior.

With a cigarette hanging out the side of his mouth, he glanced at me and said, "I don't have any work, and I don't need no bait."

I cleared my throat and said, "If you're Chad Finnegan, the harbormaster told me I might be able to charter your boat this morning to take me to Pine Isle."

He stopped wiping, looked away, then turned and squared up to me. He squinted while taking a drag, then flicked the butt into the water. "Who are you?"

"My name is Winson LeBlanc. I own Merchants Bank in Collingwood."

"No shit. You're kidding, right? Who put you up to this? That bastard Freddy!" He looked toward a boat behind us and yelled, "Screw you Freddy."

He could have been from the shipyard because his mannerisms, expressions, and language were similar to those men I had worked among.

"No, sir. I'd like to charter your boat to take me to Pine Isle. I have a map and the coordinates. Are you available?"

He cleared his throat, paced back and forth, looked out at the open water, and pointed west as he said, "See those clouds darkening up. This ain't a day for a long boat ride, mister. But we can fish around here." His raspy voice bore the strains of smoking for years.

"Sir, I don't want to go fishing. I want to go to Pine Isle. I have $200 cash in my pocket. Take me to Pine Isle and back. I just want a boat ride and to look around on the island."

"For two hundred, cash? No fishing?"

"You heard me correctly. I propose we get started to get ahead of any weather problems, as you pointed out."

He pressed his lips tightly, squinting his eyes, and his face turned hard.

"Make it $250, and you have a captain for the day."

I didn't want to give him the money and have him start out, then turn around and head back to shore. "$175 now and $75 for a completed trip and your good service when we return to the docks."

"Let me see the cash."

Pulling out a roll of bills, I spread the money like a peacock's feathers. He inspected the cash and said, "Give me the $175."

I counted out $175 and handed it to him. He took it, then turned his head away from me, folded the bills, stuffed them into his pocket, and snapped, "Get your ass in here, but you don't sit near me. Understood?"

"Yes."

When I climbed into the boat, it smelled of dead fish. Before he untied her, I gave him a paper with Clara's directions. He laid out a map of the islands, pointed to a small island, and said, "So we're going here where it says, Pine Isle?"

"That's it. How long to get us there?"

With his finger, he pointed out our route and said, "Without rough water and harsh weather, it'll take about an hour and a half. After we dock, how long ashore will you need?"

"A few hours to look around the Island."

"No more than two hours, or we won't be back until after dark. The sun sets early this time of year."

He didn't ask, and I did not want to tell him the reason for my trip.

"Let's shove off."

As we motored out of the marina, some of the other boat captains and crew started whistling at us, and one yelled, "Look at Finn, he's a rickshaw puller?"

Another jeered and said, "Hey Finny, are you now a sampan?"

He lifted his middle finger and pointed it towards them, pulled his broad-brimmed hat low across his forehead, and lit a cigarette. When we motored past the quiet area between the buoys, he said, "Better put on your raincoat," then he opened the throttle. The water furled behind us as the bow rose and the stern deepened in the water.

I put on my raincoat and buttoned it before the water spray hit me. The captain was like a mute and smoked each cigarette to a stub. He kept to himself and focused on searching the waters ahead as the boat sped forward.

Looking out to the west, the sky was darkening, and a storm seemed to be moving toward us. I yelled, "Finn," and pointed at a growing mass that was now a blackish-gray and had consumed the horizon.

He didn't look at me as he said, "I've set myself against the sea all my life and have always won. Now stay in your seat. I warned you there was a nasty storm forming."

The wind gusted. Its bite cut deep and stopped my mind from focusing on his attitude or the storm. Stretching my arms to release the tension in my muscles and neck, I noted the islands and cottages on our way, which varied from inexpensive frame buildings with wooden docks to elaborate homes with boathouses. I tried counting the islands, but there were too many.

Finn slowed the engine and pointed ahead to an island with a cottage. "That's Pine Isle."

"Can you circle the island before you pull up to the dock so I can look around?"

"Yep. When I bring her alongside the dock, you can get your skinny ass off the boat."

I was unaffected by his coarseness after the language I had heard on the ocean voyage, in the work camp, and at the shipyard.

When we docked, I got off, and he threw a rope, so I could tie her down. After I secured the boat, he leaned back in his chair, put his feet up on the side of the boat and pulled out a fresh pack of cigarettes. He lit one with a silver lighter with the image of a girl dressed in red on it and said, "I'll wait here two hours. Anything more, and I'm gone. That storm won't wait for anyone."

I doubted he would leave because I hadn't paid him the extra $75.

"Might do a little fishin' while I wait."

I was grateful to be on Pine Isle and to look for any signs that could lead me to find Caitlin and Kathleen. I reminded myself that everything was evidence.

The island was beautiful, just as Kathleen and Caitlin had described. I headed to the cottage first and searched for clues that the inspectors might have overlooked. Kathleen's suitcase was in the large bedroom, and her clothes were in the closet and drawers. When I saw Caitlin's sweater in a smaller bedroom, I clutched it to my chest. Her clothes were also hung in the closet and folded in the drawers. Their toiletries were still in separate bathrooms.

It was apparent the girls left without taking anything with them. I looked through their belonging to see if anything was unusual, but seeing nothing amiss, I explored some of the trails on the island.

Two hours later, while walking back to the boat, my failure to discover anything significant during my visit to where Caitlin was last known to be, left me so discouraged that I could not lift my head to look at the boat or Finn. Suddenly I saw something flash in a crevice between two wooden planks on the dock. If I had not been looking down, I would never have seen it.

I took out my pocketknife, opened the blade, and tried to dislodge the glass bead, but it was attached to a chain. I worked it loose and carefully worked nine more unbroken beads attached to a tiny wooden cross. I examined them, then took out my handkerchief, wrapped the beads, and placed them in the pocket of my jacket. I had seen Rhoda with a similar chain of beads which she called *rosary beads*, and often chanted a different prayer over every bead as if each bead represented a person.

Kathleen wasn't Catholic. She attended the Baptist church with Caitlin. So, did she leave them as a clue? Or in a struggle, did she drop them? Or did they belong to one of the abductors?

Scanning the horizon, I vowed to Caitlin that I would find her and would keep the beads until both she and Kathleen were safely home.

Finn yelled from the boat, "Get your sorry ass moving, and we might beat the storm back to the marina. Let's not waste any time. Let's go."

I untied her and jumped in the boat.

"Did you find what you're looking for?" Finn asked as he backed away from the dock.

"Nothing significant. Just some rosary beads."

"Whatever you're looking for must be important if you're willing to shell out $250."

"My wife and her friend were staying in the cottage, and both women have disappeared."

He didn't react or respond but looked straight ahead as he pushed the throttle to full speed, and off we went, buffeted by rough waves and a biting wind. I pulled the beads out of my pocket, opened the handkerchief, and considered what to do with them. Kirkpatrick had said that everything was evidence, so should I turn them over to him?

For me, they were my only tie to the girls, so I put them back in my pocket and fingered them during the boat ride back to Penetanguishene. I found myself praying as Caitlin and Rhoda would, and it seemed to serve as a distraction from my anxiety.

Midway back to land, the storm engaged us, rain slashed against our faces, and the waves rocked the bay boat. I closed my eyes, not against the storm, but against the pain of what I imagined Caitlin and Kathleen were experiencing.

As the storm rolled over us, I was numb, and the waves stiffened. Finn cursed, and his muscles were knotted against the strain as he fought the wheel all the way back to the marina.

When we docked, I paid him the extra money, and as I stepped off the boat, he said, "Hey, LeBlanc."

I turned to face him.

"I hope you find your wife and her friend."

When I nodded, he tipped his hat at me and said, "Anytime you need a boat ride, I'm your man."

It was still daylight on the drive back to Collingwood, and I was caught in a twilight between different worlds. When I arrived home, I was cold and wet, even with the heater blowing full blast in the car.

As I pulled into my driveway, Graham was standing at the curb talking to another man, who was leaning against an older model vehicle. Graham was stomping his feet at my car door before I turned off the engine. The other man a few feet behind was Patrick Chorley.

Graham was red-faced and smoking a cigarette.

"What are you doing..."

Graham interrupted me and said, "Shut the hell up."

Chorley handed me an envelope and said, "Open it."

There was no return address and no postage. "If this is evidence, we shouldn't touch it."

"We've already read it, asshole. Open it," Graham said.

With my handkerchief, I pulled out a folded piece of paper and read a typewritten note:

> **We have your wives and want $80,000 cash in small bills for their release. We'll be in contact to arrange an exchange. No police!**

I took several dry swallows, my throat tightened, and I fell back against the car.

"You're a total dullard," Graham yelled with a scowl on his face.

"Frank, settle down," Chorley said.

"No one's gonna tell me what to do."

Graham glared when Chorley took a firm hold of his elbow and said, "Please Frank, let's focus on getting Kathleen back. We need to work together."

"That's your choice," Graham said as he looked at me, shrugged his shoulders, and huffed.

Chorley turned to me and said, "I can't believe this has happened. This note could've been in my mail slot several days. I could kick myself for being out of touch."

"I haven't received a ransom note and they have my wife too!" I said.

"You shit, Kathleen's missing because of you," Graham said.

I bit my tongue and looked at Chorley.

"What should we do with this?" Chorley asked.

"We need to call the police."

"Like hell we do. It'll put my daughter in danger. Can't you read? The note says no frickin' police!" Graham shouted.

"You know the police are already involved," I said.

"They shouldn't be, and we need to keep them out of it from now on." Graham glared at me.

"When did you find the note?" I asked Chorley.

"I got home about an hour ago."

"I left the house early this morning. I should see if I've received the same message."

"We're coming with you," Graham demanded.

I gritted my teeth because I didn't want Graham in my house. I walked to the front door and looked at the mail slot, wondering how I would handle Graham. When I opened the door, Graham tried to push his way in, but I pushed him back and said, "I don't want you in my house."

"Well isn't that a kick in the ass....he doesn't want me in LeBlanc's house." He waved his arms around and said to Chorley, "This is his fuckin' mansion!"

"Please Frank, just wait here," Chorley said.

I stepped inside, and an envelope had been pushed through the mail slot and was lying on the floor. It was also without postage and had no returned address.

"It's the same envelope," Chorley said as he reached out for it.

I grabbed his arm and said, "Don't touch it. It might have fingerprints."

"Quit wasting time. Open it," Graham yelled from the porch.

"No." I pulled out my handkerchief, picked it up, was careful not to touch it, and headed to the office.

Chorley paced back and forth as I opened the envelope, pulled out the folded sheet of paper, and read the same message.

"It says no police, so what does it matter if we touch it?" Chorley asked.

"The police are already involved. We need their help. They're professionals and know what to do, so I'm calling now."

"I don't want to argue. I just want Kathleen back," Chorley said.

"And I want Caitlin back, but we need help."

"Let's work together to make an exchange. You own a bank. Do you have the money?"

Before I answered, Graham started banging on the door.

We both walked out onto the porch, and I said, "We need to call Chief Kirkpatrick."

"Hell no!" Graham said.

"Don't be stupid. The police investigation is in full force." I raised my voice as if that would help get through to him. When he set his jaw, I said, "I don't care what you do, but I'm going to call my attorney."

I tightened my muscles and expected to engage in a physical fight with Graham as he puffed up his chest, and when he took an aggressive step toward me, I planted my feet, clenched my hands, and said, "My wife is missing, and she's seven months pregnant."

"Then produce the money, and we can manage this by ourselves," Graham said.

"I'm not doing anything without consulting my barrister."

"Why don't we go with you to see him now," Chorley said.

"It's Saturday. I'll call to see if he's available." I went back into the house and called Clive. When he took the call, I explained what was happening. After I hung up, I returned to the porch and said, "Clive Owen will meet us at his office, 150 Hurontario. I'll meet you there. I want to put on some dry clothes." I didn't want to be near Graham.

"I don't know where his office is, so come with us. I'll drive," Chorley said. Before I could say anything, they walked toward his car.

I put the letter in a satchel, changed my clothes, locked the door, and headed to Chorley's car.

Graham was leaning against the car and barked, "Hurry your tight ass up, let's go."

I was about to confront him when I heard a growl and turned to see black lips curled back from bared teeth that nipped at me before the owner yanked the dog away.

Graham's laugh was wicked.

"What the hell are you doing?" I asked the man holding the leash and wondered if he could be involved with Caitlin's disappearance?

"He's a young dog that I'm training. He's not dangerous." He pulled hard on the leash and continued on his way.

Chorley's car was old, with exposed rust and chipped paint. I sat in the back seat amidst empty cigarette cartons and trash on the floor, and the car reeked of smoke. It looked as if he lived in the car for years. We drove to Clive's office, and none of us said anything while we waited outside Clive's office. I rubbed my thigh and the rosary beads in my pocket, nervously working them in my hand.

When Clive arrived, I introduced Chorley and Graham.

"Let me see the ransom notes."

We showed him the identical messages, and I said, "Mine doesn't have fingerprints, so look at Chorley's."

"Aren't you the smart ass," Graham said.

"Have you called Chief Kirkpatrick?" Clive asked.

"They don't want the police involved, so we came to you as a compromise."

"I'm going to call Kirkpatrick and have him meet with us to analyze the notes."

"Like hell you are, it's my daughter's life at stake," Graham said.

"It's my wife we're talking about, and I don't want to put her life at greater danger." Chorley raised his voice.

Clive studied Graham and Chorley, then said, "That's fine, but you may be charged with perverting the course of justice. We need to have the police analyze these notes. And I might remind you that Kathleen and Caitlin are in grave danger. They've been missing for four days, and the police have no substantive leads. These messages are the only contact we've had from the kidnappers. This will change the direction and focus of the police investigation."

Chorley whispered to Graham, who grunted, then nodded, and Chorley said, "Ask Kirkpatrick if he can come to your office now."

Clive called Kirkpatrick, and after hanging up, said, "He's coming right over."

It was an uneasy twenty minutes waiting for Kirkpatrick, and when he arrived, he said, "Good afternoon, gentlemen." Kirkpatrick looked at Chorley and said, "Are you Patrick Chorley?"

"Yes."

"Where have you been for the past week?"

"I was traveling from Thunder Bay to Sault Ste. Marie. I sell marine insurance for Ontario Marine and am on the road much of the time.."

"Do you have proof?"

"I have hotel and restaurant receipts. Are you accusing me?"

"No, but we need to cover all bases. Please bring them to the police station. Now, let me have a look at the notes."

Clive pointed to the notes on the table.

"I opened mine with my handkerchief."

He nodded at me in approval, then said, "Mr. Chorley, have you touched your note?"

"I didn't realize I shouldn't touch it. I didn't know Kathleen was missing."

"If any of you receive notes in the future, follow Winson's lead and don't handle them directly, and call us immediately."

"Follow Winson's lead, eh," Graham said.

Kirkpatrick put on white gloves before examining the notes, pulled out an envelope, and slid both notes in before removing the gloves.

Graham stood and said, " Nobody has anything against Kathleen." He pointed at me and continued, "but he owns a bank and a big fancy house, and you know how people around here feel about his kind. It's his bloody fault this has happened."

"Our focus is to safely rescue Kathleen and Caitlin," Clive said.

Graham raised his voice like he was in his bully pulpit. "Well, hell, look to him for the damn money. He's got it, and we don't. Let's get this over with because I want my daughter back."

I pushed back my chair, stood up, balled my fists, and my face burned. Graham was crude, had no respect for me, and now demanded that I put up all the money. Then Graham rose, followed by Chorley.

Clive took hold of my arm and said, "Winson, Mr. Graham, Mr. Chorley, we all need to remain calm. Everyone is under stress."

I was about to explode in anger, so I stepped back to distance myself. Striking Graham would not help Caitlin.

"Let's remain calm and take our seats," Kirkpatrick said. No one spoke until he added, "We'll need to discuss the ransom, but not today."

"The note says, 'No police.' Can't we do this without your involvement? It's too dangerous for Kathleen," Chorley said as Graham nodded his approval.

"Mr. Chorley, we're already involved, and everything, and I mean everything, has to go through us from this point forward. Is that clear?"

Chorley slumped in his chair and looked away.

"Is that clear, Mr. Chorley?"

He nodded.

"Mr. Graham, is that clear with you?"

"Hell."

"Mr. Graham!"

"In the interest of saving my daughter, I'll keep quiet for now. But if something goes wrong, I'm going to be looking for you."

"Mr. Graham, we need your cooperation, not your threats. There's not a lot we can do until we know the terms of the exchange. If any of you are contacted, you'll need to call us immediately," Kirkpatrick said.

"We can manage this by ourselves. If we give them the money, we'll get Kathleen back. We're not contacting you anymore. Simple as that," Graham said.

"It's not that simple. You shouldn't take matters into your own hands. You'll put yourselves in danger, in addition to the ladies," Kirkpatrick said. "I'll have the letters and envelopes analyzed. I doubt there are any detectable prints on Mr. Chorley's note, but hopefully, there'll be something on Mr. LeBlanc's. If you receive any unmarked letters, don't touch them, and contact us immediately."

"Prints would sure be helpful," Clive said.

"That'll be all for now until we receive the results," Kirkpatrick said as he picked up the evidence envelope. "Mr. Chorley, you can either come with me to the police station for questioning, or I'll send Inspector Milner to your home."

"I'm not going to the police station, and Milner better be in plain clothes and in an unmarked car because I don't want police seen with me or at my house."

"He'll be out of uniform and at your home within the hour," Kirkpatrick said. Graham and Chorley left without saying a word, and Kirkpatrick was right behind them.

Clive asked me to stay, and after everyone left, he said, "I don't want you to be alone tonight, so come home with me for dinner. I won't take no for an answer. Have you eaten today?"

"No, my mind hasn't been on food."

"That's what I thought. And I want Bitsy to look at that bite."

I was exhausted and didn't want to be in my empty house. "I accept."

Not much was said on the drive home. After I thanked Clive, he said, "You come when you're ready."

Alone in the house, I thought about the ransom payment and wasn't sure I could produce it because I had added most of my funds to the bank's capital account to offset deposit withdrawals, trying to avoid a liquidity crisis. We had lost more customers after the negative article in the *Times*, and if a deposit run developed, it would force me to raise capital quickly and discretely.

I stood in a hot shower until my bones warmed, then dressed and drove to Clive's house for dinner.

Clive and Bitsy welcomed me and led me into the parlor where Bitsy had appetizers on a coffee table and poured us wine as the phone rang.

Clive excused himself and returned a few minutes later. "I apologize, but that was a client with an urgent problem, and I'll be gone for about an hour or so, but eat without me."

He kissed Bitsy on the cheek as she lowered her head. "After all these years, I expect disruptions like tonight. But, as you know, Clive is extremely loyal to his clients. I'm glad he chose law over medicine, or I might have ended up feeling like a widow."

"You married a good man."

"He's the man of my dreams."

"I feel the same way about Caitlin."

"Our daughter went to the same school as Caitlin, so over the years, we've seen her grow into a beautiful woman. How did you meet her?"

"We met through Catherine DeVeaux's piano lessons."

"Ah, interesting." Her smile warmed my soul, but I was exhausted from the day's events and found it especially hard to talk about Caitlin.

"Clive said you haven't eaten, so please take some hors d'oeuvres."

I started nibbling and sipped wine when a clock chimed seven times. It was a large, free-standing clock against the far wall, made of walnut with intricate woodwork and a beautifully-designed face.

"That grandfather clock was a wedding gift from Clive's grandfather, Wallace, who started the law firm."

"It's magnificent. It reminds me of my grandfather. He made beautiful hardwood musical instruments, and I helped him in his workshop. I wanted to be like him."

She nodded. "Wallace was a lawyer known for his integrity, and Clive takes after him."

"Like YeYe."

"YeYe?"

"That's Chinese for grandfather." I didn't want her to open a conversation of my family, so I asked, "How did you meet Clive?"

"We met when he was in Law School, which changed my life. He's a kind man who values me."

"Tell me more."

"I'm sure I can share some of my history before Clive returns, but next time I want to hear about yours."

"Agreed. I enjoy people's history, everyone's life is unique, and it's an education for me to hear about their lives."

"It's a good character quality to take an interest in other people. I'll start with my parents, they lived in Hamburg, Germany, near the North Sea. Mother's birth name was Lazarus."

She caught the surprised look on my face. "That's right, my mother was Jewish, so I'm Jewish."

"But Clive is…"

"He's as English as they come, and my father wasn't Jewish."

"How did their marriage come about?"

"The story goes that one weekend, my mother went to a café that overlooked the Elbe River. A man asked her to dance, and three weeks later, she married him, and nine months later, I was born."

"That was fast! Mixed marriages can be difficult."

"Clive told me about your in-laws. I'm curious, how do you think your parents would've reacted to Caitlin?"

"Father would've disapproved, but Mother would've loved and accepted her, as would my grandparents. Caitlin changed my life for the better. Without her…."

She took hold of my arm and squeezed, and I took a deep breath and caught myself from becoming more emotional. Her expression was full of compassion. I barely knew her, but like Catherine's, her presence was soothing.

"In love, we realize who we want to be." She was sincere and genuine.

"Meeting Catherine and receiving her acceptance, followed by Julian and Caitlin, all turned my life around. They became my family."

"You've certainly endured difficult conditions, and you'll get through this one too. Grieving takes its toll. I'm sure you haven't been sleeping well."

"Sleepless nights have become routine."

"We all want to be in a warm and welcoming place. So our door is always open to you, day or night. Clive and I want to do everything we can for you and Caitlin."

I realized I was sharing as much as she was. She had a gentle manner, so the time went quickly as we talked. We were both surprised when the kitchen door creaked open, and we heard Clive's footsteps. When he entered the parlor, he said, "I could use a drink."

"Were your ears burning? We were talking about you," Bitsy said.

"I apologize for having to leave. My client had a thorny issue for me to address. It looks like you haven't started dinner. You must've enjoyed the time visiting." Clive said as he took her hand, and they shared a smile born from a deep love for each other.

"I've kept the food warm, so pour yourself a drink, and I'll have dinner on the table in a few minutes."

After Bitsy went into the kitchen, I told Clive about going to Penetanguishene, chartering a boat to Pine Isle, and finding the rosary beads on the dock. I pulled them out of my pocket, handed them to him, and said, "Do you think these beads might be an important clue?"

"Could be. Are the Graham's Catholic?"

"Not to my knowledge. Caitlin goes to the Baptist church with Kathleen."

"Have you told Kirkpatrick?"

"No, do you think I should?"

"They're probably not important. The police did a thorough search of the island and undoubtedly would have taken them if they were evidence."

"I held them in my hand and prayed during the boat ride back to the marina. There's a comfort holding them."

"If they help you, keep them. But you should probably tell Kirkpatrick."

Bitsy called us to dinner, and after eating, I thanked them for the food, but more for their company and support, and excused myself.

Returning home, I had a certain calm from the day and evening activities even though Caitlin's circumstances were unchanged.

Chapter Thirteen

Sunday

It was half-past seven on Sunday morning when I went to see Catherine. Although she couldn't solve my problems, I valued her council, and being with her would be calming.

I opened the front door and heard, "Winson, welcome. I'm in the kitchen with Joseph."

I knew Joseph Lawrence as a very private man when I rented the loft with Kai and Jackson. He preferred to be alone and never spoke unless spoken to. Before Wei Lei worked for him, he ate alone and kept to himself. But when Wei Lei started cleaning the house and cooking for him, he asked Catherine to join him for meals. Then he invited Wei Lei and Kai to live in the loft and asked Kai to maintain the house and the grounds.

As I walked into the kitchen, Lawrence said, "How did you know it was Winson?"

"By his scent."

Lawrence quizzically said, "You could actually smell him?"

"We all have a scent, even you, Joseph."

Lawrence crinkled his nose and let out a belly laugh. It was one of the few times I heard him laugh.

"Welcome, Winson, we're having tea. I'll pour you a cup," he said.

"Thank you."

"Do you have news of Caitlin?" Catherine asked.

When I hesitated, she said, "You can speak in front of Joseph."

"Winson, if you'd be more comfortable just speaking to Catherine, I can excuse myself," Lawrence said.

"Winson, I want you to tell Joseph about Caitlin. He was City Clerk, and before that ran a newspaper and may have some suggestions."

"Mr. Lawrence, the police told me not to tell anyone, but Catherine's one of the few people I confide in. Caitlin and Kathleen Chorley are missing."

"Oh, no. What happened?"

"They've been kidnapped. I came to tell Catherine that Patrick Chorley and I received ransom notes yesterday."

"What's the status of the police investigations?" he asked.

I told them about the initial searches and my trip to Pine Isle. "The kidnappers asked for $80,000 for their release."

"$80,000," Catherine said as she cleared her throat. "Are you and Mr. Chorley and Mr. Graham going to pay the ransom?

"Chorley and Graham don't have the money, and because of several issues, I don't have immediate access to $80,000."

"What about the money you inherited from Julian?" she asked.

"Julian's cousin, Benjamin Saez, filed a lawsuit contesting Julian's Will, which has tied up all my assets."

"Can you borrow money from your bank?"

"We've experienced an unexpected number of deposit withdrawals over the past few months, and before the Saez lawsuit, I had to use most of my inherited funds to augment the bank's liquidity. I've not taken a salary for the past six weeks, and I'll need to stop funding Wong's search for my parents. I'll meet my obligations one way or another."

"Oh, Winson, that's terribly unfair," Catherine said.

"I was surprised when I read the *Times* article about Merchants Bank last week," Lawrence said.

"Clive Owen is trying to get the paper to print a retraction. Since Julian died, we've had quite a few customers close their accounts. I've been meeting with customers every day over the past few weeks, and just when things were turning around that *Times* article came out. I suspect it was initiated by Darwin Avant, head of Simco Bank, because he met with me last Friday in Creemore and offered to take over Merchants Bank, and I refused him."

"I know Avant and expect he didn't offer you much, if anything, for the bank. He's always operated like a shark. I can't help with the police investigation, but I can provide some community history."

"Joseph has been City Clerk for decades. Before that, he ran a newspaper," Catherine said.

"Mr. Lawrence, I value anything you can offer."

"Please call me Joseph," he said with a smile.

I straightened in my chair and said, "Thank you, Joseph."

"There are, shall I say, several special interest groups, who gather together to protect their collective interests. Members are drawn from the upper and middle classes, and many join for the benefits of common aid and security. Membership includes professionals, small-shop owners, and tavern-keepers who impact the machinery of local government and administration and can exert pressure on police, magistrates, and even juries."

"I'm not naïve. I know there's part of the population that hates minorities, and I know of outside influences on the police, which result in some crimes going unpunished."

"Joseph, more than most, knows about those types of inner workings around Collingwood," Catherine said.

"I'm concerned that someone or group is boycotting the bank because I'm Chinese. A bank teller told my assistant that a customer closing his account said the only possible thing worse than having a Chink own the bank would be a Nigger."

"How bad is the situation?" Catherine asked.

In response to her question, I filled them in on what was going on at the bank.

"I might be able to help with the depositors. Let me speak to a few friends. But your primary focus should be on your wife and child," Joseph said.

"I'd gladly exchange my bank ownership for Caitlin's safe return, but my immediate need is to come up with $80,000 to pay the ransom and hopefully secure her release."

"You said Kathleen's husband can't help?"

"He sells marine insurance throughout the Great Lakes, drives a beat up old car, and they live in a rented bungalow. He found out Kathleen was missing yesterday when he returned home from a business trip, and a ransom note was in his mail slot. He didn't know what the note was about, so he called the Grahams looking for Kathleen. When he and Frank Graham came to my house, they were terribly upset. Unfortunately, neither of them have money to pay even part of the ransom."

"I can help and want to go through this with you," Catherine said. She cleared her throat. "I can withdraw the money from my trust fund, enough to pay the ransom. I don't expect or want you to pay me back."

After only a blink of hesitation, I said, "Thank you, Catherine, but that's not something I would consider."

"Excuse me!" She raised her voice along with her eyebrows. "Why not?"

"I can't let you risk your life savings and would never want you to do something that could affect your ability to stay in Joseph's house."

Joseph cleared his throat. "You'll never have to worry about that happening. Catherine has a life estate in this property, so technically, it's hers as long as she lives. Besides, I need her company, and we look after one another."

"Winson, I insist," Catherine said with finality.

I heard Julian's voice in my ear, encouraging me to receive, but I couldn't accept her money to pay the ransom.

"I'd never forgive myself if I jeopardized your future in any way."

"Father planned for my life when he would no longer be around to look after me. I seldom withdraw money from the trust because I make enough from teaching to support my lifestyle, and I watch all my pennies."

I swallowed a couple of times. "Catherine, I couldn't ask you to do that, but I'm overwhelmed by your offer."

"Nonsense. You're not asking me. I'm telling you. Besides, we all need to be pragmatic. The shadows of life are getting shorter for me."

"I don't want to think about you not being here." I couldn't bear the thought of losing her and Caitlin. It would devastate me.

"When I'm gone, the money I have will be yours and Caitlin's. So I'll go into your inheritance now to pay the ransom. But, before I pass, I want to see Caitlin safe and at home with you and your baby."

"I want you to live for a long time and won't jeopardize your future. I'll find another way to get the money."

"Now you're avoiding what I want to give you. Julian told you to be open to receiving."

I was having a challenging time dealing with her generosity and persistence. "The trust provides for your future, and I can't let you touch it."

"I'm doing it for my future, and that future is you, Caitlin, and your newborn. You're my family, my offspring, and family does for family. I'll call the bank trust officer tomorrow and tell them I want to withdraw $80,000."

Before I could say anything, she continued, "Enough said."

I leaned over and kissed her on the cheek. She took a firm hold of my arm and said, "From now on, update us daily. Is that understood?"

"Yes."

When I looked at Joseph, he smiled because he knew that there was no way to refuse her request when Catherine took a stand on an issue.

"Joseph, do you know the current editor of the local newspaper?" I asked.

"I've never met Joseph Sylvester, but I know someone who does. Like Catherine said, for a time, I was a newspaper editor and heard and saw a lot. A small-town community paper is different from a big city like Toronto because there's no investigative journalism. Instead, it's a community service to keep everyone tied together. Regarding your situation, I know of some groups who disapprove of your owning Merchants Bank."

"Because I'm Chinese?"

He nodded.

"Joseph, don't hold back. Tell him more."

"Certain parties are pressuring others to bank anywhere other than Merchants Bank. Understand that there's something sinister just out of sight. It's a stealth world beneath the surface that maneuvers in gray areas where the authorities can and do look the other way."

My eyebrows rose, and I asked, "By authorities, do you mean the police and judges?"

"Yes."

"And you know this how?"

"From a newspaper editor that I worked with years ago."

"Not all police are dishonest. Have you met the newly appointed head of the Collingwood OPP, Chief Kirkpatrick?"

"Not yet, but I've heard comments that he'll make a fine police chief. For decades around here, there's been a tradition of don't ask, don't tell. A lot of criminal behavior has been concealed."

"How does that happen?"

"Groups tend to be clannish, and when people attain a certain level of wealth and influence, they come to believe they're entitled to it and will do everything they can to protect that status," Catherine said.

"That clannishness, with its dark underbelly and dirty little secrets, has been the status quo for a long time. But because of favors, it's progressed to 'if you squeal on me, I'll do the same or worse to you,' and it's created a self-sustaining system," Joseph said.

"What do you suggest?"

"I have a retired newspaper friend named Alex Berry. He was an editor for thirty-two years and knows more about the people in this area than anyone. He might be able to give us some ideas. Come with me to visit Alex."

I appreciated Joseph's offer, but my mind was fixated on Caitlin and raising the ransom. Catherine broke my thought process when she said, "If Joseph says so, you should go with him."

Joseph gave me a look like YeYe did when he told me to do something for my own good. I turned my eyes away and said, "I apologize. I have so many issues at the bank to contend with, but Caitlin is foremost on my mind. Could we meet him today, so I don't have to take time off work?"

"He lives in Wasaga Beach and we'll be there several hours. Let me call and see if he can meet us."

"I'm ready when you are."

While we waited for Joseph to call Alex Berry, Catherine said, "I want you to open your eyes and realize that throughout history, you don't get to be the dominant class because you're nice."

"I'm experiencing that."

Joseph returned to the kitchen carrying a bottle of Jameson Irish Whiskey and Catherine said, "Get to it, men."

We got in his car, and Joseph put the box on the floorboard of the back seat. "This is a little something for Alex."

On the way, I asked, "How did you meet Mr. Berry?"

"I met Alex when he was editor of the Barrie Daily, not spelled the same, and I wrote some articles for him. We stayed in contact over the years, and then he retired to Wasaga."

When I looked out the window and saw a long sandy beach that stretched for miles, I knew we were approaching

Wasaga Beach. We turned left onto a side road that crept along the shoreline, then pulled into the gravel driveway of a wood-framed house with a small front porch bordered by white hydrangea. The setting from the front was modest, but between the houses, I could see the white sandy beachfront meeting up with the clear blue water of Georgian Bay.

When we got out of the car, a cool crisp wind was blowing off the water, and the sky was filled with puffy white clouds in the aftermath of yesterday's storm. We walked to the front door. Joseph knocked, pushed it open, and called, "Alex."

"About time, Joe, come in. The door's always open, eh."

Joseph closed the door behind us, and we entered a large room with drawn curtains that shut out the glorious view of Georgian Bay. The only light was from a small table lamp and the fire burning in a large fireplace made of river stones. The wooden floor creaked as we walked toward a man sitting in a leather recliner with a plaid blanket draped over his lap. He had high cheekbones, thinning silver hair combed back from his high forehead, and ashen skin. He had a gravelly voice, wore a shabby robe, a cigarette was in his left hand, and a cup of tea in his right.

"The wind, she's been blowing like that for three days."

Joseph sat next to Alex, gripped his hand, and said, "It's been too long my friend."

"You know my door's always open for you."

"I want to introduce my friend, Winson LeBlanc."

Alex glanced my way.

"Young man, Joe here speaks highly of you, and that doesn't come easy to him."

"Alex, I brought a little something for you," Joseph said.

"What is it?"

"Eighteen-year Jameson Whiskey."

"Ah, a man after my heart."

Alex's eyes followed Joseph as he set the bottle on a small table.

"Winson, share some of your history in Canada with Alex."

When I finished telling him how I got to Collingwood, he said, "I've heard Chinese gangs are cruelest to their own kind. By the way, call me Alex, most everyone does," his face looked pained as he repositioned himself in his recliner. "Drink?"

"I'm driving, but I'll pour one for you and Winson," Joseph said.

"Nonsense. You brought Jameson, and one should always enjoy good whiskey, eh. But save the Jameson for later. I have an open bottle of single malt in the kitchen." Alex winked at me. " Joe, bring three glasses, a pitcher of water, and the whisky bottle that's on the shelf above the counter. Misery loves company, and besides, you can drink coffee before you drive home."

"Alright, Alex."

"Winson, go and help Joe."

I passed a rectangular table with an assortment of awards, and behind it, the wall was full of mounted photos of Alex holding awards. I paused for a moment and recognized a few important people in the pictures.

I carried the water pitcher and whiskey as Joseph cradled three glasses in his hands. When Joseph poured the drinks, Alex said, "If that's mine, there ain't enough whiskey in it."

Joseph added whiskey, then Alex lifted his glass and said, "Cheers."

It had an earthy taste that lingered and was warm going down.

He stretched out his feet from under the blanket. He had on socks but no shoes or slippers. "Boys, better take off your shoes. Visiting's always better in socks."

"We'll keep ours on," Joseph said.

Alex's fingers were long and thin and wrapped around his glass.

"When did you switch to Bunnahabhain single malt?" Joseph asked.

"I'm a Scott, was brought up on it." He chuckled, then added, "A friend turned me on to it, but it's hard to come by. Some say it's an acquired taste, but I liked it from the first sip."

"Thank you for meeting with us," Joseph said.

"So Joe, our meeting today is supposed to be a secret, but it isn't because I told my girlfriend."

"I can't believe Estelle's still with you."

"Yep."

They both laughed.

"Estelle sold advertising for Alex."

"She took care of me at the paper and now. We've been together close to twenty years."

Alex turned quiet for a few moments and said, "Joe, the time we worked together was the best of my life."

"What? Rotten food and being at work by four every morning."

"But it helped pull me out of my swamp of boredom. I relished discovering newsworthy stories. Like the story we ran about the cemetery for black pioneers and how their graves were desecrated and the tombstones were stolen and used for building projects?"

"Many blacks are still concerned about going out on dark Saturday nights."

Joseph's eyes turned glassy as he looked fondly at Alex, who pointed at his empty glass, and when Joseph dutifully refilled it, he smiled.

We sat looking at the fire until Alex said, "Son, will you take a big log and put it on the fire so that it'll burn most of the night and there'll be coals to start the fire again tomorrow. You understand I can't chop my own wood any longer."

I picked up a large log and laid it on the small fire. When I sat, Alex raised his glass and said, "Gentlemen, let's toast to the criminal element! It gives reporters plenty to write about. Cheers."

He perked up in his chair, lit a cigarette, and asked, "What do you want to discuss?"

Alex laid his head back while listening to Joseph provide the background between Julian and me and Merchants Bank, the disappearance of Caitlin and Kathleen Chorley, the ransom notes, Avant's offer to take over the bank, and the *Times* article.

When Joseph stopped talking, he was quiet, and I wondered if he had fallen asleep.

After a few minutes, he said, "I wanted to be an investigative journalist, but with a small-town paper, you needed to get along and keep people together, so I had to look the other way many times. Certain groups had behind-the-scenes control, which gnawed at my sense of ethics and contributed to my alcohol indulgence. When I retired, I didn't want to see those people, and I mostly shut myself off to the world. I did succumb to my vices of drinking whiskey and playing poker."

He shut his eyes for a few moments and said, "Joe, did you say Kathleen Chorley?"

"Yes."

"Is she related to Patrick Chorley?"

"He's her husband."

"Kathleen's his only asset. Poor girl has a jerk for a father and a mother who is a saint to put up with him. I've played poker with Chorley. Seen him a few times in a weekly game with a barber who can take care of more than just your hair. Chorley revels in raising the stakes, doesn't like to lose, but then none of us do."

"Where do you play?" Joe asked.

"Mostly in the back of the barbershop, but he organizes some high-stakes games at a lodge up north. I played a couple of times in the big games, but they're too rich for my blood. I only play in the local $100 buy-in games, and figure if I lose a hundred, it's okay because it's entertainment, and you never know what interesting information you'll pick up."

"Do you mean the barbershop called Mick's outside Wasaga's city limits?"

"Yeah, that's the one. Mick's been running the shop for over thirty years, knows everything happening in town. I'm sure he's involved with more than poker and haircuts. He's a big brute with rotten teeth who wears a wedge cap, and he'll give you any haircut you want as long as it's a brush cut. Usually wears a sleeveless undershirt that hangs over his big belly with a cigarette hanging out the side of his mouth and keeps a water glass filled with gin. Wouldn't let him cut my hair if it was free, though I've been known to sit in his chair for a shave and to hear gossip."

He paused and looked at his hands as he went on, "He's very good with a blade, if you know what I mean."

He paused to finish off his glass and continued, "He came from Italy on a Navy boat through the St. Lawrence Seaway, settled in Toronto, then moved to the Blue Mountain area.

"For years, I've heard about some big money poker games in the area," Joseph said.

"Do you know anything more?" I asked.

Alex leaned toward me, and his eyes were cold as steel in winter. "You might want to have the police investigators check out Mick Mezzetti. I heard your new police chief is a straight-up guy." He fell back into his chair and shook his finger as he said, "But leave me out of it."

He closed his eyes, and his breathing became rough. "Sorry boys, at my age, after the second or third Scotch, I start to sag."

My heart started to race, and I wanted more information from Alex, so I tapped Joseph on the shoulder and whispered, "Is there some way we can ask Alex a few more questions?"

"Maybe the Jameson will loosen his lips," he whispered.

Alex opened his eyes and said, "Still here. What day is it?"

Joseph laughed and said, "I didn't bring eighteen-year Jameson to age on the shelf."

"You know I would never refuse a good whiskey like Jameson and your company. So let's drink. I'll take mine neat." He adjusted the blanket and straightened in his chair.

Joseph opened the bottle and poured three shots. Alex lifted his glass to Joseph and said, "To our newspaper days."

We each downed our shot.

"Alex, Winson is running out of time to find Caitlin. Can you tell us more about the gambling?" Joseph asked as he refilled our glasses.

Alex took a sip, curled his lower lip inward, then squinted and stared. "There's a weekly high stakes game, plenty of booze, and women. Mick's over six feet tall with a square jaw, menacing stare, and the loudest person you'll ever encounter. He controls the games and seems to bring in an unlimited supply of heavy bettors. I understand there's plenty of protection at the high stakes games, if you know what I mean. He's connected with some evil characters and knows where the action is."

"What do you mean?" Joseph asked.

He closed his eyes, shook his head from side to side, and said, "Sordid activities. I should've done something about that long ago when I ran the paper."

Alex stopped to pull a cigarette out of a Marlboro pack and light up. A giant ashtray was on the table next to his chair piled high with cigarette butts. He adjusted his thick, black horned-rimmed glasses, which made his eyes look bigger.

"What about Chorley?"

"He's a two-fisted plunger with a big ego. Mick and he are idiots and chew on each other to see who has the highest opinion of themselves, but Mick can play Chorley like a fiddle. I've only seen Chorley when I play in the local games. He wins some and loses some, like the rest of us, but he's a poor loser."

When Joseph looked at me and I mouthed, *the newspaper*, and pointed toward Alex, he nodded.

"Alex, the *Times* is running articles without verifying the facts, which are detrimental to Winson's bank. They're not open to printing retractions or providing their sources. Joseph Sylvester, the GM, won't talk to Winson's attorney, and I don't know him. Can you do anything?"

Alex didn't respond.

"Alex, I could use the favor." Joseph produced the most serious look I had ever seen on his face.

Alex pulled the blanket that covered his legs up to his chest and said, "I'll see what I can do. Sylvester owes me."

"What are those?" Alex asked as he looked at what I was doing with my hands.

Unconsciously, I had pulled out the rosary beads and was fingering them to try to calm myself.

"When I went to Pine Isle looking for clues, I found these wedged between the boards on the dock."

"Bring them closer, so I can see them better."

I took them to him, and he held them in his hand. "Mick has some just like them. He would pull them out before the last card was drawn in a game, praying for luck, I guess."

Joseph's eyebrows raised as our eyes met. Was it time for me to tell Kirkpatrick about the beads?

Alex pulled again on his blanket and stared at the fireplace.

"It's time for us to go. Thank you, my good friend," Joseph said.

Alex looked at me and said, "You owe me."

"Thank you, Alex. I appreciate your help, and you let me know if you ever need anything," I said.

"Good luck, son."

"Joseph, don't stay away too long. I don't have much time left."

Despite Alex's condition, I had the feeling he took mental note of every detail.

When we were in the car, Joseph said, "You need to ask Chief Kirkpatrick to investigate Mezzetti, his game, and his connection to Chorley. Just don't tell him where you got the lead. I'm

sorry we didn't talk more about Merchants Bank. I'll call Alex tomorrow and see if he called Sylvester."

As Joseph dropped me off at home, I said, "I don't have the words to express how much I appreciate your support."

"Call on me anytime and at any hour."

"Thank you, Joseph. And please tell Catherine what we learned from Alex."

I called Clive and told him what Alex said about Mezzetti and Chorley, Alex's promise to call Sylvester at the *Times*, and that Joseph would continue speaking to Alex about what was happening behind the scenes.

Clive told me to call and tell Kirkpatrick about Mezzetti and Chorley.

Chapter Fourteen

Monday

I had been awake for hours when the phone rang at 6:30.

"Winson, have you seen the morning paper?" Clive asked.

"I was about to leave for the bank. The paper's still outside."

"Look at the front page. I'll wait."

There must have been bad news because Clive would have told me if Caitlin had been found. I went outside, picked up the paper, and saw the headline:

Two Women Kidnapped
$80,000 Ransom Demanded

I was faint seeing it on the front page with Caitlin, Kathleen, and Merchants Bank photos. My hand shook as I picked up the phone and said, "I can't believe this is in the newspaper. How did the information get out?"

"As soon as I saw the headlines, I called Kirkpatrick, and he said, 'It was leaked and endangers the….'"

I interrupted, and my voice quivered, "Clive, I need to tell Caitlin's parents before they read the paper. I'll speak to you later."

"Wait. Who have you told about the kidnapping?"

"Ahh, ahh, Peggy, Catherine, Joseph Lawrence, and Alex Berry, but none of them would have disclosed information about the kidnapping to the paper."

"We'll deal with this. You call if you need anything."

I called Mulroney's house and could tell I had woken Maureen. I didn't want them to learn of the kidnapping from reading the paper or from friends. It was better that they heard it from me. I asked her to wake Kierian and told them about Caitlin's disappearance and the ransom note. I assured them the police were doing everything possible to find Caitlin and Kathleen. Maureen's voice was shaky, and Kierian called me a son of a bitch. Their voices were distressed, and when Maureen asked me to meet them at their home for coffee, I agreed to see them at 8:30.

Before the bank opened, I called the entire staff into the conference room, told them about Caitlin's disappearance, and showed them the morning paper. I could see the disbelief on their faces, and one by one, they offered their encouragement, thoughts, and prayers, and several expressed surprise that I could still function and run the bank.

∽

It was a short drive to the Mulroney house and a sudden chill and quiver of apprehension shook me as I climbed the front steps. I paused before knocking on the door, feeling unprepared emotionally for the conversation and Kierian's reaction. Maureen greeted me and looked over her shoulder before inviting me into the kitchen. I smelled freshly brewed coffee, but the aroma was overcome when Kierian came in from the backyard, smelling of cigarettes and liquor.

Maureen served me coffee as Kierian leaned against a counter and said, "Nice of you to tell us our daughter has been kidnapped. How long have you known?"

The atmosphere was explosive, and I understood we were all under stress. Before I answered the question, Maureen intervened, "Please, let's have coffee, and you can tell us what happened."

I started by telling them about the searches and the ransom letters.

"Why did you let her go to Pine Isle when she's pregnant and just out of the hospital?" Kierian snapped.

"Dr. Franklin said it was okay for her to go, and Caitlin insisted. I was going to join them last Thursday."

"You're an idiot. You've put her life in danger."

"Kierian, stop. You're not helping the situation. We're in this together." She stared at him like a mother with a defiant son.

Kierian opened the refrigerator and took out a pint of Guinness, popped the cap, and took a drink. No one spoke for several minutes until he shook his finger at me and said, "I blame you for Caitlin's disappearance!"

He uttered a string of swearwords, and I understood his anger because I was angry and wanted to yell profanities too, but it wouldn't solve anything. I was sorry Kierian had relapsed back into drinking. It had been challenging to build a relationship with him, and now it was like watching a dam burst.

When he made an aggressive move toward me, I rose, braced myself, and put out my hand to stop him. He turned halfway around, looked at me from the side, cocked his head, and the light showed on his hardened face, revealing his anger.

"Do you know what the fuck you are?"

I didn't respond.

"Any child you bear with Caitlin will be a half-breed. Do you know what that makes you?"

I looked at Maureen, and her face was ashen.

"Do you know what that makes us?"

Maureen rose, and stood face to face with him, stomped her foot, and said, "Stop it, Kierian. Stop now! You're not helping."

He stepped toward her, scowled, lifted his hand, and threatened a slap. She stepped back as if struck, put her hand over her mouth, and took a deep breath. I could see she was on the verge of tears.

When he turned towards me, his face was inflamed.

"Because you have money and own a bank doesn't change a thing between us. You caused her to marry out of her culture, her faith."

"You mean out of your culture and your faith."

"When she married you, she closed a bloody door that locks from the other side."

He stood and was quiet for a while before saying, "I don't want to speak to you ever again. I don't want to hear from you, understood? As far as I'm concerned, you don't exist, and I want nothing more to do with you. Maybe Caitlin will finally tire of you, come back to her senses, and return home. Now, get the fuck out of my house!"

"No, no! He's a good man. He's Caitlin's husband," Maureen screamed.

"Shut up, bitch."

She approached him, but he pushed her away, and as his cussing continued, tears flooded her face.

"Winson, please stay."

"Maureen, thank you for the coffee, but I'm only making matters worse being here. It's time for me to go."

Before leaving, I said to Kierian. "I'm sorry. I wanted to tell you as soon as I knew about Caitlin, but the police asked me not to tell anyone to protect Caitlin and Kathleen. Don't take your anger out on Maureen."

"Get out!" Kierian yelled.

I walked out and closed the door behind me as I heard Maureen weeping. Driving away from their home, I tried to process what had occurred. Kierian had reverted to who he was at the shipyards. My heart ached for Maureen because I had to leave her alone to deal with Kierian's anger, but I needed to focus entirely on Caitlin.

∽

Shortly after I returned to the bank, Anita came into my office and said that Mr. Gilpin and Mr. Mote were in the lobby and wanted a word. I went to the lobby with her and greeted them.

Gilpin said, "Ari called us early this morning and told us about your wife and Kathleen Chorley. We wanted to express our concern personally and let you know we've posted pictures of them in our businesses and ordered flyers to give our customers."

Mote added, "The flyers should be ready this afternoon. We'll have some delivered to the bank. It's not much, but we wanted to do something. If there's anything else we can do, please don't hesitate to call on us."

I thanked them, and they both hugged me and said they were praying for me. It was all I could do to maintain my composure.

A half-hour later Gene escorted Graham and Chorley into my office. Gene was holding watch over Graham.

Graham looked at me and said, "Lose the nigger."

Looking at Graham, Gene said to me, "Sir, do you want me to stay?"

"No, Gene, we'll be okay."

"I'll be outside the door if you need anything."

"Please close it behind you."

"What the hell happened that the paper printed headlines about the kidnapping and ransom demand?" Graham huffed.

"You know as much as me."

"You Chinese shit, you aren't telling us what you know!"

I didn't respond. Chorley squirmed in his chair, and his eyes wandered around the room.

"What about the money?" Graham's voice rose.

"We should each contribute," I said.

"Neither of us has that kind of money." He became red-faced, looked at his son-in-law, and repeated in a loud voice, "We told you that before. You own this bank and a fancy house. You can afford the ransom. What are you, a Jewish Chink! And it's your fault that Kathleen's missing." He stood and took a step toward me, and I could smell his rancid breath from alcohol and cigarettes. He yelled as he pointed at me, "I'll kill you if my daughter isn't returned safely."

Gene opened the door. "Are you okay?"

Anger flooded me as I stood, gripped Graham's hand, squeezed hard, and didn't let go. He winced from my grip and seemed smaller as I looked at him and said, "If something happens to Caitlin and our baby, I won't want to live, but I'm not responsible for what's happened."

It galled me that Graham treated me in such a derogatory manner. When I let go, Graham took a few steps back, pulled out a cigarette, and started to light it. I had enough and demanded, "This meeting is over, you need to go."

Graham stepped toward me again as I prepared to confront him, but Gene grabbed his arm and said, "Enough. You heard Mr. LeBlanc. It's time for you to leave."

I stepped back and leaned on my chair.

Graham continued to glare at me while trying to pull away from Gene.

"Frank, go outside and calm down. We need to stay focused on Kathleen. Nothing else matters," Chorley said.

When Graham stopped fighting Gene, he shook his shoulders.

Chorley's voice cracked as he said to me, "I'm sorry, but we don't have much money. You need to understand, my father-in-law is a burnt out old man who lives on a pension, and I'm a salesman and live off commissions." He cleared his throat, wiped his mouth with the back of his hand, and in a low voice said, "We need your help. Isn't there something you can do?"

When I didn't reply, he continued, "I apologize for our behavior."

When he said that, I looked at Graham, his eyes widened, and his nostrils flared, and he said through a clenched jaw, "He doesn't speak for me."

Chorley lowered his head and said, "We're all under stress, eh. My wife is missing, just like Caitlin, so we need to put our heads together and talk about what we can do."

He looked at Graham and said, "Frank, we need him. Let's work together."

With that comment, Graham walked out without saying a word, Gene followed him, then Patrick, in silent acquiescence, started to follow, but stopped in the doorway, turned around, came back into the office, and stood in front of me. "We need to work out something. I'll do anything to get Kathleen back."

He rubbed his bloodshot eyes and wiped his chin on his shirt sleeve when Graham, with Gene at his side, came back to the doorway incensed and said, "What are you doing with him?"

"Talking," Chorley muttered. "We need his help."

I made no promises, and they left together.

Caitlin's life was at stake, and the newspaper headline added more pressure. It was up to me to step up with the ransom, but how would I raise it? Would I have to take the money from Catherine? She wanted us to have it and called us her children. But if things went awry with the abductors, I couldn't jeopardize her trust, even with Joseph's assurances.

∽

My joints ached, the constant tension took a toll on my body, and the time with Kierian and Graham drained me.

I had a pounding headache, unusual for me, and needed to clear my head, so I told Peggy I was going home for an hour or two to get my mail and check on a few items. Before entering the house, it had become my routine to walk the grounds and check the house's perimeter. Without seeing anyone, I opened the front door and picked up the envelopes on the floor that were pushed through the mail slot. One envelope had a Taiwan stamp, which I recognized immediately.

I checked the locks on all the doors and windows and went into Julian's office, opened a cabinet, took out a bottle of Macallan Scotch, poured a shot, drank it, and enjoyed the burn all the way down my throat.

Sitting at the desk, I poured a second shot, took out Julian's letter opener, slit the envelope, and pulled out Mr. Wong's letter. With trembling hands, I read:

Dear Mr. LeBlanc,

I am so sorry to hear about the passing of Julian LeBlanc. I will continue to work for you under the same arrangements. Regarding your inquiry about the probability of getting your father released, Pai contacted a person in authority. In his discussions, $5,000 was mentioned to attempt his release. Unfortunately, an illicit market exists for this type of engagement, and we have no leverage, influence, or assurances.

If you want to pursue his release, I will need this additional money, but I stress that there is no guarantee.

Pai said it was too risky to locate Kai's parents because of his grandfather's military service to Chiang Kai-shek. There is a bounty for his capture and death to anyone who assists him.

There is no added information regarding your grandfather. In all probability, he has passed away. We haven't been able to locate your mother, because it is challenging to check all the villages in the remote mountain regions, but she is likely teaching peasants.

We did find that your sister is in the service of Lin Biao, an army military leader, but we have been unable to find her location.

> *I am sorry we do not have better news, but such are the conditions we face with our own families.*

> *Sincerely,*
> *Howard Wong*

I wanted to tell Mr. Wong to continue his searches, and payment would continue as in the past, but I was not in a position to send money under the circumstances. I put off writing a reply, and, when I thought about going to China in the future, realized that I would be arrested as a criminal.

After all that had transpired, I needed to be comforted and not with a bottle of Scotch. I was empty of physical and emotional reserves.

Nights were the worst. I hurt for hours, both emotional and physical, and the pain wouldn't go away until I dozed off, and even then, relief was temporary. My sorrow was spreading to all areas of my life.

I poured the remaining Scotch down the drain, and despite my misgivings, I went to see Catherine to accept her offer to pay the ransom. I drove to the Lawrence house, and when I entered, Catherine was alone in the parlor and wore a pink floral dress which I had never seen her wear.

"Winson, just the person I wanted to see. Have a seat next to me."

I kissed her on the cheek, and told her she looked beautiful.

"Tell me, what do you hear about Caitlin?"

"No news."

"Oh no. I hope they're okay."

My voice was shaky. "How are you?"

"I've had a rough morning. Everything's been a bit of a struggle."

She didn't have her customary poise or composure. Her hands rested on her knees and were open to the sky. There were long moments of silence, and she moved in an unsettling way in her chair, then went about straightening her sweater and working a button open and closed.

"Is everything okay?"

"It made me feel useful when I planned to help Caitlin and Kathleen. But this morning, when I called the bank that administers my trust and told the secretary that I wanted to withdraw $80,000, she needed to discuss the request with the trustee. She called back an hour ago and explained that what I wanted to do was prohibited by the terms of the trust. Father was particular in how he established the trust to protect me from my own actions and from others who might want to take advantage. I told her that I was leaving my assets to you and Caitlin in my will. She said that despite my will and the request being noble, I could only legally withdraw money for my health or maintenance. I said it was my money, and I wanted to break the trust's provisions. She apologized and said that was not possible."

Catherine lost her voice as tears flooded her face. I tried to console her and said I had other sources for the funds, but whatever I said didn't stop her pain. I gave her my handkerchief as she muttered, "I'm so sorry."

I had never seen her this emotional. I tried to get her to drink water, held her, and said, "I love you."

She kept repeating that she had failed Caitlin and me. So I stayed with her.

When she regained her composure, she wiped her eyes and said, "Joseph read me the newspaper article this morning. I was surprised to see the ransom demand in print."

"The police are investigating the source for the article. It had to be a leak from within the police or RCMP. I hope it won't affect Caitlin and Kathleen's treatment by the kidnappers."

"Do the police have any promising leads?"

"Not yet."

"Oh my. I'm praying for our dear girls and baby. I hope they're okay."

"We need all your prayers."

"How are you holding up?" she asked.

I told her about my encounters with the Mulroney's, Graham and Chorley, and Wong's letter.

"I know this is all very painful for you. Everything is out of your hands. You know I'll always be here for you."

"You can't imagine how comforting it is for me to be sitting here with you."

She cleared her throat.

I rubbed my eyes, took a deep breath, and said, "I'd like to stay, but I must return to the bank."

"You're in no condition to go back to work." She took hold of my arm. "I can feel the tension in your body and in your voice. You need encouragement."

Even though she was blind, she saw through me.

"Stay a little longer. You know when I set my mind to something, I get my way."

I didn't speak while she hummed a tune to herself that I didn't recognize.

"Have you told Ruth and Miriam about Caitlin?"

"I haven't had time."

"You should talk to them. I'm sure they saw the newspaper headline."

"I will. They're wonderful ladies. I'll stop by the church on the way back to work."

I kissed her on the check and she said, "I love you, my son."

Walking out of the house, I wiped my eyes with the back of my hand. By the time I got in the car, I told myself to toughen up and focus on the ransom because I needed to find another way to get the money.

When I walked into the Seventh Avenue Church, Ruth was cooking in the kitchen with several other women. She greeted me with a hug and invited me to stay for lunch.

"Do you have time to talk to me for a few minutes?'

"Of course. Let's step outside and talk. We'll be serving soup and salad for lunch in about 30 minutes if you want to stay."

We sat at a picnic table, and I told her about the kidnapping. She wiped a tear from the corner of her eye, and a low moan came from her throat as she prayed for Caitlin, Kathleen, and the baby to be safe, for me to have peace and be able to raise the ransom, for the kidnappers to be kind to the women, and for the police to find them before the ransom was paid. "Miriam and I will continue praying until Caitlin is safely back home. In fact, the whole church will be praying. Caitlin and Kathleen are in God's hands wherever they are. Now you know, God is good."

"I remember what you taught me. God is good, all the time. All the time, God is good. But there are times when it's hard to see the light for all the darkness."

"I know, but the day always follows night."

After visiting with Catherine and Ruth, I was encouraged and thankful for their support and prayers.

∽

It was almost noon when I returned to the bank, called Miss Jerome, and detailed the recent turn of events. There was silence for a few moments, and I thought the line went dead.

"Winson, what I'm about to share is to be kept in the strictest confidence. Do you understand?"

"Certainly." I didn't know what to expect next.

"We researched and discovered that Superior Court Judge Oliver Irving Sinclair allowed an interim judicial release of Tak, and the Moran Law Firm acted on his behalf and put up surety. Daniel Chan is a Parliament Member from British Columbia, and he's an ex-partner of the Moran firm. There are other ties of Chan to Dung, which I can't go into, but we hope this investigation will help us close in on Dung and Tak and their organization. I requested the assignment of an Ottawa-based RCMP undercover agent, who happens to be Chinese, to investigate Dung's Vancouver operations. Our office will keep Chief Kirkpatrick informed. We'll find Caitlin. Don't hesitate to call me anytime. Do you still have my home number?"

"I do, and thank you for the update and your optimism."

But I didn't share it, and after the call, I couldn't sit still, so I went to see Clive. I told him about my conversations, and we also discussed my call with Miss Jerome in the strictest of confidence. Clive reminded me that anything we shared would be protected by solicitor-client privilege and said, "Let's update Chief Kirkpatrick together on your call with Ellen Jerome and see where the investigation stands."

"Unfortunately, I can't share what Miss Jerome told me about Tak, but she said they were keeping Chief Kirkpatrick in the loop."

"Have you told Kirkpatrick about your meeting with Alex Berry?"

"I left him a detailed message last night to look into Mike Mezzetti."

"Let's see if we can meet with Kirkpatrick."

Clive called and asked Kirkpatrick to meet us. He said he was terribly busy and asked us to come to the police station. When we arrived about fifteen minutes later, he joined us in the conference room and asked, "Is there something new I need to know?"

"I talked with Ellen Jerome today, and the RCMP has been looking into why Tak was released and Dung's business operations. She said she'll keep you updated on the progress of their investigation. Did you check into Mike Mezzetti after my phone call?"

"First, thank you for the information about Mezzetti. I'm new to the area, so I pulled and read a long file on the Mezzetti family. The OPP has tracked them for years, yet no one has been prosecuted. Who provided you this information, and what's the connection to the kidnapping?"

"I would like to tell you who it is, but I promised not to reveal my source. I'm not sure there's a connection, but Patrick Chorley has played at some of his poker games."

"Young man, we need to know your source." His probing eyes were trying to pull an answer out of me as he drummed his fingers on the table. His manner was thoughtful, and he treated me with respect even when asking tough questions. I liked him.

"Our friend has known him for years, and if you knew the source, you would trust whatever he disclosed. I'll put my reputation on the line on this issue. Isn't it enough of a lead to pursue?" Clive intervened.

Kirkpatrick pursed his lips and gave me another hard look, exerting a subtle form of pressure, and said, "You're not going to tell me?"

I shook my head. "I wish I could, but I made a promise before he would give me the information."

"It would be helpful to have that information, but we'll proceed without it. I can't talk to you about Patrick Chorley, but we're looking into his history, just as we looked into yours. I'm aware of Miss Jerome's investigation and hopeful she can make progress to bring charges against Dung and Tak. At the present time, they're our most likely suspects."

"Did you send anyone to Tobermory Friday night since you wouldn't let me go?"

"That's an ongoing part of our investigation, and I can't discuss it with you at this time. Now, let me review the status of our suspects. We have contacted Darwin Avant and will take his statement tomorrow. We'll question him about his knowledge and affiliation with Taylor and Cheek."

"Can you ask Avant about the newspaper article condemning Merchants Bank after he tried to force me to sell the bank to him for almost nothing?"

"We can question him about your meeting with him, but from what I understand, he has an extremely sharp and protective attorney who won't let him answer questions that could be detrimental to him."

"But he's trying to force me out of business."

"Winson, this conversation won't help us find Caitlin. Let's focus on suspects," Clive said.

"We've opened a file on Benjamin Saez, and I sent Detective McGee to speak to him. He claims you stole his rightful inheritance and knows nothing about Caitlin's disappearance. He's confident the courts will rule in his favor. We had him followed for a few days, and he went about his activities in a normal manner. Do you have any other reason to suspect Mr. Saez?"

"No, just what we've told you."

"We've quite a file on Jay Metzger. He's a contemptible person who lives off facilitation payments. He won't talk about his activities or contacts and definitely dislikes you but says he committed no crime. We're watching him for the time being."

"He tried to rape my friend Wei Lei."

"Hmm. Did she file charges?"

"She's a poor Chinese girl. Who would believe her?" She was industrious and Metzger was indolent.

"I'll note to look into that." After writing in his notebook, he said, "McGee interviewed Hollis Fitch, who's been terminated as President of Simco Shipbuilding. He received a severance package from the company and moved to Toronto. If he's involved in the kidnapping, it's from a distance, but he remains on the list."

"Have Chorley and Graham provided their suspect lists?" Clive asked.

"Mr. and Mrs. Graham insist that no one they know would harm Kathleen. She has been the perfect daughter and has only friends, no enemies. Chorley has given us a list, but we can't discuss it with you, and we don't discuss your list with him."

"If you don't have any more questions for me, I need to show you this." Kirkpatrick pulled the Toronto newspaper from under his file folder and pointed to the headline:

Two Collingwood Women Abducted
Police without a Clue

Clive and I looked at each other. Neither of us had seen the paper. Clive read the article then handed it to me.

"We were disappointed to see the Collingwood newspaper article but were even more surprised the Toronto paper picked up the story. We didn't want this to happen, and we're concerned about the abductors' reaction to seeing police involvement."

"How are the newspapers obtaining this information?" Clive asked.

Kirkpatrick shook his head, put up his hands, then looked away.

"There must be an inside leak from someone who's feeding the newspaper information," Clive said.

"I was told by those who wanted me appointed chief that there had been corruption within the department for years. So I accepted the position to clean up the department, but that doesn't happen overnight. I have my suspicions, and there's an internal investigation."

"Do you have any theories?" Clive asked.

He pursed his lips, shook his shoulders, closed his hands, and said, "Several, but I'm not at liberty to discuss our internal affairs."

"Is Sergeant Ellarby on your list?" I asked.

"I can't comment on that."

"What am I to expect in a country where laws don't work the same for everyone? Sergeant Ellarby has been against me without cause since the first time I met him."

"I need to have solid grounds to take action against an officer, and it takes time to build a case. If Ellarby is behind this, he'll be punished."

"But this leak threatens Caitlin and Kathleen," I said.

"I know, son. My heart goes out to you, but know that Milner, McGee, and I are doing everything we can to find them."

The meeting adjourned, and driving back to work, I replayed what Alex and Joseph had shared about how the town functioned. Drott was waiting for me in the lobby when I entered the bank, and after an exchange of pleasantries, I took him into my office, and he said, "Winson, I know this is a challenging time for you, with your wife missing, but I need to talk to you about business. You know I've been buying materials from Imperial Lumber. I pay for half the invoice upfront and the balance after delivery, but I haven't received a lumber shipment for three weeks. My cabinet customer is hounding me to stay on schedule, and when I call for Dung, I'm told he's not in the office. I should sue Imperial, but in the meantime, I need a loan to purchase lumber from another supplier to meet my contract obligations. My father started this business over seventy years ago, and I worked with him since I was ten, and we've never experienced this situation."

"Mr. Drott, how much do you need?"

"$20,000."

Making a loan to Drott was untimely because increasing loans with the deposit runoff would exacerbate our loan to deposit ratio. But putting the customer's interest first and making the loan was what Julian would do.

"Merchants Bank is glad to help. You and your father have been valued customers for a long time. Come with me, and I'll have Peggy draw up the loan documents on the same terms as your last loan. The money will be available in your account tomorrow morning."

As I walked him to Peggy's office, he grabbed my arm, stopped me in the hallway, and said, "Doing business with you makes me feel like Julian's still here."

I told him how much I appreciated his comment. When we entered Peggy's office, I told her what documents Drott needed to execute and then wondered what might be behind Dung's failure to deliver Drott's materials.

Leaving Drott with Peggy, I was exhausted. So much was happening that I felt sick and decided to go home and rest for an hour. When I pulled into the driveway, I noticed the back door ajar. I shivered because I hadn't left the door open when I went to Catherine's. I looked around the rear, then circled the house and looked in the windows but didn't see anyone, and there was no sign of anything out of place.

I entered through the back door, into the service porch and laundry room, and looked for something to defend myself. I picked up a broom and heard an odd hollow sound coming from the kitchen. As I tightened my grip on the broom handle, the kitchen door swung open, and in front of me stood Wei Lei.

"You look like you've seen a ghost! What are you doing with the broom?" She started chuckling.

Before I could respond, I heard boots clacking on the hardwood floors and saw Kai, who said, "Good to see you, brother. What's with the broom?"

I was speechless and relieved, and all I could do was hug both of them.

We went into the kitchen, Wei Lei put on the kettle, and we sat at the table.

"I'm so glad to see you, but you scared me half to death. How did you get in?"

"We thought Caitlin would be home, but when she wasn't, I remembered that you kept a spare key under the flowerpot," Kai said.

"Is Caitlin teaching piano?" Wei Lei asked.

I swallowed hard.

Wei Lei put her hand on my arm, "What's happened?"

"She's been kidnapped."

Wei Lei screamed, covered her face with her hands, and sobbed. Kai stood up, knocking over the chair. His eyes flashed with anger. He closed his hands and was breathing hard as he paced back and forth.

I took a long breath and exhaled, then rose and walked around the kitchen, attempting to relieve my stress. Wei Lei rose and embraced me. We held each other, and what energy I had drained out.

I don't' know how long we stood there when Kai asked, "When?"

I asked them to sit while I relayed what happened, the police investigations, the bank confrontation with Tak and Eng, the Tobermory messages, the ransom notes, and the encounters with Graham and Chorley.

Wei Lei choked back tears while Kai shook his head, pulled a rolled-up cigarette out of his pocket, and cursed. I asked him not to light it in the house. He glared at me when a loud whistle from the tea kettle broke the tension between us. I knew his anger wasn't directed at me.

Wei Lei rose and said, "You probably aren't eating. I'll fix the eggs and bacon I saw in the refrigerator."

I couldn't remember if I had eaten, then realized I only drank a partial cup of coffee at the Mulroney's and some Scotch.

While Wei Lei cooked, Kai asked, "It's Dung and Tak, isn't it?"

I went through the list one by one. When I mentioned Metzger, Wei Lei said, "I hate that man and his wife."

"Winson, you and Caitlin should have left Collingwood with us. I knew when Tak found us, he and Dung would never let us live in peace. Like locusts, they'll devour us," Kai said.

"Kai, our life is here in Collingwood."

"I hate this country."

"You can't color an entire nation by the acts of a few."

"But those few get away with too much."

"It's shameful that our own people, our blood, prey on us," Wei Lei said.

"It's tribal."

"What do you mean?" Kai asked.

"Like what happened to us and the Koreans who were sold to Dawson Creek?"

"Our fathers were wrong to send us here," Kai said.

"But you know what Mao has done to our families and homeland."

"Kai, we can't return to China," Wei Lei added.

"Even if we were free from Dung and Tak, all Canada wants from us is our labor, to work on the railroads or mines or the worst jobs at the lowest pay," Kai said.

"At least we have each other," Wei Lei said as she put her hand on Kai's shoulder. "What else can we do?" she asked me.

"I don't know," I said in despair.

Wei Lei put her arms around me while Kai said, "It has to be Dung and Tak who have taken Caitlin."

"What can we do for you?" Wei Lei said.

"Sit with me. Your company helps."

"We're here for as long as you need us," she whispered. "Let me serve our meal and tea."

She poured hot tea into cups and put a generous portion of bacon, eggs, and toast in front of each of us. I hadn't had a home-cooked meal in weeks and hadn't eaten much since Caitlin's disappearance. I didn't have much appetite, but I forced myself to eat since Wei Lei went to the trouble to fix it, and food might help settle my nerves.

"What happened in Timmins?" I asked Kai.

"Wei Lei worked two jobs, cleaned houses during the day, and worked in a restaurant at night. I found a job in the mines, which was worse than the logging camp. My body ached from swinging a pick all day, and I sweated through filthy clothes that never dried out. There was no latrine, and the bosses would drive us so hard, we'd soil ourselves. It was miserable work, and we were treated worse than animals. I'd rather slop hogs on my family's farm."

He hung his head and slumped his shoulders. His hair was in a long ponytail and reminded me of our time at the logging camp.

"They kept small birds in the mine to detect gases. A few weeks ago, Kai came home early because the birds died," Wei Lei said.

"It was like when *Montebello* went. We were trapped and had to run to escape before we couldn't breathe. The next morning, I couldn't make myself go into those shafts," Kai said.

"I got Kai a job doing dishes and repairs at the steakhouse where I worked. But the owner made advances toward me. I tried to avoid him and not offend him because we couldn't afford to lose our jobs. Then, late one night, he tried to assault me sexually. He said I owed him for Kai's job."

"When I came around a corner and saw the owner pawing and groping at Wei Lei, I became furious and couldn't control myself. I nearly beat him to death. As I hit him, I was also striking at the mine bosses and Dung and Tak." Perspiration erupted on his face. Wei Lei got up and hugged him, and when I handed him a towel, he looked at me and said, "Winson, you t..t..told me not to go, not to work in the mines. You w..w.. were..."

"It's okay, Kai."

"I couldn't go down that hole any longer. The darkness closed in on me."

"We needed a change. Early on, I shouldn't have tolerated the owner's advances, but we needed the money." Wei Lei said as she put a glass of water in front of Kai.

"I should have killed the bastard." Kai raised his voice and pushed the glass away.

"We don't know if the owner is alive. When I pulled Kai off him, he was unconscious but still breathing. We went home, told my parents what had happened, packed, and walked to the bus station because Kai would never receive a fair trial in Timmins."

Wei Lei's eyes turned glassy, I reached for her hand, and she put both her hands on mine and said, "I may never see my parents again. All we could think of was coming back to Collingwood and asking you and Caitlin for help."

"Why do we always have to leave?" Kai lamented.

She choked up, so I said, "There's plenty of room upstairs. You can move into a bedroom and stay as long as you want."

She let go of my hands so she could hug me. Kai managed a smile and nodded at me.

Then Wei Lei put her head in her hands and said, "We need to find work where we can maintain a low profile because of what happened in Timmins and especially if there's a warrant issued for Kai's arrest."

"Joseph, I mean Mr. Lawrence, and Catherine, told me how they miss both of you, and he hasn't found anyone to replace you. There's a good chance he'd consider hiring you back. And working there, you would be out of the public eye."

"You called him Joseph. Are you on a first-name basis?" Kai asked with a smirk.

"We've become friends, and I've spent time with Catherine and him since Caitlin's disappearance. They've both been supportive of me with all that's happened."

Kai tapped his empty cup and said, "Do you have any of Julian's liquor?"

I hesitated but seeing the look on his face and remembering that I tried to comfort myself earlier with alcohol, I went to the cabinet and pulled out a bottle of Scotch. Wei Lei didn't drink, but Kai downed a shot, then took the bottle and poured another. When he poured a third, I said, "That's enough."

"You've changed, no smoking, no drinking. What happened?" Kai raised his voice.

"I drink in moderation."

"I'll drink to that."

I laughed, and it helped ease my tension.

"My uncle would say, 'Your name's your destiny, change it, and you change your future.' We shouldn't have changed ours. Look what's befallen us." Kai said as he glanced around the room and said, "I need a smoke."

He went out the back door, and I sat with Wei Lie as she sipped tea and ate sugar cookies.

"This is hard on him, Winson. He hasn't adapted to Canada as you have."

"Does he have a drinking problem?"

She nodded.

"Is he smoking opium?"

She nodded again.

Looking out the window and seeing a cloud of smoke hanging in the air, I said, "I worry about his drinking."

"Talk to Kai. He needs a job and something good to happen. You know he's a good person."

I nodded, went out the back door, and Kai was sitting on the bench by the blue spruce engulfed in a haze of smoke, and on the ground around him was a scattering of cigarette butts.

When I stood in front of him, he slurred, "You could achieve anything you want in an open country, but here we're at the bottom of the ocean." His face was red, and he was sweating. "I can't work like a mistreated dog for another day." He inhaled, and as he spoke, smoke leaked out of his mouth. "What I have going for me is that I'm big and strong. I can work for Dung to track those who owe them, and in return,

I can provide for Wei Lei and protect her family, then we wouldn't be looking behind us anymore, and I could be the hunter instead of the hunted."

His lack of English imprisoned him and was a limitation I had endeavored to avoid from the time I left China. If he offered himself to Dung, he would be like a caged animal.

"Is that the life you want, to live in the shadows?"

"That's where I live now."

"Do you want to hunt others, like you and I have been hunted?"

He squinted his eyes at me.

"If you join them, you'll never get out."

"What choice do I have?"

"We always have a choice."

"When did we have a choice about leaving home?" he scowled.

"Answer the questions?"

"Look, our lives are burning up like cigarettes," he scoffed. "If it weren't for Wei Lei, I would have killed myself by now. I've made up my mind. I'm going to offer myself and be a Snakehead."

"You can't go against your people, your own blood."

I sympathized with his situation and understood his deep sadness and tormented soul. We both faced a future without hope of ever seeing our families again. But that was the past, and to think otherwise was dreaming. After several moments of silence, I put on a brave face and asked, "Would you come after me if Tak told you to?"

His eyes widened. He stood up, paced about, stopped in front of me, grimaced, and continued walking as he finished his cigarette and used it to light another. Glassy-eyed, he sat and said, "Why did my father send me to live in hell? It would have been better to stay in China and live under Mao. At least I would have family."

"Your father and grandfather despised Mao and wanted a better future for you."

"But I can't tolerate constantly looking behind me and being pursued. Besides, with Dung, I'd be with people who speak Mandarin, our kind, and Wei Lei wants children but living the way we are, there's too much stress, and we won't have any. So we'll die with no future."

I put my hand on his shoulder and squeezed. "Would your father approve of working for Dung and Tak? Is that the hope for a better life they intended for you?"

"But they have power."

"They use their money and influence to take advantage of people. What they do is simply wrong. They destroy lives. Do you want to participate in that?"

He closed his eyes and hung his head.

"I know you can see what my life has stood for. You've stood by me when I needed you. We've tried to do what's right and seek justice."

He looked me in the eye.

"There's a line that separates us from Dung and Tak. Two of them on one side of the line, and two of us on the other side. You decide with whom you want to stand."

He frowned and put his head in his hands.

"Which side would your father or Wei Lei want you to stand on?"

"I need another drink."

"Would you have respect for yourself?"

He lit another cigarette.

"I know what constant anxiety does to a person, and I understand why you drink and smoke. I do both when the stress gets to be too much. We have no roots, no stability, but we have each other, and we have our common memories of China and those we left behind. We have to move forward and do the best we can. We are both fortunate to have wives who love us, and we have each other. Use your memory."

"I remember the times on the ship when you smoked and drank."

"Why are you and I here?"

"What do you mean?"

"You saved my life back at the camp. Now I want to save yours. I'll be back in a few minutes."

I went back inside and said to Wei Lei, "He talked about working for Dung and Tak because they would protect him and your family."

"On the way here, he said he didn't want to have to live with my parents in a small room anymore. He hated that we spent our wedding night with them."

"Kai isn't thinking clearly. Dung and Tak are predators, scouring the landscape to feed their greed." I closed my eyes for a moment and said, "Excuse me for a few minutes while I make a call in my office."

She put her hand on my arm and squeezed as her lip trembled.

When I returned to the kitchen, Wei Lei was washing the dishes and turned toward me.

"I called Mr. Lawrence. He'll hire both of you and wants you to live in the loft. I told him you would be over first thing in the morning."

"Oh, Winson." She wiped away her tears with a dish towel and said, "Thank you." She took a moment to look around the room. "But looking at you and the condition of the house, we need to stay with you until Caitlin returns." She wrapped her arms around me and said, "Can we stay here?"

"With all the attention on me, you'll be better off staying in the loft. The police know where I live, and I don't want them to find Kai."

"But we want to help you."

"Maybe you can. Do you know a Lysa Wu from Timmins?"

"Lysa, with emerald green eyes and plum-colored hair?"

"Yes. What do you know about her?"

"She came to the restaurant, always expensively dressed and wearing a lot of makeup. Most of the time, men escorted her, some Canadian, some Italian, but never Chinese. Once, she came with her parents, and we talked. Her family escaped from Dung and Tak, and when Tak found them in Timmins, he put her to work to pay off their debt, which she thought was paid, but Tak said if she didn't cooperate, he would turn them in as illegals to the RCMP. I shared our story with her. Why do you ask?"

"She's in Collingwood and came to the bank, gave me a note from you, and said she knew you and Kai."

"I told her about you and Kai's history with Tak, how you helped us, and that you run a bank and married an Irish girl. I hadn't seen her for a few weeks, and when I asked her mother about her, she said Tak had a job for her out of town. I didn't write her a note. Did I do something wrong?"

"No. No, not at all. Let me tell Kai about Lawrence. You wait here for us to come back in."

I went back out, sat next to Kai, and said, "I called Mr. Lawrence. He wants to hire both you and Wei Lei, and you can live in the loft."

"Are you serious?" he asked as he rubbed his eyes with the back of his hand.

"He definitely wants you back. He's missed you and Wei Lei. You can start tomorrow morning."

Like the first rays of sun breaking through a storm, a grin cracked and consumed his face. He stood up, threw away his cigarette, put his arms around me, and hugged me as tight as he could as Wei Lei came out of the house and joined us.

I pushed back a little and said, "Kai, stop. I appreciate the hug, but I have to go back to work and can't smell like cigarettes."

"Forget what I said. If Tak sent me after you, I couldn't do it."

"If you cut Tak open, he wouldn't bleed."

We all laughed.

The tightness in my chest relented, and if not for Joseph's offer, Kai might have chosen a path down a dark tunnel. He put his hand on my shoulder and said, "We'll work for Mr. Lawrence, but we'll stay here with you until Caitlin comes back."

"The police are watching my house. It would be better for you both to stay with Joseph."

He nodded.

"Don't take offense, but have Wei Lei cut your hair."

He stroked his ponytail and said, "I haven't looked in a mirror for a long time, and Wei Lei hasn't said anything about my hair. Remember back in camp when we tied our hair in pigtails?"

We all laughed.

"Thank you for looking after me. You're my brother." Kai's expression softened.

"And I'm yours."

As we all went inside, Wei Lei winked at me.

"Make yourselves at home, and I'll see you about 6:30. But don't answer the door or the phone. I don't' want the police to ask who you are, and if Tak or Dung calls, I don't want them to know that you are here."

"We understand, and we don't like leaving you, but under the circumstance, it makes sense for us to stay with Mr. Lawrence," Wei Lei said.

Each of us, in our way, was like a fly caught in a bottle.

∽

Returning to the bank, I received a phone call from Chief Kirkpatrick. "Milner located Lysa Wu, and we have her at the police station. I want you and Clive to meet here as soon as possible."

I called Clive, then let Peggy know I'd be out for the afternoon, and took the car to the police station.

Kirkpatrick, Clive, and I entered a locked room at the station, and Lysa was sitting at a long table. We sat directly across from her, and when I caught her looking at me, she dropped her eyes.

Kirkpatrick addressed her, "You know Winson LeBlanc, and this is his attorney, Clive Owen."

She nodded as she fidgeted in her chair. "Why am I here?"

"We want to ask you a few questions."

"I haven't committed a crime."

"You're not under arrest."

"Do I need an attorney?"

"That's up to you, of course, but we want you to tell us what you know about two Chinese men who are known as Dung and Tak."

She cleared her throat.

"If you can help us, we'll do all we can to protect you and your family."

She took a moment before she said, "You would protect my family?"

"That's correct, Miss Wu."

"Why would you do that?"

"We need evidence to convict Dung and Tak."

She pursed her lips.

"We believe that you, like Mr. LeBlanc, thought you were coming to a sponsoring Chinese family when you arrived in Canada. Instead, we know you and your parents entered Canada under false documents prepared by Dung through agents in China, just like Mr. LeBlanc. To pay your debt, we believe you became involved in criminal activities involving Dung and Tak."

"What do you want from me?"

"We need information about Dung and Tak's operations which could lead to their arrest."

"But if I talk to you about them, they'll find my family and me and kill us."

"We can put you in a protection program, change your names, move your family to another province, and provide jobs."

"We've already moved from the west coast to several provinces and more recently to far northern Ontario, where

Tak still found us. Would you be sending us to Nunavut or the Northern Territories to live among the Inuit people?"

"We would work together on where to relocate your family."

"What's fair in this world?"

"We want to lock up Dung and Tak and put an end to their intimidation and oppression."

The door opened, and in walked Milner. After settling into a chair, he opened his briefcase, pulled out a file, paper, and pen.

She looked at him, then around the room, and appeared agitated.

"Miss Wu, why don't you begin by telling us how you met Dung and Tak."

"May I have some water."

Kirkpatrick poured her a glass, she drank most of the water, then spoke cautiously. "Dung indentured my family when we arrived in Vancouver from China ten years ago. My father arrived six months before my mother and me." She slumped in her chair as she said, "I was thirteen when they forced me into prostitution and my parents into hard labor."

She paused, drank the rest of the water in her glass, looked at me, and asked, "Can I please have more water."

Kirkpatrick refilled her glass, and she took several sips.

"We were only supposed to work for three years to pay off our travel expenses, and then we would get our immigration papers, but they never let us go. Three years ago, we escaped and fled to northeastern Ontario and felt safe until last year when Tak started operations for Imperial Lumber in Ontario." She took several dry swallows and sipped more water. "Tak saw me in Timmins and demanded money. I told him we were barely surviving. He threatened to force me back into prostitution to earn money to pay them and, if we didn't pay, he would turn all of us into the RCMP."

She looked at Milner, who was taking notes of her statements.

"For a while, they didn't return, but then a month ago, a man named Eng showed up in Timmins and demanded payments from us."

Her eyes turned glassy.

"When we told Eng we didn't have money to pay, he said he would tell Dung. When he returned a few days later, he said Dung wanted me in Collingwood, and I was to get close to Winson LeBlanc, owner of Merchants Bank, and pass information about him to Tak. If the information was valuable, he would release our debt and not turn us into the RCMP."

Her eyes filled, and she looked directly at me, "I didn't have a choice. I hated what I had to do."

She wiped away the tears and said, "I'm sorry,"

"What kind of information did they want?" Milner asked.

"He wanted to know about Mr. LeBlanc's circumstances, habits, and whereabouts."

"So, what did you do?"

"I tried to eavesdrop on conversations, and Tak wanted me to meet with Mr. LeBlanc outside of the bank. But that didn't work because Mr. LeBlanc is quite private and would not meet with me alone."

"How do you contact Tak and Dung?" Milner continued his questioning.

"I receive a phone call every few days from someone from his organization."

"Did you speak to Dung?" Kirkpatrick asked.

"The last time I spoke to him, he said he got more information from the newspaper than me and threatened to turn me into the RCMP."

"We've discovered that Dung's operation receives a bounty from the government for turning in illegals, so those who have paid off their debts, he turns over, while any that owe money and continue to work for him, he leaves alone," Kirkpatrick said.

Lysa appeared upset by Kirkpatrick's comment and began shaking.

I took out my handkerchief, reached across the table to offer it to her, poured her another glass of water, and said, "Take a few deep breaths, and take your time."

"With Dung's connections, how can you protect my family? He'll never let us go." Her mascara ran as her eyes overflowed. "We can't outrun him."

I had first-hand knowledge of how Dung corrupted certain police officers, arranged Tak's bail, and understood her concerns.

"With your help, we hope to arrest Dung and Tak and put them in jail for a long time, but we need solid evidence," Kirkpatrick said.

She folded her arms and pressed her lips together.

Kirkpatrick leaned forward. "Miss Wu, are you aware that Mr. LeBlanc's wife has been kidnapped?"

She shook her head then looked at me.

"Dung and Tak are prime suspects."

Her body stiffened.

After a minute of silence, she blurted out, "I don't know anything about a kidnapping, but I know Dung is vindictive and has power and political influence."

"How do you know?" Kirkpatrick asked.

She bit her lower lip and remained silent for a few moments. "They forced me to sleep with judges and politicians to gain their favor and access to information."

"Do you have names?" Milner leaned forward and pressed his pen hard into the paper.

Tears flooded her face.

Kirkpatrick waited until she settled and asked softly, "Why did he target Mr. LeBlanc?"

"I don't know, but I think he wants involvement in Merchants Bank." She bit her lip again.

Detective McGee entered the room and handed a folded note to Kirkpatrick, which he opened, read, refolded, and put in his coat pocket.

He turned toward Lysa and said, "Miss Wu, you're free to go, but we need you to remain in town. Don't tell anyone in Dung's organization about this meeting. Keep working as you were told, and see if you can arrange a meeting with Dung and Tak. There'll be undercover officers following you to provide protection. Detective McGee will escort you back to your hotel, and you are to let him know your whereabouts from now on. Is this all clear?"

"Yes, Sir."

"If you have names of judges or politicians connected with Dung and Tak, we would like that information."

She nodded, put my handkerchief up against her nose, then placed it in her purse, and avoided looking at me as she rose and followed McGee out of the room.

Clive and I stood up, intending to leave.

"Gentlemen, I need you to stay, so please take your seats," Kirkpatrick said.

We looked at each other, anticipating some news.

"McGee just returned from a visit with Patrick Chorley. He received a phone call from the abductors. They're angry about the newspaper headlines, accused him of going to the police, and demanded an additional $20,000 be delivered in the next twenty-four hours. McGee told Chorley to get Graham and come to the station immediately. I want you to wait here until they arrive. Milner, see if they're here and bring them in."

When Milner left the room, Clive asked Kirkpatrick, "Why did the kidnappers call Chorley?"

"I don't know. They may have called Winson first."

I was numb and sat silently.

When Milner entered the room with Chorley and Graham, Graham exploded, "Damn you. They said if we went to the police, we'd never see Kathleen again. What a mess you've gotten us into."

"Mr. Graham, calm down. We need to work together to get your daughter and Caitlin home safely," Kirkpatrick said.

Graham was red-faced, a vein protruded from his temple, and he took quick, hard breaths. We all looked at him as Kirkpatrick poured him a glass of water, then turned to Chorley. "Mr. Chorley, tell us exactly what was said. What was the sound of the voice, and was there an accent? Was the caller old or young, male or female? Did you hear any background sounds? Any information that might be helpful."

"It was a man's voice. I couldn't tell his age, and the call was muffled, so I didn't hear background noise."

Graham pounded his fist against the table and glared at Kirkpatrick. "Hell, man, they have my daughter! He gasped and stammered, "She's my only child. They said no police. No police! Do you hear me? They'll kill her if we don't have the money available in twenty-four hours."

"Mr. Graham, we're working around the clock and doing all we can. But if any of you receive calls from the kidnappers, you need to contact us immediately."

"Hell, no."

"You don't have a choice, Mr. Graham."

"You police should put up the ransom."

"That needs to come from the three of you."

"Get it from the man wearing the black and white railroad striped suit." He pointed at me. "Patrick and me, we don't have money."

"Winson, do you have the cash?" Kirkpatrick asked.

"I'm working on it."

"You gotta do more than work on it, boy," Graham erupted.

"I don't have ready cash like that available."

"You've known for days. You live in a mansion and own a bank. We have twenty-four hours, so take or borrow what we need." Graham squirmed in his seat.

"It's not that simple."

"Yes, it is. Either you produce the cash, or we lose Kathleen and your wife, and their deaths will be on you!" It was hard to be in the same room with him.

Kirkpatrick interrupted. "No one in this room is at fault for what happened to the women. And finger-pointing will serve no purpose."

"Bullshit," Graham snorted.

"Enough, Mr. Graham. If you can't stay calm, I'll have you removed from the room."

Graham narrowed his eyes, then pushed back in his chair.

Kirkpatrick shook his head, looked at Chorley, and said, "Did they say how they would release the girls?"

"No."

"What else did they say?"

"It was a short conversation. They kept repeating that we needed to have the money, and no police at the exchange or the women are dead."

"Winson, we need the cash for the ransom by noon tomorrow to have time to mark the bills before the transfer," Kirkpatrick said.

"Kirkpatrick, hooray! You're finally waking up, man," Graham said tersely.

"Won't they know if the money is marked?" Chorley asked.

"It's a chance we have to take," Kirkpatrick said.

"As soon as we know the details of the exchange, we can plan for it, but we need the ransom money," Milner said as he frowned at me, intending to show me his displeasure.

As I headed home, my mind raced because now I had a deadline to raise $100,000. With the house, the bank stock, and my funds tied up by liens filed by Saez, I couldn't refinance or borrow against my assets. If I withdrew money from the bank, I would risk a prison sentence for the illegal withdrawal of funds and likely end up in prison, like my father in Shanghai.

It was a bad gamble, but one I was willing to take it to rescue Caitlin. Besides, if I didn't have her, my life wouldn't be worth living.

I reconsidered who was likely to have motives to kidnap Caitlin, besides Dung and Tak.

Remembering Taylor's note to Peggy where he said she would be sorry for siding with me, the reference to my losing everything dear to me, and his departing vow to kill me, perhaps

Avant was working with Taylor. The abduction could be part of Taylor's plan for revenge. The police never located him or Cheek, and Taylor communicated with Avant, who wanted the bank. But Avant wouldn't pay $100,000, or hardly any amount because he schemed to ignite a deposit run that would lead to a liquidity crisis so he could step in while conspiring with Taylor and take over the bank for almost nothing. Taylor could be running out of money, living as a fugitive in some backwoods area in the States and need the $100,000 to survive.

When I recalled how Hollis Fitch pointed at me in the Towne Terrace Café, the thought that he aligned with Avant and Taylor kept pricking me.

Then, I still couldn't get Saez out of my mind because of the evil I saw in his eyes and his vow of revenge against Julian.

With Kai and Wei Lei returning to town, I remembered how the Metzgers had abused her and exerted their influence with Officer Ellarby, who trumped up a charge that I assaulted Caitlin. They had been too quiet and had nefarious connections within the police force, courts, and newspaper. I'm sure the thought of a man from China running a Canadian Bank incensed them.

Nonetheless, whoever was behind the kidnapping demanded cash that I needed to provide. From what Lysa said, Dung wanted ownership in the bank, but with the RCMP investigating him because of Miss Jerome's influence, how would that be possible? The Ministry of Finance would never allow Dung to directly own or invest in a Canadian bank. Furthermore, Dung operated in illegal markets and would not want any transaction to be of public record, which could be advantageous. But how could I contact him? And I couldn't meet him if Tak was with him, who I needed to avoid at all costs, and I couldn't take Gene or anyone else with me for protection. So if I met with Dung, it needed to be on my turf. But how could that be arranged?

To raise the ransom cash by tomorrow, I had two alternatives, Dung or theft from my bank. Every molecule in my body told me to avoid Dung, and if I took depositor money from the bank, I would spend years in jail, and if sentenced to Kingston Penitentiary, I would never get out alive.

A transaction with Dung would be quick, private, and, more importantly, removed from public and governmental scrutiny. But, with Dung, I was consorting with the devil.

But, if offering an interest to Dung could return Caitlin to me, it was worthwhile. Besides, he would need someone like me to front as president and operate the bank.

I avoided discussing this alternative with Clive because he would try to talk me out of it, but he wasn't in my shoes.

∽

During dinner with Kai and Wei Lei, I was distracted and excused myself to make a phone call. I left a message for Detective McGee, and the phone rang a few minutes later.

"This is McGee. What do you want?"

"I want to see Lysa Wu. Can you tell me how to contact her?"

"Why?"

"I think she can lead me to Dung."

"I'll pick you up in ten minutes and take you to her hotel, but I want to be there when you meet with her."

"I think she'll be more open if I talk to her alone. If you tell me where she is, I'll call you after I talk to her."

"No way. I'll take you there and wait in the car, and I want immediate feedback of what she tells you."

I agreed, then let Kai and Wei Lei know I'd be gone for an hour and waited at the curb for McGee.

He picked me up and drove to the Dorchester Hotel. He parked and waited outside. The lobby was empty except for a thin man in a tweed suit standing behind the reception counter. He was craggy-faced, fine-boned, and said in a high nasal voice, "How may I help you?"

"I'm here to see a hotel guest named Lysa Wu."

"Who should I say is calling?" he asked as he arched his eyebrows.

"My name is Winson LeBlanc."

I pulled out a business card and handed it to him.

He looked it over and said, "This says your President of Merchants Bank. Is that correct?" He tilted his head back and looked at me through the top of his thick glasses.

"Yes, Sir. Merchants Bank on Hurontario."

"Winson LeBlanc, it says here on this card." He cleared his throat. "I knew Mr. LeBlanc. He wasn't Chinese, eh."

I didn't want to get into this but had no choice. "He adopted me."

"Now, why would he adopt you?"

"Sir, I need to see Miss Wu, and I know she's a guest in your fine hotel. You can't have that many Chinese women staying here so please ring her room."

"She's a fine-looking lady." He raised his brow and stared. "Just your type, eh."

I clenched my teeth and repressed an urge to say something ugly.

He opened a drawer, pulled out a pen and paper with the hotel name across the top, and slid it across the counter. "Miss Wu left the hotel. You can leave her a note."

My feelings were raw, but I needed to get a message to Lysa. I asked her to come to the bank in the morning because I had something important to discuss. I folded the note and slid it across the counter.

"Thank you for your cooperation."

He didn't say anything but kept fingering the business card as he watched me walk out the door. I was certain he would read the note, and the only way I would know if he delivered it was if Lysa met me at the bank in the morning.

McGee was leaning against the car and annoyed when I told him Lysa was out and I wanted to walk home.

"What do you mean out? She's under surveillance, and no one told me she left."

"That's what I was told."

"I'll drive you home, and the police will search for Miss Wu."

On the drive home, I thought about Lysa's situation and found myself having compassion for her circumstances. It was best not to let Lysa know that Kai and Wei Lei were back in town. I didn't want her to tell Dung their whereabouts.

Back at home, Kai and Wei Lei shared their excitement about working for Joseph, and then Kai talked about some of our experiences at the logging camp and the train ride to Collingwood. We talked about things he had not shared with Wei Lei. They did their best to keep my mind off of Caitlin.

Wei Lei apologized for keeping me up late, and Kai said, "Let's have a drink before we go to bed."

He went to Julian's cabinet, pulled out a bottle of Scotch, and poured us a shot. Hoping it would help me sleep, I took a few sips and excused myself as Kai poured himself another shot.

As I sat on Caitlin's side of the bed, I put my hand on her pillow and looked at the dresser with pictures of our wedding. I opened the night table drawer where she kept a stack of notes and cards we had given each other. Reading them, I wondered if I would ever see her again. I replayed events and conversations throughout another sleepless night.

Chapter Fifteen

Tuesday Morning

When I entered Clive's office early Tuesday morning, he was alone and in the kitchen with the kettle on and Bitsy's maple scones on a large plate. I smiled and said, "Good morning. I see Bitsy's been baking."

His brow furrowed, and he didn't greet me with his normally pleasant demeanor. "I was hoping for a better start to the day. Look at this."

He opened the morning newspaper, laid it on the table, and pointed to a headline on the business page:

Ministry of Finance Audited Merchants Bank Last Year for Regulatory Violations

There was silence for a few minutes while I read the article.

"I need something to eat. Can I offer you tea and a scone?" He looked tense over my situation, and I appreciated how much he cared.

"I don't' have an appetite."

"When I'm under stress, I eat."

He put two of Bitsy's scones on two plates, offered one to me, and I politely waved it off. "Clive, I can't take funds for the ransom from the bank without facing criminal charges, and with Saez filing liens, I can't borrow against my assets and only have about ten thousand dollars of ready cash."

"You're in a demanding situation. I wish I had the money to give to you."

He finished eating the maple scone, and icing was at both corners of his mouth.

"What if I have an investor interested in buying some bank stock?"

"Because of the Saez lawsuit, it would need to be an unrecorded transaction, off balance sheet to avoid notice by the bank examiners. But if you can sell an interest, it should only be a minority stake, so you retain control. Do you have anyone in mind?"

I choked out, "Dung."

Clive's eyes widened. He sat back in his chair and put his hand through his hair, then rose and paced about until he stood and gazed out the window for a few moments.

Clive shook his head, mumbled to himself, and said, "I wish you didn't have to consider Dung. Do you think Avant would be willing to pay $100,000 for an interest in the bank?

"After his interference with a potential run on the bank, which he tried to accomplish by tipping off the *Times* with false information, he wants to take over the bank for a pittance. Today's paper is further proof of his challenges. If he did pay $100,000, I doubt it would be for less than full ownership. I would be out, but I would do it for Caitlin."

"What other alternatives do you have?"

"Catherine offered to give me the money from her trust fund, but the trust stipulates money can only be distributed to pay for Catherine's health and maintenance, and the trustee refused her request."

"Julian's trust is the same. The money can only be used for stipulated expenditures. I'd loan you the money if I had it, but like you, I only have a few thousand in ready cash. I guess that leaves Dung. Have you been in contact with him?"

"Lysa Wu said he was interested in the bank. I left her a message last night at her hotel to meet me at the bank this morning."

He took hold of my arm, and his eyes were full of compassion.

"Kirkpatrick had said that everything we discover becomes evidence, and his comment has been gnawing on me. It has become so loud in my head that I need to tell him about the rosary beads."

"Let me call him for a meeting."

He called, spoke to him, and after hanging up, said, "He'll see us at eleven-thirty at the station, and he'd like you to have the ransom money with you. I'll meet you there."

This put more pressure on me to make something happen with Dung. I left and on my way to the bank, I saw Metzger in a wide-legged stance, standing on a corner with another man in a dark pin-striped suit staring at me as I entered the bank. I ignored them and spent the morning consumed with considering every alternative to raise the ransom. Despite my anxiety and exhaustion, I tried to maintain a professional attitude with the staff.

It was a few minutes after 9:00 when Anita knocked on my door and said, "Sir, Lysa Wu is in the lobby and asked to see you."

"Please show her in."

When she walked in with Miss Wu, I said, "Thank you, Anita."

"Do you want me to stay?" I'm sure Peggy had spoken with Anita about Lysa, and I appreciated her consideration, but I needed to talk privately, so I said, "Thank you, but that won't be necessary."

She looked puzzled, and as she left, I closed the door. Lysa wore a form-fitted dark green dress that complimented her emerald eyes, a wide black belt, and spike-heeled black leather shoes. Her skin appeared even smoother and creamier than the first time I had seen her.

She sat and looked directly at me as she said, "Your note said you wanted to talk."

"I wasn't sure the hotel clerk would give you my message."

"It was pushed under my door last night. I was there all the time, but I asked not to be disturbed."

I smiled to myself, thinking of McGee scouring town reasoning she had evaded his detectives, and all the while, she was in her room.

"Thank you for coming. May I offer you tea or coffee?"

"Black coffee, four sugars."

I went to the kitchen, and when I returned to my office and handed Lysa the coffee, the scent of her lavender perfume was reminiscent of my mother.

"Do you want to know if I'll cooperate with the police?" she asked.

"No. I asked to see you because I want to meet with Dung."

Her eyes widened as she studied me.

"What's in it for me?"

"Maybe I can help you and your family."

She raised her eyebrows and leaned toward me. "What do you want in return?"

I saw from her posture and because of her background in forced prostitution, that her immediate thought would be that I wanted a liaison with her. "Please don't misunderstand my intentions. I need information. I'm desperate to save my wife and child."

"Your wife is pregnant?"

"Yes."

She narrowed her eyes and studied me, then said, "Wei Lei said you're not like other men, and you fight for an individual's rights. Why do you do this?"

I was taken aback by her question, but I decided to tell her straight. "Because every person is important. My life is important to Caitlin, our child, family, and friends. And to the immigrants trying to establish a new life in a new world. It's important to those who came before me and will matter to those still to come. I try to stand up for the truth and be a person of character."

Although her expression hardened, a tear left a wet line on one cheek.

"Is Dung in Ontario?" I asked.

She shifted her position in the chair, uncrossed her legs, then recrossed them.

"Would he meet with me?"

She bolted out of her chair and walked toward the door.

"Please don't go." I didn't know what to do. Had I pushed her too far? Should I get up and stop her?

She put her hand on the door frame, took a deep breath, then turned to face me, and said, "Dung and Tak were in Tobermory. Dung had me in a hotel, where Tak was to bring you so they could drug you and take naked pictures of us together."

"What do they want from me?"

"Like I said yesterday, ownership in your bank. I've listened to your conversations and reported everything I heard to Dung. That's what I'm supposed to do."

She looked at her shoes and fidgeted.

"Would you be able to arrange a meeting with Dung in my office?"

"Is it for the money to pay the kidnappers?"

"Yes."

"You would take money from Dung to protect your wife and child?"

I rested my chin on my hand and said, "I may have to."

"The newspaper said $80,000."

"It's now $100,000."

"You own a bank. Don't you have access to that kind of money?"

I didn't know if she was getting ready to ask me for money. "Not at this time."

"So, you need me." Her stare was intense.

My need was exposed. Lysa was in control and could do what she wanted with my emotions. "Yes. I need your help."

She searched my face. I was exhausted and had little resistance to her probes or for whatever she was about to ask me.

"You said you could help my family. How?"

I wasn't surprised by her question because she did what she needed to for her family.

"As part of any agreement I make with Dung, I'll ask him to release you and your parents from your obligations to him. But Dung can't give you Canadian citizenship papers."

"Why?"

"Because he doesn't have them to give. You'll need my assistance to work with the Canadian government. I've been appointed to a special committee in Parliament to grant citizenship to Chinese who entered the country illegally. So you and your parents could receive a pardon."

"Why would you do this for us?"

"Because I need your help, and you need mine."

"The police chief said he would provide protection for my family."

"He can do that, maybe give you a new identity and move you to a different province, but I can still help you gain your citizenship."

Arching her hands in front of her chin, she studied my face. "You know I'm being watched by the police and can't contact Dung directly."

"I hope you'll work with Chief Kirkpatrick and provide information that will convict Dung and Tak."

"I have my own plan to kill them." She shook her shoulders, and her expression turned cold.

My eyes opened wide. "Let the police do their work."

"Do you know how many times I've seen how the police have a hand in his pocket and look the other way?"

"There's a Parliament Member, Miss Ellen Jerome, who oversees an ongoing investigation to obtain evidence to convict both Dung and Tak."

"I've never heard of such a woman. What type of evidence would she need to convict them?"

"Names, places, dates, illegal acts."

"I have a black book with all the tricks I provided for Dung. Dates, places, a client list, and their preferences. And I made a backup and gave it to my mother as a bargaining chip in case something happened to me."

"Are you willing to speak about your black book to Miss Jerome or Chief Kirkpatrick?"

She squinted her eyes as if she was sorting out her thoughts.

"I have a close relationship with Miss Jerome, and she's working with the RCMP to shut down Dung's Vancouver operations and the politicians he's corrupted."

"Will she secure our freedom and citizenship in exchange for my information?"

"She can do more than anyone I know, and as a woman, she can understand how Dung has abused you."

She shook her shoulders, stuck out her chin, and asserted, "I still want to kill Dung."

"If you do, someone else will take over and continue his brutal tactics. His organization, his network, needs to be shut down."

Her expression turned intense. Then, she rose, bowed to me, and said, "I'll consider our discussion. You'll hear from me or Dung, or you may never see me again."

She turned and walked away.

I sat with my head in my hands, reflecting on what just happened when Anita appeared and said Patrick Chorley was in the lobby waiting for me.

"Please bring him in."

He extended his hand, and it was clammy.

"I came to apologize for my father-in-law, eh. He's a crusty old guy, and Kathleen's his only child, but he shouldn't speak to you or act the way he does." He had puffy eyes with dark pouches underneath, food stains on his shirt, and his hair was disheveled. His cheek quivered as he said, "I want to contribute somehow, but I don't have money."

"I'm trying to raise the ransom. Without that, we'll never see our wives again." I swallowed hard.

"They said they'd release our wives after receiving the ransom if the police aren't involved."

"But they're already involved."

"But the kidnappers said they'd kill Kathleen and Caitlin if the police were contacted."

"We can't do this on our own Patrick."

"What if I give myself to them as collateral until Kathleen and Caitlin are returned."

"That's a noble suggestion, but we need to include Kirkpatrick or Milner."

He wiped his chin with his shoulder, then stood and said, "We may never get them back alive if we do that."

Then he walked out.

Chapter Sixteen

Tuesday Afternoon

I went to the police station and found Clive with Kirkpatrick and Milner. "I have something to show you." I took out the rosary beads and put them on the table. "I found these on Pine Isle, and my anonymous source said Mezzetti fingered rosary beads like these when he played poker."

Milner crossed his arms and said, "Bloody hell! We told you that Pine Isle was a restricted area. When did you go? And why didn't you tell us about the rosary beads when you found them? How long have you known about the beads and the connection to Mezzetti? We should charge you with withholding evidence!"

I turned my full attention on Milner and said, "Your people didn't find this rosary even though they searched the island for days. I did. And now you want to threaten me for doing something you and your men couldn't do."

"Why, you bloody sneak," Milner sputtered. "I ought to lock you up right now." He jumped to his feet and started toward me.

"Milner, back off. This bickering isn't helping the situation," Kirkpatrick shouted. Then he leaned toward me and glared, "Winson, we're following every lead, but we need you to do your part. What were you thinking when you didn't tell us about what you'd found? It doesn't make sense that you wouldn't tell us about this."

"Illogical as it may seem to you, it was a connection with my wife and baby. And I thought…"

"You shit, you see yourself as a detective!" Milner said.

"Do you have the ransom money? I asked Clive to have you bring it with you," Kirkpatrick said.

There was a lump in my throat, and I struggled to find my voice. I tried not to flinch, so I glanced toward Clive, who must have seen my expression, as he answered, "We're working on it."

Kirkpatrick had been sitting at the table, but he got up, went to the window, and looked outside for a moment. "Winson," he said in a voice so low that I could barely hear it, "when will the funds will be available?"

He turned and looked at me before I had a chance to answer. "Look, son. I know you're worried about whether your wife's even alive right now, but we have to assume that both she and Mrs. Chorley are still okay. Now is not the time to hold back."

I was under tremendous pressure. "That's not the reason I don't have the money." My nerves were raw, and I was on the verge of losing control. "I'm working on something and hope to have money later today."

Kirkpatrick looked at me intensely and said, "All right, Winson. Let's get back together here at four o'clock to see where we are. Are you sure you don't have anything else that might be relevant to our investigation?"

"Patrick Chorley was just in my office. He's concerned that if the police are involved with the money exchange, we'll never see our wives again. Can you find a way to do the exchange where it does not appear that you're involved?"

"It depends on where and how the exchange takes place. We'll do everything in our power to protect the women. It would be foolish for you or Chorley to make an exchange without our knowledge and presence. I'm surprised they haven't contacted either of you with instructions."

When we were outside the station, and alone, I said to Clive, "I don't have any other alternatives. As you said, selling or mortgaging my house is out of the picture with the Saez liens."

"I can call Avant to discuss a quick sale, but he won't pay anything, especially if he's behind the newspaper leaks."

"I don't see another alternative but to go to Dung and arrange for an unrecorded transaction."

"I don't want to see you do that. Do you want me to discuss a settlement with Saez by selling him either the bank or house for $100,000 today only?"

"I would dishonor Julian if I settled with him."

"Julian specifically excluded Saez in his will, but he would understand if you did it to save Caitlin."

"We don't even know if Saez has the cash, and he wouldn't do me any favors."

"So you're seriously considering approaching Dung?"

"I know from Lysa Wu that he's interested in the bank." I swallowed hard. "What else can I do?"

"What if Dung has taken Caitlin in revenge for imprisoning Tak?"

"I've contemplated that. I could be giving him an interest in the bank in exchange for the money to pay his ransom, and if he's behind the kidnapping, he gets his own money back and an interest in the bank for free."

"That's ingenious."

"Dung would devise such a scheme and would do it so it couldn't be traced back to him."

"He knows how to work the system."

"I could accept Dung's money and live under his control or take money from the bank and go to jail for stealing depositor funds."

Clive said, "If our situations were reversed, if it was Bitsy, and those were my options, I would take..."

I cut him off and said, "Dung has cash, and it would be an unrecorded transaction. My decision comes down to a sacrifice for a sacrifice."

"What do you mean?"

"I give up my freedom and work for Dung in return for the cash to save Caitlin's life."

He raised his arms with open hands to the sky.

✑

Shortly after I returned to the bank, Peggy came in my office and said, "There's a Mr. Dung in the bank lobby asking to see you. The man with him was here before when you were threatened. They're making everyone nervous."

I took a deep breath and said, "Have them come into my office and ask Gene to join us." I didn't want to meet them in the lobby and was afraid Tak was with Dung.

"Should I alert the police?"

"No, that won't be necessary. But tell Gene to come into my office, and make sure he has his gun."

Dung entered wearing a black silk shirt and matching pants. He had aged a lot in the fourteen years since I'd been imprisoned at the logging camp. His skin had greyed, his nose was red, and his hair had thinned. He was accompanied by

Eng, his big thick-chested guard with a pock-marked face, who was carrying a black briefcase. Dung looked me over and was silent as he cast his eyes around the office, looking through his horn-rimmed spectacles as if making a mental note of everything.

He squared up in front of my desk, looked me in the eye, and said in Mandarin, "Well, well. My little shoemaker has become what I can never be, owner of a Canadian bank."

His arrogance was brutal for me to take, I wanted to retch, and a chill fell over me. My soul was shuddering, my insides were churning, and I hated being near him. I fought to control my nerves and was concerned that my desperation would make me do something I wouldn't consider under normal circumstances. There was a knock, and Gene was standing in the doorway.

"Gene, please come in." He closed the door as Eng and Gene took a measure of each other.

"Why do you need the darkie?" Dung asked in Mandarin with a raspy voice, which gave me the impression he was in poor health.

"Why do you need Eng?" I asked.

He snorted. "Aren't you going to offer us a drink?"

"Would you like tea or coffee?"

"I can see liquor in that cabinet. We'll drink Scotch. Pour three shots, but not for the darkie."

I didn't want to make an issue of his request, so I said, "Everyone, take a seat." As I went to the cabinet for the Scotch, Dung walked behind my desk, pulled open one of the drawers, and when Gene took a step to stop him, I said in English, "Dung, as a bank, we adhere to privacy laws. So, shut the drawer and take a seat."

He squinted at me, and when he closed the drawer, Gene backed off.

Dung walked the room, studied the plaques on the wall and the pictures on the credenza one by one, then sat next to Eng and said in Mandarin, "Why are you speaking in their tongue?"

"I want Gene to understand."

"He's nobody."

"He's no different than you or me."

"Hah. If you say so."

I put two shot glasses on the desk. I filled Dung's, and Eng looked me in the eye and nodded as I filled his glass.

Dung stroked his slicked-back hair and said, "We're here to do business. Drink with us."

"I don't drink when I'm at work. It's not professional."

"Make an exception."

I went for a shot glass, filled it, then he lifted his glass and said, "Ganbei," (dry your cup), which I repeated as did Eng. In China, only the host was to make such a toast, and it was considered rude if anyone besides the host made the first toast, but I let the offense pass as we drank the shot in one gulp.

The roof of my mouth tingled, and a slow burn followed. Dung pointed at his empty glass. I poured second shots for them, then Dung pointed at my glass, I filled it, then he repeated "Ganbei." We drank the shots, and this time there was a fiery warmth all the way down my throat.

Dung glared at me, and I knew his insult was intentional. It was a power play in my face and in my office. Gene was standing near the wall watching nervously, while Eng had a mocking grin on his face.

Dung pulled a gold case from his pocket, snapped it open, pulled out a cigarette, inserted the cigarette in an ivory holder, and clenched it between his teeth. Eng was instantly ready with a lighter.

The smell stirred my nerves as I remembered the haze of stale smoke that hung in the air in his office at the logging camp.

"Ashtray?" Dung asked in English as he looked toward Gene.

"Sir, we don't allow smoking in the building," Gene replied.

Dung ignored him, so I reached behind me for another glass. "Use this as an ashtray."

Dung flicked ashes into the glass, took a drag on his cigarette, and said, "Now shoemaker, let's get to business."

He studied me as if he wanted me to say something, but I remained silent.

He waited for a moment and said in English, "I understand you need capital."

He motioned to Eng, who lifted the briefcase onto my desk, took keys out of his pocket, unlocked the latches, opened the case revealing crisp bills in tightly wrapped stacks with a thick blue wrapper around each stack.

Dung rubbed his large fleshy hands together, looked directly at me, and said, "Have you ever seen $100,000 in cash?"

His lifeless, cold eyes were probing for a reaction. I took a deep breath. Dung was cruel and ruthless. Did he have Caitlin and Kathleen? Was he offering me $100,000 to pay himself? He was a Snakehead and an evil man. Could I accept his blood money? I needed to know more, so I probed, "What do you want in return?"

He narrowed his eyes, scrutinized me, clutched the arms of the chair, and said in Mandarin, "I propose we grease each other's palms." He rubbed his hands together with his polished nails. "Federal authorities will never allow me to own a bank, so I will become a silent business partner. I will move deposits here to earn dividends and attend meetings but not be an owner of record or an official board member, and you will have me for guidance and a watchful eye."

His deposits would certainly help avert a liquidity crisis. But if I accepted, I would be like a horse with a bit in its mouth, and he would ride me long and hard. Should I allow Dung to run the meeting or my business, even if I needed his money?

"Let me make it clear that you would be a minority investor, and you can't control the bank."

He covered his mouth with his hand, then rubbed it for a bit. "Look around at this office." He waved his hand at the walls. "There are plaques of recognition from the community, pictures of you with local dignitaries. Is that the old man?" He pointed to a specific picture sitting on the credenza.

"That's Julian LeBlanc."

"He's dead now, yes, and you're alone."

"Death ends a life, not a relationship."

He squinted his eyes at me.

"You and LeBlanc built your lives around doing good, and I want to be part of that public image."

He arched his eyebrows as I pushed back in my chair.

"You have chosen your path, and it's not one of doing good for others. Banking is about serving the community and building a reputation of trustworthiness, as you can see from the commendations." I took measure of his reaction, but his plastic face revealed nothing. "Are you willing to give up illegal logging, trafficking, and prostitution?"

"I support politicians and the police. So, shoemaker, why can't I do it all?" He laughed, and when he looked at Eng, they both laughed.

I wanted to tell him that greed and power consumed him, but he banged his glass on the table, then lifted it toward the liquor cabinet. It wasn't the right time to push him too hard, and I needed his cash, so I refilled his shot glass but not mine as I still had a lingering roughness in my throat and wanted to maintain a level head.

I watched him as he lifted his glass and said, "To doing good, Ganbei." He downed the shot, and his eyes watered.

When he put the glass down, he took a deep breath, coughed hard, clutched his stomach, and grimaced. There was pain in his eyes as he continued coughing, and he pulled a black silk handkerchief out of his pocket and held it to his mouth, coughing violently. Through reddened eyes, he looked at the thick phlegm tinged with red and rolled his head from side to side.

I filled a glass with water and handed it to him.

"Are you trying to save me again like you did from the snake at the camp?"

What was going on inside him? He had never acknowledged my saving him.

Eng moved uncomfortably in his seat, his eyes fixed on Dung. Gene's eyes were wide as he shifted his weight from one foot to the other.

"You saved my life, yet I hated you for it." He grimaced again and closed his eyes. "You need money." He tapped his chest. "My money."

He started coughing again and put the handkerchief to his mouth.

"Eng, papers."

Eng plopped two newspapers on my desk, and Dung pointed to the headlines. One about the bank, the other about the kidnapping.

Was he setting me up? I needed to know.

"Do you have Caitlin and Kathleen?"

He looked away as he said, "This cash will solve your problems."

"I don't know that. I might be taking this cash from you and giving it back to you as a ransom for my wife."

He remained silent.

"Do you have Caitlin and Kathleen?"

He pinched his lips together.

"If you do, you'd receive an interest in the bank for free?"

"You have no reason to believe me if I say no, but without the money, you'll never get her back. The cash is right in front of you. I'm offering it off the balance sheet and as an unrecorded transaction. What I want is a partnership, off the record and out of sight."

He waved his hand in a circular motion and said, "So everyone can get what they want."

"Do you have my wife?" I repeated.

He squinted and gave a slight grin.

"Do you?"

He pointed at me. "I invest in operating partners who are good at running their businesses. What you've achieved is much like how I've become successful. I'm buying an interest in you."

He wasn't going to tell me, I wasn't surprised, and we were light and dark in our values, how we treated others, and how we became who we are. Taking a long look at Dung, his face was starched with a forced smile, but I knew the cruelty of which he was capable.

He coughed until he spit out more phlegm, then motioned to me and said in a serious tone, "We're men from China on a continent that only allows us in if we will work for half of what others are paid. The white class sees us as inferior, as pack animals, but you and I have evolved."

He shifted his position, motioned toward Gene, and said, "Who else can you speak to in Mandarin? Not your wife, or your customers or employees."

I sat back in my chair and tried not to show any emotion. However, I was frightened because I was dealing with a demon and faced a long, dark tunnel that I had warned Kai about when he considered offering himself to Dung. And now, here I was, about to do exactly what I told Kai he should never do.

"I'm here to offer you a working partnership," Dung said. "I'll need you to continue operating the bank and being successful, but I'll want my share of the profits."

I looked at Gene, who had a puzzled expression on his face. We were mostly speaking in Mandarin.

"Can we do business together?" He leaned toward me and pressed his hands on the desktop between us.

From what Suk had told me about Dung's history in China, he was trying to strike back at forces that made him feel ashamed of what happened to his family and the torture he endured at the hands of the Japanese. Retribution could never erase the harsh feelings he experienced. It was an illusion that he could overcome those feelings by exerting control over others.

"Partners should understand each other, don't you agree?" I asked.

He cocked his head and narrowed his eyes.

"Partners are like family."

"I don't understand that."

"Family have to be equal, to get along in a state of harmony and to treat each other with civility and respect."

"The Japanese destroyed my family."

He looked past me. I remained silent and watched him. Everything in him seemed to constrict. His voice started softly, then rose in intensity, as he said, "I have power, and what they did to me, I'll do to everyone who crosses me! Including you, if necessary."

I was taught we are a composite of good and evil and to look for the good in everyone. Still, some individuals are just evil and are too broken emotionally, spiritually, and morally to the extent that their soul, their spirit, cannot be repaired. I wanted to see goodness in Dung, but I needed to see him for who he actually was and not through lenses of my hopes and expectations.

I would contend with constant disappointment if I couldn't deal with the real person at his core. I had been quiet, and I started to realize that my silence made Dung uncomfortable.

"The Japs killed my older brother when he tried to protect my mother," he muttered through clenched teeth. Wiping his mouth with the back of his hand, he stared into the distance and squirmed in his chair.

"You said, civil! Where was civility when I was beaten by the Japs? You said, respect! Where was respect when I watched my mother raped and saw my father and brother murdered?" His nostrils flared, and color filled his pasty face. "Where was respect then?"

He stood and forcefully pointed at me. "I'll show you their civility."

He looked at Eng, then at Gene, who put his hand on his gun. Both stood and faced each other as if expecting something violent to unfold.

"Do you want to see what they did to me when I was little?" Dung pulled open his elegant silk shirt to reveal scarred skin that was dark reddish-brown and looked like hardened sores.

I tried not to show any reaction, as I faced a gale of unrestrained rage that erupted from his soul and was vented at me. "Japanese bastards!" he yelled. He was breathing hard, and his face was glistening from sweat. He started another coughing fit. "I thought I could protect my family. But I had no power. I was too young and had no control."

He staggered and steadied himself against the chair. "They treated us like livestock. They were brutal and waged a savage war, and my family received the worst of it. I was desperate to save my life and my little brother and sister. Mother's last words to me were to take care of them."

He dropped into the chair. Gene and Eng both had apprehensive expressions and looked uncomfortable.

"My sister disappeared. I roamed the villages with Chukee, looking for her. We were starving when we found her; she had been taken by a gang that had food and money. I started hanging around them because of her and never told them we were related. She was always in the company of men. I became a pest, ran errands, did whatever they asked, so they gave me and Chukee food scraps, which kept us alive. I was industrious, like you. Years went by, and I moved up in the organization until I was offered my own territory in Canada. I could do to others what the Japs did to my family and me. Revenge is sweet."

He licked his lips, then pinched them together, blood filled his face, arteries in his neck were swollen, and he said, "When I could treat others like livestock, that's when I knew I had power. There's privilege that comes with power.""

"Some things follow you through life. There's always a desire to have more than we did in childhood," I said softly.

"I never saw my sister again," he muttered.

I looked at Eng and then Gene, who stood motionless, not knowing what to expect. I knew Dung had become vulnerable in front of us, and when he looked at Eng, he unleashed a torrent of cursing in Mandarin.

Eng shook, staring at Dung, and waited for the tempest to run its course.

When Dung continued cursing in Mandarin and English, I said, "I'm sorry for what you went through."

"I don't want your pity!"

The force of his anger startled me, and in a surreal sense, it was as if I had taken the place of the Japanese.

When he stood up, I didn't know what to expect as he walked about the office taking short, quick strides. Eng and Gene watched him and each other.

It took a few minutes until he settled down, but there was too much tension in the room. We were all were on edge, and the meeting needed to end.

"I want to consult with my attorney about how to do what you are suggesting, and I need to make a decision today. How can I contact you?"

He turned slowly, narrowed his eyes, and looked at me as if I were naked. "Are you playing with me?"

Even though his penetrating stare was unnerving, I took a deep breath and calmly said, "I would like until tomorrow morning to make my decision."

He stuck out his jaw, and we stared at each other, like two bulls facing off.

"Why didn't you kill me in your office when Tak wanted to?"

"I don't know." His mouth twisted. Then he turned away from Eng and whispered through gritted teeth, "You were the only one who treated Chukee with respect."

His statement caught me by surprise.

"One more thing," I said.

Dung stared at me.

"As a condition for accepting your money, I want you to release Lysa Wu and her family."

"Why? What's that whore to you? You like her? Does she remind you of your mother?"

My face burned, but I said, "Either you agree, or there'll be no deal. And if you don't follow up on our agreement, I'll find out, and our arrangement will be off."

He squinted his eyes and stared past me before he grunted, "Done."

"What about the details of the note?" I asked.

"We don't need a note. You don't want a recorded lien, do you?"

I shook my head, and he motioned to Eng, who closed and locked the briefcase. They walked out without another word, and Gene followed them until they were out of the building.

I was exhausted, soaked with sweat, and unsure if I was sober or drunk. I wanted to go home and shower as if that would wash off the slime from being in the room with Dung.

Gene returned and said, "Sir, I ain't never seen anyone like Mr. Dung and anything like what happened in this room. Are you okay?"

"I think so. Thank you for staying, Gene."

"It ain't nothin, Mr. LeBlanc."

As Gene left, I reflected on how Dung saw the Japanese abuse his family, and to survive and protect his sister and Chukee, he became entangled with criminals. He must have been in so deep with the organization that there was no turning back. Out of love and loyalty for his family, he became involved in a gang, became obligated, and it hardened and transformed him. And when presented with the opportunity to suppress others like he had been, he seized upon it.

Was I taking the same path? Would a partnership with Dung eventually turn me into someone like him?

Peggy broke my thoughts when she came into the office and asked, "What happened?"

"He wants to help us." I couldn't believe my words.

"Well, that's good news," she said with a surprised look on her face.

I headed for the break room and some coffee to sober up.

∽

We had agreed to reconvene at four o'clock in the police station's conference room. Sluggish from drinking with Dung, I arrived late, and when Milner saw me, he looked at his watch and scowled. I didn't have an opportunity to tell Clive about the meeting with Dung and his proposal as he walked in a few minutes after me and took a seat.

Kirkpatrick said, "Ok, Milner. What you got?"

Milner opened a file folder and pulled out a paper. "One of our undercover detectives played golf in Wasaga Beach with two guys who gamble in high-stakes poker games. He told them he was interested in playing and asked who runs the games. They said it's the barber."

"Where do they play the card games?" Kirkpatrick asked.

"They move around. We're tailing Mezzetti around the clock, hoping he leads us to a game."

We covered some other logistical updates, and when the meeting was adjourned, Clive approached me in the hallway away from the others and whispered, "Did you know about Mezzetti's poker games?"

"Not until Alex Berry said something. I've never met Mezzetti. Do you think that…."

Clive interrupted, "Winson, you've got to stop keeping things you find a secret. Even if you think some detail is insignificant, you've got to start sharing what you find. Tell me, did you meet with Dung?"

"Yes. He offered the cash I need for an interest in the bank as a silent partner, but we both know he won't remain silent."

"What did you say?"

"I didn't give him an answer. I told him I needed to talk to you. I need the money, but I'm struggling. Am I making a mistake that I'll regret for the rest of my life?"

He tilted his head to one side and said, "I can draft a promissory note with terms so you can pay it off."

"Dung doesn't want a note. He wants a silent partnership."

"That's to his advantage."

"I don't think I have a choice. It feels like being back at the camp where he has all the control. I did ask him if he has Caitlin and Kathleen. He said I wouldn't believe him if he said no, so he never gave an answer."

"Did you tell Kirkpatrick and Milner about Dung before I joined the meeting?"

"No, because I wanted to talk to you first and didn't want to complicate getting Dung's money by telling them. I have until tomorrow morning to decide."

Clive clutched my arm, nodded, and said he needed to return to his office.

I had time to return to the bank before closing. Peggy intercepted me as I walked in the door.

"One of the Chinese men who came in earlier today, the bigger one, left a briefcase on your desk. I put the keys in your lap drawer and have been watching to make sure no one entered your office."

Sitting on my desk was the black briefcase that Eng had carried. I put on gloves not to leave fingerprints, and my heart began to race as I unlocked the case and saw bundles of cash. I counted out $100,000 in cash, which I needed for the ransom demand.

Dung was forcing my decision, which was another of his control tactics. On the one hand, I was relieved to be able to deliver the ransom payment, but I wasn't ready to take the money. On the other hand, if I accepted Dung's money and had to concede to his conditions, which would surely follow, it would be a rejection of what I was taught about character, and I would surely disappoint my family. I was at a crossroads. Could I choose going down a path that I admonished Kai not to take?

I wondered what decision YeYe would make if confronted with the same choices. I closed my eyes and sighed heavily, and all of a sudden, I sensed YeYe's presence. He stood before me with a gleam in his eyes that buoyed my spirits. But when I opened my eyes, he was gone.

What was I going to do with the money? I didn't know how to give it back to Dung, and I didn't want to accept it. I locked it in the vault for the night.

I needed fresh air, so I headed toward Sunset Point Park. As I walked, I turned my thoughts to Caitlin. Oh, how I remember blushing while trying to catch glimpses of her when we first met and hoping she wouldn't see me. I loved walking along the shoreline together at the end of an evening, leaning against a railing, and watching the dazzling hues of red, yellow, orange, and purple in the sunset. In those memories, I found hope that she was still alive.

Entering the park, I walked to the bench where Caitlin and I watched children play and often discussed our future. She chastised me for working too much, and we had argued about my not going with her to Pine Isle. Were those to be our final words? That conversation didn't represent our love for each other. But that regret hung on the walls of my heart like the weeping willows in the park.

Out of the corner of my eye, I saw a large man in a black leather jacket walking toward me. I looked around, and unusual for this time of day, the park was almost empty.

As he drew closer, the sun was behind him, and his shadow fell across me.

"May I sit?"

"Sullivan, of course." I finally recognized his broadly jawed and bearded face that looked like he'd been in too many saloon fights.

"Can we talk?"

"Sure. What's on your mind?"

He wrung his hands and looked around with a blank stare. He hesitated before he said, "There's no way I can make up for hurting you the way I did. Sorry, man."

"Your apology is accepted. I appreciate what you did for me at the Towne Terrace."

"And I owe you for what you did for my mother."

"What was that?"

"Your efforts helped her survive after pop was killed in the *Montebello* accident."

I nodded. "Are you still working at the shipyard?"

"I work half shifts. Business is off this year."

Sheepishly, he looked away, and I wondered why he was even speaking to me.

After a short while, Sullivan cleared his throat, spit on the ground and started speaking softly. He was wringing his hands and looking out at the lake with a concerned expression as he said, "I wouldn't expect you to know about the ugly side of life here because of who you are and all, but there are people here you don't want to cross. I work for a man named Mezzetti up in Wasaga Beach.

"I'm ashamed of what I did to you and what I gotta do to others, but you gotta understand that I take care of my family by using my muscles. It's what I do. It's how I was born."

He couldn't stop fidgeting. "Ya see, Mezzetti's been running games at a private lodge up north. He puts girls in the cabins and cards in the lodge. That combination brings in the players.

"And some of those players, they lose big time, and they owe him lots and lots of money. Some of 'em would do just about anything to keep me away from 'em, eh. One of those guys is Patrick Chorley. He owes Mezzetti over fifty grand. I was going out to collect from him one way or another when Mezzetti told me to back off. He's never done that before. I don't know what he's up to, but I don't trust him about anything. Maybe it's because Chorley's wife's missing, and Mezzetti may have backed off because he's personally involved.

"When I heard about your wife and Chorley's wife, I thought I should tell you what's happening. Mezzetti is where I would start looking for your wife. He's mean and money-hungry enough to do anything."

"Where's this lodge?"

"At the Chute."

"What did you say?"

"Big Chute. And don't tell anyone where you got this." Then he pulled out a billfold from his back pocket, opened it, lifted out a card, and said, "Mezzetti's address is on the card."

I read it and started to hand it back.

"Keep it. It don't do me no good." His eyes darted about as if deciding which direction to take, then he pulled up his collar and said, "I gotta go," and walked away.

I was tight as a piano wire. My muscles were stiff, but a surge of energy coursed throughout my body. As I walked away from Georgian Bay, the sun backlit the rock formations of the Niagara Escarpment in such a way that they rose against the sky and lifted my spirits along with them.

I knew time was of the essence and was so anxious I even considered driving to Mezzetti's shop myself. I deliberated asking Gene to go with me, but instead, taking a few deep breaths to clear my mind and reset my emotions, I ran to the nearest phone booth and called Clive at his office. He asked where I was and said he would meet me at the park entrance.

I was waiting next to the road when Clive picked me up.

"What's going on?" he asked.

I recounted the Sullivan conversation and said, "I want to meet Mick and was going to take Gene with me."

"That would be two murders for the paper to cover. Absolutely not. We're going to the station and tell Kirkpatrick and Milner what Sullivan told you."

I gritted my teeth and knew Clive was right.

"Where's this Big Chute?" I asked.

"There's a Big Chute on Highway 34 about an hour north of Wasaga Beach."

"What is it?"

"It's a marine railroad that physically lifts boats out of the water and over a hill on a track system, then launches them back into the water on another lake. It's part of a canal system that connects Georgian Bay with Lake Ontario. There are private lodges and small cabins near the Big Chute."

"Sullivan said Mezzetti sent him to collect from Chorley. Is it possible that Mezzetti could be involved in the kidnapping?

"He's a hoodlum." There was anger in his voice. He started driving faster and said, "Did Sullivan say how much money Chorley owed Mick?"

"About fifty grand. Apparently, Chorley played in the big-money games Alex talked about. Sullivan called on the losers to collect their debts."

"If Mezzetti is involved in the kidnapping, he probably had thugs do his dirty work."

"What about Graham?" I asked.

"I don't understand."

"He's always defensive of Chorley. Why is that?"

"Perhaps because they are two of a kind. Both bullies."

As we pulled into the parking lot of the OPP, I said, "Clive, before we go in, I want to tell you about …"

"Tell me later. We need to get inside now."

We hurried inside and met with Kirkpatrick and Milner, who were waiting for us. I repeated what Sullivan told me, and then Milner opened a file, thumbed through it, pointed to a document, and said, "A man named Childress operated the boat transfer at Big Chute for decades. He retired last winter without notice, and a Toronto company took over moving boats back and forth through the Chute."

"Milner, enough history, what does that have to do with anything?"

He narrowed his eyes at Kirkpatrick. "I researched it a while ago. One of our undercover officers is invited to a game, and we're setting up surveillance."

"When is it?" I asked.

"That's police business," Milner snapped.

"That's enough, Milner. Winson, thanks for giving us this information. We'll take it from here." Kirkpatrick said as he dismissed us.

Outside the station, I told Clive about Dung's maneuver and the briefcase full of cash locked in the bank vault.

"Without an agreement?" Clive said.

"Dung didn't want anything to be recorded. I told him I would give him my decision tomorrow."

"This isn't good. You'll never get Dung out of your life."

"I know. Dung's reputation will be a stain on me, and being in frequent contact with him will be like receiving ant bites filled with acidic venom."

Chapter Seventeen

Wednesday

I was surprised to see Kirkpatrick when I arrived at Clive's office. He was seated at the conference table and asked, "Do you have the ransom money?"

I looked at Clive for advice.

"Tell him everything. Caitlin's life is at stake," Clive insisted.

"I met with Dung yesterday afternoon."

"And you didn't tell us? Are you withholding information on purpose? Are you trying to thwart this investigation? Are you working with Chorley without us?"

"I'm sorry I didn't tell you about Dung. I'm not withholding information on purpose, and I'm not working with Chorley."

"Then explain yourself because from where I'm sitting, your position doesn't look so good."

"I thought if I could talk to Dung, I could find out if he had Caitlin and Kathleen. Dung came into the bank about one o'clock yesterday with a bodyguard named Eng and a briefcase with $100,000 cash. He offered me the money for an unrecorded partnership interest in the bank."

"Why didn't you call me while he was there? You know we want him for questioning."

"I thought he might give me answers that he wouldn't give you because he wants something from me."

"Did you ever think he might have Caitlin and Kathleen, and he'll get his own $100,000 back if he returns the women?"

"Yes. I even told Dung I thought he was doing that. He neither denied nor confirmed my suspicion. He very well could have them, but I had to take a chance."

"So you took the money from him?"

"No."

"But you said you have the money?"

"While I was at the police station with you yesterday afternoon, Eng left the briefcase with Peggy Bailey. But I told Dung I needed until noon today to make my decision. I was surprised when the briefcase was on my desk last night. It was late, and I didn't know what to do, so I put the briefcase in the vault overnight. I'm sorry if I've made a mess of things. Maybe I'm not thinking straight."

I closed my eyes. "I can't imagine my life without Caitlin, and I'm desperate to get her back." I looked at Clive and then at Kirkpatrick. "I don't want Dung's money, but I don't know how to return it. He said he'd call me at the bank at noon today for my decision. It's just like Dung to manipulate me by sending the money early. What should I do now?"

"You need to stop trying to be an investigator. I'm having you tailed from now on. We need information faster than you're giving it to us. You withheld the rosary beads, you're talking to Chorley about the ransom, you won't give us the names of your information sources, and now this. I'm more than a little disappointed. You know I trusted you even though Milner told me not to."

"I'm sorry, Chief."

"I'm sending an officer to the bank to pick up that briefcase."

"But it's not my money, and if I can't use it for the ransom, I want to return it to Dung."

"That's not your decision. The money is evidence in this case, and I'm going to hold it at the police station." He stood for a moment, ran his fingers through his hair, then walked out the door.

"Clive, what can I do? I don't want Dung's money. I just want Caitlin back."

"You must give the briefcase to the police, and if you want their help, you'd better cooperate. I think you should go to the bank before the police arrive."

≈

It was still early morning as I walked to the bank. I was feeling low and confused for making such a mess of things. At Clive's office, Kirkpatrick didn't update me on the investigation, and it had been more than twenty-four hours, and we hadn't heard from the kidnappers. Why hadn't they contacted us, and why did Dung show up at about the same time as we should have heard?

Suddenly, my left arm was squeezed, and the barrel of a pistol was pushed into my back. My mind was in a spin as I glanced over my shoulder and saw the image of a man in a dark shirt.

"Yell, and I'll shoot."

I couldn't believe what was happening, and I strained against his grip, and as I struggled to pull away, the barrel pressed harder against my body, and my muscles cramped.

"You avoided death working the logs, and Dung could've let me kill you in his office. I would've shot you behind Parliament Square, but the guard showed up, and I would've shot you and your wife in Ottawa or pushed you in front of the train, except for the detectives. I waited for you in Tobermory, but you didn't show. You've run out of lives. There's no one to help you now."

Tak's voice was a low growl. I imagined myself getting shot and bleeding on the ground, and I shivered uncontrollably.

"You think you're better than me!" You're just a shoeshine boy!"

My eyes darted about looking for help, but the street was empty.

"There's no one to help you. I'm gonna put you in your place. Dung thinks he wants you as a partner, but I don't want any part of you in our organization. This morning you die." He put the cold barrel hard against my hot neck.

"Tak, let's…"

"Shut your face." He pressed the gun against my neck. "Start walking, normal-like. Any struggle from you and I pull the trigger right here on the street."

"Please, Tak. I don't want to be partners with Dung."

"Shut the fuck up." The pistol clicked as he cocked it.

"I want to return the money to him. Put the gun down, and I'll give you the money."

"You'll give me the money, all right. Where is it?"

"At my house, in the safe." I don't know why I lied, but I couldn't take him to the bank and endanger other lives.

Tak stood behind me as I turned and walked toward home. "After you kill me, will you release Caitlin and Kathleen?"

"Ha! You'll never know. You'll die never seeing your wife and her friend again. But you'll be seeing your friends Suk and Biyu today."

He moved the pistol up to my temple as he sneered, "So the money is at your house. But you will never tell me where it is. Will you?"

Sweat beaded on my face.

"All I need to know is that it's at your house. I'll find it."

He pushed me up against the wall of a building, and three shots rang out. The tug of his hand pulled my arm as I fell to the ground.

Everything went white, and time had no meaning until I heard 'Mr. Leblanc,' and there was a hand on my shoulder.

"Mr, LeBlanc, are you hurt?" a voice asked.

"I don't know. Am I dead?"

"Dying doesn't hurt. It's quicker than falling asleep."

I looked up and blinked several times.

"But, no, you aren't dead. But you do need to sit for a bit and let me look you over."

"Detective McGee, where did you come from?"

"Chief Kirkpatrick called me on the way to the station. Said you were at Mr. Owen's office and for me to shadow you. I saw this guy jump you with a gun in his hand, and I've been watching for the right opportunity to shoot. Who was he?"

"Was? Is he dead?"

"Unfortunately, yes. I couldn't risk warning him with that gun pointed at you."

"It's Tak."

I tried to collect myself but couldn't muster the energy. "Thank you for saving my life," I mumbled.

"Just following orders. It looks like I winged you on your left arm. I hope you're right-handed."

I saw blood on my sleeve and a tear in my jacket. "It stings but doesn't hurt much."

"Let me look at it." He gently took hold of my arm and said, "It's a bullet wound. You'll be okay, but you need to get treated."

"You're a good man."

He cracked a small and quick smile. "Can you wait here for a few minutes while I call the station for backup and an ambulance for you?"

"Yes. I'll be okay."

I watched him walk around the corner, then turned my head and stared at Tak. He was face down in a pool of blood with a bullet hole in his head and another in his back. He lived a violent life and died a violent death.

My mind went back to the first time I saw Tak outside the Vancouver Immigration station. There were so many bad memories of him and no good ones. I was sorry for his wasted life, but would his killing become the death of Caitlin and Kathleen? Would Dung take his revenge out on my wife?

After a short visit to the emergency room, five stitches, and my left arm in a sling, much of the day was spent at the police station answering questions. I wanted to be at the bank at noon for Dung's call, but Chief Kirkpatrick didn't trust me. He had an officer pick up the briefcase from Peggy before the bank opened. Clive drove me home in the afternoon with orders to get some sleep.

I saw McGee and another officer several times that afternoon roaming around the grounds around the house. I didn't know if Dung had called the bank for me. I was in the dark, exhausted, and under the influence of pain medicine.

I laid in bed, not understanding what was happening. Everything was a blur as I fell asleep.

Chapter Eighteen

Thursday

Kirkpatrick's call woke me at half-past twelve in the middle of the night.

"I have an update. Mezzetti was arrested a few hours ago on a criminal charge of conducting illegal gaming activities and is under questioning, but so far, he's refused to answer any questions from our officers. If he doesn't break his silence, we'll offer him a plea bargain if he leads us to the women. In the meantime, we're conducting a coordinated search of the cabins and area around the Big Chute. We're fully engaged."

"Have you notified Chorley as well?"

"I called you first."

"I won't be able to sleep after your news, so be sure to call when you know more." I was so keyed up all I could do was pace. I showered, dressed, and packed a change of clothes for Caitlin. Only able to use one arm, everything took longer. I sat in the office for a while, and when my arm started throbbing, I went into the kitchen, took two prescription pain pills, and put the kettle on for tea.

When the doorbell rang, I thought it would be McGee, Kirkpatrick, or an officer with another report. I was surprised when I opened the front door and saw Chorley standing in front of me, unshaven and wearing a scruffy shirt.

"Patrick, what are you doing here?"

"I need to see you."

He was clearly in a state of distress.

"Come in, and tell me what's wrong." I led him into the parlor, where he sat in a chair, and I sat across him on the sofa.

He pointed at my left arm in the sling and said, "What happened to you?"

"I was shot. Detective Magee killed a Snakehead gang member who had a gun to my head. I don't know if it had anything to do with the kidnapping."

"Are you okay? Can I do anything for you?"

"I'll be okay." I didn't tell him I was on pain pills and completely exhausted.

Placing a cigarette in the corner of his mouth, his long fingers searched the outside pockets of his jacket. Not finding a match, he pitched the cigarette on the floor in disgust.

"Did you hear from the police?" I asked.

"Kirkpatrick called me, and I thought it was good news until I received a call from one of the kidnappers. Shit, they said if they don't get the money by nine in the morning, they'll throw Kathleen and Caitlin in the lake. Damn, we have to do something." He looked at me with a hostile glare.

Would they do that to my wife, my child? Who are these brutes that would harm innocent women? This can't be happening, but it is. When and how would it end? What a nightmare! "The police said they would negotiate with Mezzetti if he knew where our wives are being held," I said.

"You don't understand! I've played poker with Mezzetti. He's a bloody parasite. He sets up the games for the players to lose. He'll never lead the police to our wives." He said through gritted teeth.

"But Kirkpatrick said he'd offer Mezzetti a plea bargain for any information leading to Caitlin and Kathleen."

"If he bargains with the police, the crime ring he's involved with is ruthless, and he won't live long. Unless you produce the money now, our wives will die." His cheeks flushed, and his facial muscles became rigid.

"Then you think Mezzetti knows where they are?"

"Bloody hell! I just know you need to give me the money for the kidnappers before nine." His eyes flashed with anger.

"Patrick, we need to stay calm under pressure."

"You're right. I got the call and got all worked up, then came straight here. I've played in their poker games and seen what they do to guys who don't pay up. We're running out of time. I just want this all to go away." His voice slowly grew louder, and he pounded his fists on the arms of the chair. "I know we're both under stress, eh. But you're not listening to what I'm telling you." His voice cracked. "I'll do anything to get Kathleen back. We need to work out something. You must have money?"

I didn't want to tell him about Dung's money, but I didn't want to lie. I was lightheaded and not thinking clearly as I blurted, "I gave the money to the police."

He sat up in the chair, "If you gave them the money, then why aren't the police arranging for a money drop and exchange?"

"All I know is that I got shot this morning, and Kirkpatrick called me like he did you, to tell us that they're closing in on the kidnappers who must be panicking if they called you right after Mezzetti was arrested."

He stood up, paced around the parlor, and a vein in his neck seemed to swell. Like me, I was sure he was feeling frustrated and helpless. He pointed around the room and said, "Your house is filled with fine furniture and paintings. LeBlanc made lots of money, and you just stepped in as his son and inherited it! Why can't you do something to save our wives?"

We had been struggling. We were both exhausted. I could see the impact stress was bearing on Patrick as his eyes welled with tears.

He was different from Graham. He had apologized for his father-in-law, even called him crusty, and said it was hard to have a good relationship with him. Patrick openly said he didn't have the money, but how could he afford to play in high-stakes poker games? Seeing his old rusty car and knowing he lived in a rented bungalow, I knew he wasn't flush. I admired the fact that he offered to give himself up as collateral, which was something I would do. Looking at his puffy, bloodshot eyes and seeing his cheek quiver, I could empathize with him. We were both clinging to hope.

"Patrick, the stress is getting to both of us. We're doing everything we can, and I know how you feel, I've shed many tears, not knowing if my wife and child are still alive. I've been in a state of total panic and desperation, grabbing at any opportunity that might change the situation and bring Caitlin and Kathleen safely home. My life will be destroyed if Caitlin doesn't come home."

Obviously agitated, Chorley walked to the far corner of the room, stood in front of the record player, and started fiddling with the needle arm.

"Patrick, the police have Mezzetti in custody and said they're close to finding our wives."

"Like hell they are."

His face turned red, his jaw was set, and he glared as he walked toward me. My arm was uncomfortable from pain, and my jaw clenched so hard that I thought it would shatter.

He stopped, picked up the metal-framed photograph sitting on the table next to his chair, walked up to me, and held it for me to see, as he asked, "Who's this?"

"That's Julian LeBlanc and his wife, Ruthie, before their accident."

He shook the picture in my face as he said, "There's money in this house, but you're not going to tell me where it is, are you?"

"I told you, I gave it to the…" he swung the picture, hitting the top of my left arm with the metal edge of the frame. He struck my arm a second time, and the glass shattered. I shrieked as I tumbled to the floor, writhing in pain. Broken glass was in my hair, on my clothes, and my head spun as I tried to keep from passing out.

Chorley looked at me and said, "I'll find the money myself if I have to tear this place apart."

I lifted my arm at the elbow, hoping it would ease the pain as it continued to throb. I lay on the floor and watched him walk into the office and heard books and glass crash against the floor. Why would he attack me? Was he irrational from stress and futility?

Then I heard the bedroom door bang open and heard him rummaging through our things. His aggressive attack on me and my home was clearly motivated by other intentions. I was beginning to feel that I may have been taken in by him.

But it was still possible that the constant stress of the kidnapping was causing his behavior. Each of us handles stress differently. In addition to the abduction, he was in serious debt to Mezzetti to the tune of $50,000. Alex had told me that Chorley was a plunger as a gambler because of his big ego, and he often got into it with Mezzetti.

When he came out of the bedroom, he didn't even look at me when he went from room to room as if I didn't matter to him. He stomped past me on his way into the kitchen and I heard drawers and cabinet doors banging, and glass breaking. I put my head against the floor and looked up at the ceiling. My wife and child's future were at stake, and it wouldn't be long before he came back after me. My body was like a string, pulled to its limit and about to snap. When I looked at Julian and Ruthie's broken frame and photo, I knew I had to get up and stop him.

I struggled to my feet, leaned against the wall to steady myself, and knew I must be strong. I had overcome many threatening situations and found the will to survive. Before I walked into the kitchen, I didn't know what I would say or do, but I needed to stop his madness.

When he saw me in the kitchen, he turned and said, "I'm gonna burn this house down if you don't give me money."

"I told you, I gave it to the police. Call Kirkpatrick, and he'll tell you."

"Bullshit." Chorley picked up a butcher knife from the contents of a drawer he had spilled on the floor and pointed it at me.

"It won't do you any good to hurt me. It's the kidnappers you're angry with."

"No, it's an insignificant pissant who inherits money, and a bank, and a mansion, and doesn't have to sell himself each day to make a living."

With a wild look in his eyes, he started toward me, swinging the knife wildly through the air threatening with every swing to injure or even kill me. I stepped back until I was up against the stove as he came at me.

My life, wife, child, house, everything was going to be destroyed. I was in total panic and desperation and needed something to defend myself. I leaned away from him, felt the heat from the stove, and remembered the tea kettle. It was still boiling. I had put it on to make tea and had turned the burner down, but not off. It was all I had to defend myself against this maniac.

I reached behind me with my right hand as he yelled, "Now, for the last time, tell me where you hide your money?"

I managed to grab the handle, swung it around, and flung it at Chorley. The lid opened, and scalding water splashed across his face and shoulder.

He shrieked, and the knife clattered to the floor as he stumbled backward and fell to the floor. "I can't see, I can't see," he screamed.

He was rubbing his face with the back of his arm as he shrieked and rolled on the floor.

I kicked the knife away from him and looked at him in disbelief over what had happened. Then I heard sirens blaring, followed by pounding on the front door. The door was forced open, and someone was yelling my name.

"In the kitchen," I said as loud as I could.

McGee burst into the kitchen with two officers as Chorley screeched, "The bastard blinded me on purpose. Arrest him."

"Chorley tried to kill me with that knife. He's torn apart the house looking for money and threatened to burn the house down."

"LeBlanc couldn't do all this damage with one arm. Cuff him," McGee said.

McGee took out a handkerchief and picked up the knife as evidence. The two officers cuffed him, and as they dragged him out of the house, he yelled, "Mezzetti coerced me. It was Mezzetti. It wasn't me. It was Mezzetti," he kept saying over and over.

"Are you okay?" McGee asked.

"I've been better, but I can't tell you how relieved I was to see you."

"This has been quite a night for you, eh," McGee said.

"How did you know that Chorley was here?"

"Our tailing officer lost him earlier, but then we received a call from a patrol officer who spotted Chorley's car in front of your house, and I rushed over with backup."

"Do you think he knows where Caitlin and Kathleen are?"

"He'll be questioned at the police station, but I think we'll find your wife soon."

"I hope so and thank you. In the past twenty-four hours, you've saved my life twice. If I have a son, I should name him McGee."

"Don't do that."

"I owe you my life!"

"Surveillance work is one of the more thankless tasks for any police officer, so it's nice to be appreciated. I'm going to leave an officer here for a while, but you call me if you need anything."

When McGee walked out the door, the flashing lights of the police cars bathed the house in red. There was still a police officer taking pictures of the damage, who asked me not to clean up until he was through.

My arm throbbed, so I took another pain pill, even though it was too soon, and tried to settle myself. I was still worried and thinking about what Caitlin was going through.

About an hour after McGee left, Kirkpatrick called and said, "Great news. Caitlin and Kathleen are safe and with Milner."

My heart was thumping so hard that I thought it would burst out of my chest. "Am I dreaming? Are they really okay? It's been some night!"

"Yes, they're okay and being taken to the hospital in Midland."

"Hospital?"

"Just a precaution. Milner said they're okay."

"The baby, what about the baby? Do you know anything about Caitlin's condition?"

"Milner didn't say. I'm sure they're exhausted from their ordeal."

"What about Mezzetti."

"We're holding him on charges of illegal gambling. Hopefully, we'll have enough evidence to charge him with kidnapping too. "

"I hope he's convicted. And he shouldn't be able to get away with his unpunished crimes."

"We'll do our best to see him incarcerated."

"How did events unfold?"

"Our undercover agent was at a late night game at the Big Chute Lodge. He had notified us that Mezzetti was running a game, and before we arrested him, we set up surveillance and saw two men approach the lodge from the rear. Mezzetti came to the door, and they argued. The two men waved their hands in disgust at him and walked away. Two of our plain-clothes officers followed them at a distance. Excuse me for being so excited about what happened with my officers, but catching bad guys is what motivates me about police work.

"It was a moonless night, and they trailed them through a forested area, thought they'd lost them until they heard swearing, and followed the voices to an isolated cabin. The officers waited and watched for a while. Then approached the front of the cabin, broke in the door, and one of the officers shot one of the men when he went for his gun. When the man fell to the floor, the other man immediately threw his hands in the air and said, 'I ain't' reachin' for no gun.' They cuffed them and found Caitlin and Kathleen locked in a back bedroom."

"Thank God they're safe."

"McGee told me what happened at your house with Chorley. Are you okay?"

"I am now that Caitlin and Kathleen have been found."

"I'll get back to you later in the morning as soon as I know when the doctors will release them. Unfortunately, they'll need to answer some questions and fill out police reports before they can return home. We'll bring them to Collingwood as soon as possible. After what you've gone through, you need rest."

"I can't thank you enough."

Clive was the first one I called to break the news. He and Bitsy were overjoyed. When I called the Mulroney's, Kierian answered the phone. "Who the hell calls at two o'clock in the morning."

"Kierian, it's Winson. I just received a call from Chief Kirkpatrick that Caitlin has been rescued and is safe."

"Where is she?"

"Midland Hospital. It's a precaution for her and Kathleen."

I could hear Maureen saying, "Who is it? What's happening?"

"It's Winson."

She must have pulled the phone away from Kierian because I heard her soft voice, "Winson, what have you heard about Caitlin?"

"Caitlin and Kathleen are safe."

"Oh, thank God, I've been praying day and night. Do the Grahams know?"

"I don't know if the police called them, but it looks like Chorley's involved."

"Oh no! Clara will be devastated."

"I'll let you know as I know more."

"God bless you, Winson."

It was too late to call Catherine and Joseph, so I made a mental note to call them and Miss Jerome later in the morning.

I wondered about the health of Caitlin and the baby and fought the urge to drive to the hospital. I was too excited to go back to sleep, and my mind churned as I paced the floors, wishing Kai and Wei Lei were here to keep me company. I would need their help to clean up the mess in the house before Caitlin got home.

Regardless of what Kirkpatrick said about questioning them and bringing them back to Collingwood or that the doctor told me to rest for a few days, I decided to drive to Midland. After a quick shower, I was dressing when the phone rang.

"Mr. LeBlanc, McGee here. Chief Kirkpatrick wants you to know that your wife is being transported to Barrie because of her condition."

"Chief Kirkpatrick told me they were exhausted. What's happened?"

"All I know is that an ambulance is taking them to the Royal Victoria Hospital in Barrie."

"Thank you for letting me know. I'm going to the hospital."

"You may not be able to see them until after they've been examined and treated, and you shouldn't drive if you've been taking pain pills."

"You're right. Thank you for reminding me."

I hadn't seen my wife for weeks and had an adrenalin rush from all the excitement. I needed to be with my Caitlin and didn't want to wait for someone to give me a ride. I made a strong pot of coffee and set out for the Royal Victoria Hospital in Barrie, thankful that the police officer had departed.

It was a moonless night, and I was ecstatic that the women were safe, but my heart was sad for Kathleen, and I didn't know how I could tell her what her husband had done or what I had done to him.

My thoughts alternated between excitement and exhaustion. What an ordeal we had all experienced. I had many challenges in my life, but Caitlin missing had consumed me, and not knowing her or the baby's current condition elevated my anxiety.

Without warning, the car started sputtering, and the engine stopped. I looked at the gas gauge, and it was empty. With all the excitement of Tak, Chorley, the meds, and the rescues, I had neglected to check the gas gauge. All around me was farmland, and no vehicles were on the road. I walked toward the nearest town. About fifteen minutes later, headlights appeared behind me, a truck pulled up next to me, and a man in a cowboy hat lowered the window and said, "Looks like you could use some help. Is that your car about a mile back?"

"Yes, I ran out of gas."

"No gas stations open this time of the morning. Want a ride?"

He was alone, and I couldn't tell much about him. In my experience, most people didn't give rides to Chinese, but here he was, offering me a ride, and I was anxious to get to the hospital.

"Thanks, I'm indebted to you."

"Mostly farmers out this time of the morning. Where you headed?"

"Barrie. Royal Victoria Hospital."

"For your arm?" he asked, looking at my sling.

"My wife was rescued from kidnappers a few hours ago. She's also seven months pregnant. I was so anxious to get there that I didn't look at the gas gauge."

"My name is Cody Larson. Hop in."

"Winson LeBlanc."

"I'm headed to Toronto for supplies. How about I drop you at the hospital in Barrie? It's on the way."

"I would like to pay you for your trouble." I reached into my pocket to get my wallet.

"I'm not doing this to get paid. Never know when I'll need help myself."

"Thanks. I'll remember what you've done, but I still want to do something for you. I'm the President of Merchants Bank, and when you're in Collingwood, please come in."

"The Merchants Bank that's been in the newspapers lately."

"We're trying to get the wrongful articles retracted."

"Looks like you've had more than your share of trouble."

We rode in silence for miles.

Barrie was quiet when we arrived at the Royal Victoria Hospital. There was an ambulance in the driveway and a black and white Collingwood police vehicle behind it.

Cody stopped his truck near the emergency room entrance.

I thanked him, gave him my business card, shook his hand, and told him he was a godsend.

"I hope your wife and baby are okay. I'll put gas in your car on my way home. Always carry an empty can in the back of the truck."

"You're too kind. Let me at least give you money for the gas."

"That would take away my reason for helping." That was his last word before I watched him drive away.

I entered the hospital through double glass doors and walked up to the reception desk. An older woman with black-framed glasses and salt and pepper hair in a bun looked at me when I said, "I'm looking for Caitlin LeBlanc and Kathleen Chorley. My name's Winson LeBlanc, Caitlin's my wife. They were rescued from kidnappers and brought in by ambulance not too long ago." I knew I was rambling.

"The police said no visitors at this time. They're being examined by our medical teams."

"She's been missing for over two weeks. I need to know she's okay. The police told me she would be here."

"Sir, she's with the doctor. You can take a seat, and I'll let him know you're here."

"Can you make an exception and let me see her now?"

She gave me a stern look.

"Detective McGee of the Collingwood OPP called me and said she was brought to this hospital. Please, I need to see her and hold her hand."

"We have rules here. I don't know how things work in China, but here we follow protocols."

"If you were pregnant and taken hostage and now were hospitalized, wouldn't you want to have your husband by your side?"

She remained silent.

The critical issue was that Caitlin was safe. I bit my lower lip and tried to be diplomatic. "Would you please explain these circumstances to the doctor?"

"Sir, the Collingwood Police said no visitors."

"If Detective McGee is here, tell him Caitlin's husband wants to see her."

"I'm sorry, but I can't leave the reception desk. If someone comes out, you can ask them." She avoided making eye contact and thumbed through the papers on her desk.

I wanted to burst through the doors that said Medical Staff only but didn't want to run the risk that she would call security. I paced and sat, paced and sat, and watched the clock mark time.

When the doors to the Emergency Room swung open, Kathleen was in a wheelchair being pushed by a nurse. "Oh my God. Winson," Kathleen screamed as she tried to get up from the chair.

The nurse put her hand on Kathleen's shoulder. "Please don't stand up. You can visit your friend from the wheelchair."

Kathleen extended her arms, inviting a hug.

Overcome with emotion, I held her tight and asked, "Are you okay?"

"I will be. I'm too exhausted to think."

"I'll leave you two to visit, but Mrs. Chorley, please stay in the wheelchair until you're released. It's hospital policy," she said as she pushed Kathleen to the back row of chairs in the waiting area. I sat next to her as the nurse went through the double doors and back into the exam area.

"Where's Caitlin? Is she okay? And the baby?"

"An obstetrician is examining her. Caitlin told me the baby's still kicking. Hopefully, everything's okay. I'm so sorry, so sorry."

"You're safe now."

"I feel responsible." Her voice cracked, and she had difficulty continuing until she finally said, "An officer told me about Patrick's gambling debts. He never told me. I'm so ashamed." Tears filled her eyes.

"It's not your fault. I know you love Caitlin and would never do anything to endanger her."

"It was my husband who put us through hell."

"It was more my fault than yours. I should have gone with you to Pine Isle."

"None of this is because of you." Kathleen squeezed my arm. "Caitlin and I have done a lot of crying over the past weeks, God has brought us through this ordeal together, and we'll be stronger for it."

"I prayed for your safety." I pulled the rosary beads from my pocket and showed them to her.

"Where did you get those?"

"On Pine Isle. I vowed to keep them as my lifeline to you both until you were safe."

"They're mine. I had the beads in my hand when the kidnappers wrenched me into the boat, I dropped them. I took it as an omen that we weren't going to make it."

"I prayed for you every time I held them. The beads ended up being a clue because they were a connection to Mezzetti, which helped lead the police to the Big Chute. So here, they're yours once again." I handed them to her. "And they kept you safe."

She kissed my hand and then cradled them against her heart.

"Rhoda had rosary beads, and she's Catholic, but you're not."

"Patrick is. He gave them to me as a gift when he proposed. I kept them in my pocket when he was out of town." She started sobbing and muttered something under her breath.

"What did you say?"

"Patrick, the bastard! I'm glad he's in jail and hope he won't be out for a long time. Now that I know about his gambling debts, I'm going to divorce him." Then she gave me back the beads, folded her arms, and said, "I don't want these anymore, and I didn't know about Mezzetti."

"He lives in Wasaga Beach, runs high-stakes poker games, and is part of a crime ring. I was told he sets up the games for the players to lose, and I talked to someone who collects money for Mezzetti. The collector said he called on Patrick several times to collect on his debts, but then Mezzetti recently told him to lay off."

When tears streamed down her face, I handed her a handkerchief. She regained some composure and said, "He traveled so much, I suspected there were other women."

I was embarrassed for her.

"Did Caitlin ever tell you anything about Patrick?"

I shook my head.

"He's emotionally and physically abusive." She bit her tongue. "My marriage has been over for years, but I didn't want to admit it."

I didn't know what to say.

"Daddy's filled with so much hate, and he sticks up for Patrick. He was best friends with Patrick's father, baptized Patrick, and treated him like the son he always wanted. I married a man just like my father. I love my mother, but I need to get away from Daddy."

"Kathleen, look at me." I took her hand. "I understand how you feel. You're upset right now and may reconsider staying with them, but in the meantime, you're welcome to stay with us."

"You should talk to Caitlin first."

"You know what she'll say. You're like sisters, and she probably wants your help once the baby arrives."

"Thank you." She shook her head as she said, "Patrick had vices, but I never thought he was capable of doing this to us. The gambling may have started small, but certainly got out of control, for it to end up the way it did."

I reached out to hold her hand, and she leaned over and kissed my cheek.

"How in the world could Patrick have been a part of what happened to Caitlin and me? We had just finished dinner Monday night and were about to do the dishes when the front door was kicked open, and three hooded men forced their way into the cottage. They blindfolded us, bundled us with the sofa blankets, and put us in a boat. It seemed like hours before we docked. The men didn't speak to each other. But one of them said we would be shot if their demands were not met within seventy-two hours." She started to chew her nails. "We decided that the only way to survive was to cooperate and say as little as possible."

"Did you ever see who they were?"

"No. They wore woolen masks over their faces. When they brought in our food, it wasn't much, and we had no appetite. I knew Caitlin needed nutrition for the baby. I ate to encourage her to eat."

Her hands shook, and I took hold of them to calm her.

"We were locked in a small bedroom with boarded-up windows. We shared a double bed and had a toilet and sink for a bathroom. We didn't know night from day, but we knew we were captive more than three days and our nerves were raw. They'd bring us food, and we tried to ask questions, but they never answered. I'm sure God was with us because we're here now. It helped both of us to sing to the baby."

She put her hand to her mouth, took several slow dry swallows, and looked at something far away. I was relieved when the ER doors swung open, and a young nurse dressed in a starched white uniform and cap asked, "Are you, Mr. LeBlanc?"

"Yes, I am."

"Your wife can see you now."

I took hold of Kathleen's hand. She smiled and said, "You go. I'll be okay. They called my mother to pick me up. She's on the way. I'm glad they let me talk to you before I left the hospital."

She let go of my hand and motioned me down toward the corridor that led to Caitlin. Passing several drawn curtains, the nurse opened the last one in the row. Caitlin was in bed, her eyes were closed, and she had pulled her legs up as far as her swollen belly would allow. Her arms were around her belly as if protecting our unborn child.

I gently pulled the blanket around her neck and kissed her cheek. When I softly said, "Caitlin, I love you," her eyes opened wide, a bright smile spread across her face, and she threw her arms around my neck.

I held her close, nuzzled her hair, took long, deep breaths, and whispered, "Are you alright?"

"I am now that you're here. I kept asking to see you, but the nurse said I needed to rest."

"I'm here, and I'm staying."

"I just need you to be with me."

"You're all I ever need. I can't get enough of you and don't ever want to be away from you again. I'm so sorry I didn't go with you to Pine Isle."

"Hold me tight." Her tears were on my cheek. We held hands, and she closed her eyes.

"There're no words for how much I love you," I whispered.

She squeezed my hand and winced.

"Are you in pain?"

"No, but our little one moves and kicks without warning."

"How's our baby doing?"

"The doctor said the heartbeat's strong. Put your head here." She touched her tummy, and I lifted the blanket and placed my ear against her skin. The heartbeat was strong, and I moved my hand over her belly and talked to our child.

"I'm tired. If I go to sleep, promise you won't leave."

"Promise."

I pulled up a chair and held her hand. She didn't say anything, and I worried about her condition.

The doctor came through the curtain about an hour later and checked on her. He motioned me to follow him.

He led me to the nurses' station and said, "Your wife's been through an ordeal. She's dehydrated, and we're running several tests and want to keep her for observation. The baby's heart rate is good, and her pregnancy appears to be normal."

"Can I stay with her?"

"We have rules against…"

He looked at my feet, and I was tapping them rapidly.

"Under the circumstances, I'll make an exception."

I thanked him and was at Caitlin's side day and night for two days, except when I went to the reception area to call Catherine and Miss Jerome to let them know that Caitlin and Kathleen were safe. I held her arm as she walked and slept in a chair next to her bed.

On Saturday morning, Maureen came and wanted to stay during the day and told me to go home. Before leaving, she pulled me aside and said, "I'm embarrassed by my husband's treatment of you. There's no excuse for his actions. He has a terrible temper. I wish I could make up for his behavior."

She took hold of my arm and said, "I appreciate you and apologize for all he has said and done to you. But I hope you know that doesn't represent how I feel toward you. I love you and am looking forward to being a grandmother. Kierian puts Caitlin on a pedestal, and when he couldn't do anything to save her, he directed his anger at you. I pray you can find it in your heart to forgive him again?"

"He's Caitlin's father, and I'll do whatever makes her happy." I accepted her hug.

I took a taxi back to my car. There was gas in the tank, and the engine started right up. Cody was a man of his word, and

I was thankful for his goodness and compassion. Had Julian or YeYe sent him?

Chapter Nineteen

On Sunday, Caitlin came home from the hospital, and Kathleen moved into an upstairs bedroom.

They went for medical exams together, and both had lingering fatigue from the trauma they had experienced. They suffered stress from the shock of the kidnapping, and Kathleen's grief was compounded by her husband's actions.

Since Tuesday, I had not been to the bank, but Peggy said we had several new deposits and loan applications. The best news was a letter from the Ministry of Finance notifying me that the bank audit was canceled.

Clive told me the court hearing for the Saez lawsuit was scheduled for a week from Friday.

Kathleen filed for divorce, and I helped her collect her things, close up her home with Patrick, and move in with us. Caitlin and Kathleen were inseparable, and Kathleen found renewed purpose in being a helper for Caitlin, for which I was thankful.

Maureen insisted on being at the house with Caitlin while I was at work, and Kierian snuck in and out before I came home.

I still needed to deal with Kirkpatrick and Dung and the $100,000. The police did pick up the briefcase from the bank, and the money was in their possession. When Tak was shot and killed, the money became part of that investigation. I was on edge, wondering when I would hear from Dung, anticipating hostile behavior and a cycle of retaliation against me.

On Monday morning, I met with Clive and Chief Kirkpatrick to discuss the situation. The Chief suggested we include Miss Jerome in the conversation, so we called her, and the first comment was asking about Caitlin and the baby.

After I updated her on their condition, Kirkpatrick told her about the search and rescue operation. "You know our investigation included Dung and Tak as possible suspects." He told her about the $100,000 that Dung had delivered to the bank and Tak's death. "We're in possession of the money, but it won't be part of the kidnapping charges. Hopefully, it can be used as evidence in charging offenses against Dung."

Kirkpatrick asked me to discuss Lysa Wu.

"Lysa Wu told me she has a black book of judges and politicians she escorted on behalf of Dung and Tak. If we can protect her and offer her and her family citizenship, I think she'll testify against them."

"Chief Kirkpatrick told me about Miss Wu. The RCMP picked her up for questioning on Friday. She turned over her black book, and we're keeping her and her family in hiding until Dung and his organization are brought to trial. I'll have an RCMP agent pick up the briefcase and money. We can hold it as evidence against Dung in our investigation of his illegal operations. We've issued a warrant for his arrest."

"Do you know Dung's whereabouts?" I asked.

"Not at present. We had a raid on the work camp Saturday, and the operation has been shut down. There were twenty-five illegals living there, and many were teenage boys. The adults were taken into custody and the boys are being cared for by an orphanage for the time being. We suspect he fled the country."

With these actions, I put thoughts of Dung aside and was content knowing that Caitlin was healthy and our child was doing well.

"Miss Jerome, Merchants Bank received a notice that the bank audit was canceled. I believe I have you to thank."

"Winson, you don't need to worry about the bank examiners for a while because they'll be busy spending time with Mr. Avant, conducting an extensive examination of First Simco Bank's asset quality, capital liquidity, earnings, and consumer compliance. Also, we'll be interrogating Avant about his contact with Taylor."

Clive thrust his fist in the air, and Kirkpatrick had a broad grin.

"How are conditions at your bank?" she asked.

"I've promoted several female staff members whose efforts have accounted for new accounts and deposit growth."

"You know that I'm pleased to hear about empowering women."

"Miss Jerome, I want to add that the *Collingwood Times* will be printing a retraction of the previous articles about Merchants Bank, although it won't make the front-page headlines," Clive said.

"Let me make a call and see if I can encourage the paper to move it to the front page. But, gentlemen, if there's nothing else to discuss, I've a meeting to attend."

We thanked her, and justice was being served.

∽

Before going to court on Friday regarding the Saez hearing, I visited Julian's grave. The well-maintained site had a large maple tree that provided shade for Julian's resting place and was among other clustered tombstones that all faced east. Ruthie's and Joseph's graves were on each side of him. The family monument was etched with six-pointed lilies carved into the stone above the name 'LeBlanc.' Below Julian's name and dates of birth and death was the inscription, "He loved unconditionally."

In Jewish tradition, I gathered some small smooth stones and placed them on top of the headstone in memory of my beloved father. He was in the hands of God but not forgotten.

I spoke to him about recent events, and from somewhere within me came vivid images of YeYe, mother, father, and Lijuan. They were in front of me, then moved in a circle around me, and when they stopped, I bowed three times to each of them. After that, the part of my heart filled with the pain of loss seemed to dissolve and feel lighter.

YeYe's image lingered for some time, and I sensed that he had slipped across the limits of this world and into the edges of the world to come. He believed this world and the next were connected. From what Wong had written, I knew my family suffered greatly under Mao and hoped YeYe's suffering was over. He had brought knowledge and light into my world and others that he touched. China would be darker for his absence. I was blessed to live in the shadow of two great men, YeYe and Julian. I hoped to be a small reflection of them both.

Looking at Julian's grave and speaking to him about his cousin, I heard an inner voice say, "You've been forced to leave your home, culture, and country. Yet, there's a buoyant spirit that courses through you and gives you the ability to rebound. Life is nothing but transitions."

I was at peace that Julian's intentions would prevail. My life was complicated, but so was humanity. Caitlin would tell me to count my blessings.

At the preliminary Saez hearing, Clive requested a summary judgment and outlined the reasons in detail, including my adoption papers and Julian's letters to Clive requesting exclusion of Benjamin Saez and his family from the will. There was also a statement from Julian's doctor affirming his mental capabilities to the date of his death.

Saez's attorney filed papers authenticating his relationship to Julian LeBlanc and death certificates for Julian's wife and son. He documented dates and times spent with Julian and tried to show a close relationship. He also accused undue influence on my part as Julian's caregiver. The judge took the pleadings under advisement and would alert the attorneys about his decision to schedule a hearing.

Monday morning, about ten o'clock, Clive called and said he had news he wanted to discuss over lunch. We met at the Towne Terrace Café and sat at a corner table. Clive ordered pints of Guinness.

After the waitress served us, Clive lifted his glass to mine and said, "To justice!" We clanked mugs, and he said, "This morning, I received notice that Saez's challenge of Julian's Will has been dropped. This is cause for celebration, and lunch is my treat!"

"Thank you for all you did, Clive. You never gave up on me."

"When Julian passed away, his friendship was irreplaceable. But I told Bitsy this morning that through you, Julian's still in my life."

"Thank you for your kind words. I've enjoyed getting to know Bitsy. She's been wonderful to me."

"She's looking forward to spending time with you and Caitlin as a couple."

"That would be our pleasure."

"I'm curious, was there any explanation in the notice why the Will contest was dropped?"

"His attorney probably advised him to drop the suit. I think Saez was looking for an offer to settle, and when it didn't come, he realized his challenge would be expensive. But enough of that, congratulations."

I hugged him and didn't know if the wetness on my cheek was from him or me, but it didn't matter. My shoulders relaxed, and my soul seemed to float.

That night, I shared the good news with Caitlin.

"I knew his suit was without merit, but that didn't change the anxiety I endured or the issues caused by the liens."

"I would live with you in a tent in Timmins," Caitlin said.

"When your arms are around me, I 'm home."

We laughed and cried tears of joy and relief.

"Caitlin, this calls for a celebration. What would you like to drink?"

"Sit with me first. There's something I want to discuss."

We sat on the sofa, and she took hold of my hand. "Don't you think it's about time to pick a name for our baby?" Caitlin asked.

"Whatever name you choose is fine with me."

"If it's a boy, I like Winson Julian LeBlanc after you and Julian. If it's a girl, I like Catherine Aria because Catherine and music brought us together, and Aria is a self-contained piece of music for one voice."

I agreed with both names. We played Julian's music on the record player and danced. Thankful for many things, our lives together, Winson Julian or Catherine Aria was on the way, and the litigation over our assets was behind us. We were so loud, Kathleen came into the parlor and said, "What's all the celebration about?"

When we told her the news, she took hold of our arms, and we swung in a circle until Caitlin needed to sit.

"You two sit while I pour us drinks to celebrate."

We toasted to Julian and Clive. I lifted my glass to Kathleen's and said, "I'm glad you're living with us. We'd like you to be godmother to our child?"

"Caitlin, is that okay with you?" Kathleen asked.

"Of course, Winson suggested it to me days ago, and I agreed."

"I want to meet someone like Winson," Kathleen said as I blushed.

"It's been a stormy period for all of us, but the sun is coming out from behind the clouds," Caitlin said as she took hold of Kathleen's arm.

⁂

The next day, I stopped by the police station to thank Chief Kirkpatrick for saving Kathleen's, Caitlin's, and our baby's lives and to give him a basket of sweets.

"Just performing my duty."

"What you do for the community is one of the most important careers one could have and will never be properly acknowledged. I value your efforts. You live a life of integrity."

"I appreciate your comments. I got into police work because I believe in the justice system."

"Speaking of justice, what's happened to Chorley and Mezzetti?"

"Chorley's in custody and being held without surety awaiting a court hearing. Chorley asserts Mezzetti fixed poker games, extended credit at usurious interest, and sent collectors to threaten his life if he didn't pay. He claims Mezzetti schemed to take the women hostage, collect the ransom, pay off Chorley's debt, return the women, and when he refused Mezzetti's plan, he was strong-armed into participating. Mezzetti isn't talking, based on his attorney's council. He posted a surety, so he's been released from custody.

"Kathleen and Caitlin identified one of the kidnappers but could not identify the other two. The one they identified is Robert Jackman. His attorney is negotiating with the Crown attorney for immunity in exchange for testifying against Mezzetti."

"What about the newspaper leak regarding the kidnapping?"

"We think one of the kidnappers leaked the information to try and get more money when they realized Caitlin was your wife and you owned Merchants Bank."

"Do you think Mezzetti will be prosecuted?"

"It's an embarrassment that he has a long record of charges without convictions. So many people, including a few politicians, know of his illicit activities but have kept mum for decades and looked the other way. We're trying to bring that to an end through the offer of immunity."

"Let's hope the charges convict him this time."

"It remains to be seen how Chorley's testimony will turn out in court. But between the two of them, it's every man for himself."

"Is there any news on Dung?"

"He's on a *Most Wanted List* but hasn't been found. I agree with Miss Jerome that he's left the country."

"He had connections in China and Korea."

"Who knows where he is?"

ᗡ

When I returned home, Caitlin said a letter from Howard Wong was on my desk. I opened it and read:

> *Dear Mr. LeBlanc,*
>
> *I am so sorry to report that I will no longer provide information regarding your family. I received news that Pai was arrested and executed for activities conducted against the government. I worked with Pai for many years and will be unable to continue working on your behalf because of this tragic event. It is increasingly difficult to conduct searches in China.*
>
> *I am sorry to terminate our relations, but such are the conditions we face in these uncertain times.*
>
> *Sincerely,*
> *Howard Wong*

Mr. Wong was a good man, and I promptly wrote a letter expressing my sorrow over losing his friend, Pai, and for what his family was facing. I thanked him for his diligent service and sent money for his and Pai's family for all they had risked trying to locate my family.

My family's search was now without legs. Was there any hope of ever finding them? I took a shot of Julian's Scotch and silently saluted Pai and Wong. Then, as YeYe taught me to do for NaiNai, I chanted for the dead.

I lost track of time and was startled when Caitlin took hold of my arm.

"Are you okay? You were speaking in Mandarin."

I handed her Wong's letter and said, "All I need is right here in this room. You and our child complete me."

"I love you. We love you."

"I've been many things, a simple boy from Hangzhou, a devoted son and grandson, a curious teenager, an idealistic student, a rebellious traveler, a prisoner, and a human chattel. Everything changed when Catherine and Julian became surrogate parents for me, and my world became complete when I met and fell in love with you."

We embraced, and she led me into the dining room, where we had dinner with Kathleen, Catherine, Joseph, Kai, and Wei Lei.

In my life, there had been heartache and pain. I had traveled so far because of my parent's hope to change my future, and I couldn't stop the force of their decision. Looking around at our extended family and the peace and tranquility that encircled us, I remembered the blind man on Hangzhou's docks. Before I boarded the ship for Canada, he placed his wrinkled hands on my bowed head and chanted to instill in me noble truth, perseverance, and to be eyes for the blind. As I sailed across the Pacific in that ungodly ship, I had no idea what life had in store for me.

I learned that nothing was certain in life, and that character cannot be developed in ease and comfort, but only through persevering, adhering to one's value system, and maintaining personal integrity.

Chapter Twenty

Catherine called on Saturday and wanted to see Caitlin and me. It was late afternoon when we entered the Lawrence house and found Catherine alone in the dining room having tea.

"My beloved children are in the house. Everything is as it should be."

We kissed and hugged her.

"Pour yourselves some tea. Wei Lei made scones, and there's a jar of Sandie's blueberry-peach jam."

"Yummy, I'm eating for two, and Winson could put on a few pounds," Caitlin said.

After sipping her tea, Catherine pushed an envelope toward Caitlin and said, "I want you to read the letter inside."

Caitlin opened it and read to herself as her eyes welled with tears. "Oh, Catherine, how exciting."

"What is it?" I asked

"It's from Yves. He's proposing marriage."

Catherine put her hands one over the other on the table like a little girl. We met Yves when he came to town for the presentation of the Order of Collingwood to Catherine. She usually cut off any conversation involving him with a sad expression on her face. This time was different. There was joy in her voice and a smile on her face.

"What are you going to do?" Caitlin asked.

"By the look on your face, you're going to say yes, and I say it's about time," I added.

She stuck her chin out, closed her eyes, tilted her head back, and said, "I was born in 1899, at the end of the Victorian age. My father had guilt for causing my blindness and doted on me, and consequently, my aunts' opinions were that he spoiled me rotten."

We both laughed and looked at each other.

Catherine pointed to the floor and said, "This beautiful Persian rug is from Aunt Tinny, and I can still feel her presence here. The glass lamps with beaded shades in the parlor are also from her." She shifted uncomfortably in her chair and winced.

"Are you having pain?" Caitlin asked.

"I've been sitting too long. Let's go outside for some fresh air. My children, getting old isn't for the faint of heart!"

I chuckled over her defiant attitude.

"Caitlin, are you up for walking a bit in the backyard?"

"I would like to. I've wanted to see if the wild Primrose is blooming."

As I helped Catherine up, she took hold of my arm, and we made our way out of the house, down the back porch steps, and strolled along the path lined with long shiny green-leafed plants with a rigid stem that supported tiny succulent white bell flowers.

"Don't the Lilies-of-the-Valley smell wonderful?" Catherine commented.

"I love the sweet fragrance, but they can be poisonous if eaten. I'll need to keep the baby away from them," Caitlin said.

We passed the carriage house, which in years past housed horses but now was empty. As we walked, Caitlin said, "Catherine, you're very quiet."

"I know, and I haven't answered your question about Yves' proposal. For weeks, I've been consumed praying about you, the baby, Kathleen, and thinking about life. I'm glad I'm blind rather than deaf. Music has been so much of my life. I don't know how I would've negotiated without the ability to hear music. Music brought you and Yves into my life."

Her voice was strained, and then she stopped talking and seemed agitated.

"Are you okay, Catherine?" I asked.

"It's emotional pain. You see, my brothers died from heart failure before their forty-second birthdays. So, I've been without family for quite a while." She sighed and said, "I'm ready to return to the house. Let's sit in the parlor."

Being in the parlor with Catherine was so peaceful. It was filled with her scent, which floated like her fingers over the piano keys. She sat in her rocker, and we were on each side of her.

"Despite my blindness, I've toured the world, Jerusalem, Switzerland, Spain, and Great Britain. Gone to many castles, plays, operas, and art museums."

She reached out for Caitlin's hand and said, "You've been of great support to me in so many ways, but especially when I dictated music for you to transcribe in braille."

"Catherine, we know you love Yves. Are you going to say yes?" Caitlin asked.

She remained silent.

"Why are you hesitating? You know how much he loves you," I asked.

"At one time, I could've seen spending all of my life with him. But now, my life's almost over."

"You've many good years left. Why don't you spend it with someone you've always loved?" Caitlin encouraged her.

"I never wanted to be a burden to him or to hold him back because of my handicap."

"Obviously, he doesn't think you're disabled, and neither do we. He said he never found another Catherine. He's devoted to you," I said.

Catherine huffed. After a few moments of silence, she said, "Winson, go up to my room, open the lower drawer of the dresser on the right-side of my bed, and bring me all the envelopes that are tied together."

I went to her room, opened the drawer, and picked up several stacks of envelopes.

Caitlin had a surprised expression on her face as she said, "Are all those from Yves?"

"Yes. Yves wrote to me regularly, regardless of whether I wrote back. You're welcome to read them. They go back to the first year I returned to Collingwood from Europe."

She paused as Caitlin unbundled one of the stacks, and open the envelope on top, pulled out the letter, and started reading to herself.

"I've lived alone for so long, I'm not sure how I would manage marriage, but I'm finally giving in to the love we have for each other."

"Does that mean you're open to his proposal?" I asked.

"Look at it as a new musical arrangement," Caitlin added.

A broad smile spread across her face, and she laughed.

"I guess even a blind person can see how much he loves me. How stupid would I be to ignore the love we share? I guess you two have opened my eyes."

We started to laugh but waited until Catherine giggled, then we joined in.

"Caitlin, would you write my reply to Yves? Winson, get my stationery and a pen." Her voice was like a lilting little girl's.

Catherine possessed an incredible mind and saw the world through her music, her friends, and what she read. She was a character and a beautiful human being. If not for the blindness, she would have had an incredible life outside of Collingwood. But because of it, she blessed the people of Collingwood with the music she taught to so many.

When I returned, she cleared her throat and dictated:

My dearest Yves,

You've always been the only man for me. So let me start by saying, yes, definitely yes, I will eagerly marry you at your earliest convenience.

There, it's finally out of my mouth. I feel relieved and excited. Hallelujah!

Now, let's start planning and consider details.

We should marry at the Collingwood Inn, in their courtyard under a canopy, with a beautiful array of white gardenias because I like the fragrance. Caitlin will be my matron of honor, and Winson will walk me down the aisle. The Episcopal Reverend Phillip Thornier will perform the ceremony. I'll leave it up to you to choose your best man.

For music, a violin ensemble will start with Vivaldi's Four Seasons, followed by a list of some of our favorite compositions, which we'll choose together.

> *On to the menu. Champagne and appetizers,*
> *followed by a seated four-course dinner of shrimp cocktail,*
> *green salad, chateaubriand with grilled asparagus and*
> *lyonnaise potatoes, and ending with wedding cake. One*
> *layer must be chocolate.*
>
> *We'll work on the guest list together. I 'd like to*
> *invite some of the musicians who played with us for so*
> *many years, the students I've taught, and our family and*
> *friends.*
>
> *Yves, you will look fabulous in your white dinner*
> *jacket. My dress will be a surprise.*
>
> *Come to me as soon as you can, and we'll plan the*
> *rest together.*
>
> *With all my love,*
> *Catherine*

"Oh, and Caitlin, I'll need you to take me shopping unless Mrs. Williamson can make me a dress. After that, I'll need Mrs. Weldon to do my hair and nails."

Her skin was pale and delicate but quite lovely. As she dictated, she would pull her blouse smooth and finger each button.

"I must call Mr. Stromberger, find out what dates are available, and make arrangements with him."

I squeezed her arm, and her face brightened. Caitlin and I grinned from ear to ear.

✧

Four weeks later, the wedding took place on a sunny, cloudless Saturday afternoon. Catherine and Yves had been together for the previous three weeks, and they looked as happy as any couple I had ever known, except for Caitlin and me.

The arbor in the Canterbury Inn courtyard was covered in white gardenias, and the fragrance filled the air as a hundred guests from all over the world were seated in white chairs waiting for the ceremony to begin.

As we waited, Caitlin said, "Catherine, the setting for your wedding is wonderful! Mr. Stromberger has outdone himself. There are white roses and gardenias along the aisle, and your groom is very handsome in his white dinner jacket. This is the fanciest wedding I've ever been to."

When the violin ensemble played Vivaldi's Four Seasons, I noticed Caitlin put her hands on her back.

"Are you okay?" I asked.

"It's a small contraction, don't worry. The baby isn't due for a couple more weeks."

"It would be exciting to have a wedding and a baby on the same day," Catherine said.

"That would be too much excitement for me," I said and kept my eyes on Caitlin as she slowly walked down the aisle. She was so worried about how she looked in her rose silk maternity dress, but to me, she was the most beautiful woman in the world.

"Catherine, are you ready? Your handsome groom is waiting at the altar for you."

She took a dry swallow and said, "I feel like a little girl."

When the ceremony was over, I stood with Caitlin in the receiving line. She whispered in my ear that she had several contractions during the ceremony, but they weren't at regular intervals, and not to worry.

As the guests mingled, waiting for dinner to be announced, Caitlin asked Kathleen to walk with her to the restroom.

A few minutes later, Kathleen came back and took hold of my arm. "Winson, come quick."

"What's wrong?"

"Her water broke."

"What does that mean?"

"She's going to have the baby today. We need to take her to the hospital. She's waiting in the lobby."

Joseph Lawrence stood alongside me and said, "Go, take care of Caitlin. I'll tell Catherine and Yves what's happening."

"Thank you, Joseph. Would you call the hospital and tell them we're on our way, then call Maureen Mulroney, and let her know? Catherine knows the number."

"Certainly, now you go, and quickly."

Kathleen and I helped Caitlin into the car's back seat, and we rushed to the hospital. Caitlin's pains were getting harder and closer together. Kathleen kept telling her to take deep breaths and exhale slowly. As we pulled into the hospital's parking lot, we saw a nurse waiting with a wheelchair. Joseph must've had some connections. Kathleen and the nurse helped Caitlin into the chair.

"I love you," Caitlin said as the nurse rushed her through double doors, and I stood in front of that dreadful sign that read, *Medical Staff Only*. I had spent a lot of time pacing in hospital waiting rooms. Hopefully, this would be a joyous occasion. I didn't know what Caitlin was going through or how long we'd be waiting.

"She's going to be fine. She and the baby are both healthy. You're going to be a daddy soon!" Kathleen encouraged.

Maureen arrived minutes later, and the three of us waited together. It was torturous waiting and not being with Caitlin.

I was thankful when Kai and Wei Lei joined us. Wei Lei said, "Any news?"

I shook my head and said, "Sit with us."

I was bouncing my feet when Kai said, "We left the reception before they cut the cake. Joseph gave a wonderful toast on your behalf to the bride and groom."

I didn't have much to say as all my thoughts were on Caitlin.

A few hours later, Yves walked in with Catherine on his arm.

"How's Caitlin doing? Did we get here in time for the arrival?" Catherine asked.

"The nurse said it shouldn't be much longer. She's almost fully dilated." Kathleen said.

Kierian walked in the door and sat in the far corner of the waiting area when Dr. Franklin came out and said, "All went well. Winson, you can come with me to see mother and child." I'm sure there was a lilt in my step as I walked through the double doors.

My wife had the sweetest look on her face holding our baby.

"Meet Catherine Aria LeBlanc. She's perfect."

"A girl?"

"Do you see your daddy with a big smile on his face?"

"You're both beautiful. I'm so proud of you. How do you feel?"

"I couldn't be happier. I can't say it didn't hurt, but she was worth every pain."

∞

Life is about perseverance, and YeYe taught me to always choose to do the right thing and that our capacity for change is like the resilience of bamboo. It doesn't matter if someone cuts it down because it grows again, and no matter how strong the wind or how rough the storm, it is far more flexible than one would ever imagine. And so are we.

In the beginning, I did not know whom to trust, where to find help, or the confidence to make the right decisions. Eventually, I found kindness and even friendship in the most unexpected places when I opened myself to others. People from different backgrounds went out of their way to help me become like a stalk of bamboo.

If I had closed myself off to others and relied only upon myself, there is no way I could have succeeded as I have done in my life. I would not have my home, my job, or my beautiful wife and daughter.

Addendum

Collingwood Series Historical Context

During the 1800s and 1900s, China's troubling political and social circumstances stimulated immigration to North America. Over 44,000 immigrants arrived in Canada between 1858 and 1923, initially to work in mining, agriculture, and factories. In 1881, the Canadian Pacific Railway brought in 15,000 Chinese workers and paid them half of their Caucasian co-workers' wages, which intensified anti-Chinese sentiment.

These Chinese workers had no negotiating power over their wages, but they needed to send money back home to support their families and repay loans to the merchants who paid their passage to North America. At the same time, Caucasian workers pressured Parliament to ban Chinese workers because their need for higher wages caused them to resent the Chinese who were squeezing them out of jobs.

After the Canadian railway was completed in 1885 and the large number of Chinese workers were no longer necessary, Canada's first Prime Minister, John Macdonald, passed the Chinese Immigration Act, which stipulated that all Chinese entering Canada must pay a CA$50 fee, referred to as a Head Tax. This fee increased to CA$500 in 1903, two years of salary for an immigrant worker. In addition, the Chinese Exclusion Act of 1923 prevented Chinese immigration except for businessmen, clergy, educators, and students and was in effect until 1947. As a matter of interest, Australia and the U.S. passed similar laws.

During the Head Tax era in Canada, many illegal immigration schemes existed where adults and children came with fraudulent papers and assumed a false identity of someone entitled to return to Canada. These children were known as "Paper Sons or Daughters." Merchant brokers and crime rings acted as middlemen, and widespread trafficking flourished. Many Chinese families paid exorbitant sums to these men who promised them opportunities for a good life for their children in Canada. But when these children arrived, the unscrupulous middlemen in Canada claimed they owed more money and sold them into indentured service. The Chinese middlemen told others, like our character Winson's family, who couldn't pay, that they were sending their children to sponsoring Chinese families. But when they arrived, the traffickers forced them into hard labor.

In 1960, the Royal Canadian Mounted Police started a crackdown investigation of this widespread wholesale illegal smuggling of Chinese immigrants into Canada. The RCMP suspected a massive syndicate of providing fake documentation to "Paper Sons and Daughters." During the crackdown, the RCMP offered a bounty for illegal immigrants. Traffickers, like Dung, often profited a second time by reporting the "Paper Sons" who had paid their "debt" but were not legal citizens.

After months of investigation, squads of under-cover police converged on businesses and homes from Vancouver to Montreal with the assistance of Chinese police officers brought over from Hong Kong to secure documentary evidence such as 'coaching' papers, passports, and visas. The campaign, known as 'Kin for Hire,' investigated over 20,000 names. As a result of the investigation, which revealed the immensity of the problem, the government instituted a Chinese Adjustment Statement Program in 1960 to provide amnesty to all the "Paper Sons and Daughters."

The seed for the Collingwood Series came from my meeting an Irish Canadian woman who shared her story of falling in love and marrying a Chinese "Paper Son" in 1950. Then, I met a group of Chinese immigrants in their twenties who shared their knowledge of human trafficking into Canada through a crime ring known as the Snakeheads, whose operations began in the 1960s. Unfortunately, human trafficking still exists today in North America and is a multibillion-dollar industry.

Acknowledgments

A heartfelt thank you to two special people in my life. First, to my wonderful wife, Karen, for her willingness to review, comment, discuss, restructure, and edit the story, and for her constant and steadfast encouragement and love. She brought light and pure love into my life from the first day we met.

And to Dr. Lew Spurlock for offering his friendship, literary guidance, and mentorship, which significantly contributed to writing this book series and furthered my development as an author. Lew pushed and prodded me to unlock what lies within me, which is a great gift to an aspiring author.

I also want to thank my many gifted proofreading and editing partners, who have graciously given me constructive criticism and sound advice.

Thanks to Doug Burlock for his permission to use one of his wonderful Collingwood photos, *Weeping Willows*, for the book cover.

About the Author

George Fillis is an internationally known author of the Collingwood Series whose works are featured in Midwest Book Review and California Book Watch. A graduate of Trinity University, he lives in San Antonio, Texas, with his wife, Karen. He discovered his passion for writing after careers in securities, real estate, and biotech. Inspired by travels to China and Canada, he heard a remarkable story about a 'paper son,' which was the seed for *A Heart To Survive* , *An Unexpected Father,* and *Unpunished Crimes*.

He hopes this book series generates awareness about human trafficking and what it means to stand alone in the face of overwhelming odds, the importance of character, always choosing to do what is right, and understanding what it is like to live outside of one's comfort zone. All of which come at a cost.

Made in the USA
Columbia, SC
15 March 2022